The Highlande

Book 1 in The Highlander's Bride

series

By Cathy MacRae

AMAZON KDP EDITION

2nd EDITION

PUBLISHED BY
Short Dog Press

www.cathymacraeauthor.com

The Highlander's Accidental Bride © 2013

Copyright Notice

DEDICATION

I would like to dedicate this book
to the people who have cheered me on
from the first day I decided I would become an author.
Rayleen Hendrix, Abby Iwanski,
and my friends at Heart of Dixie Romance Writers
who celebrated each stage of the journey with me.
You guys rock

BOOKS IN THE SERIES

THE HIGHLANDER'S ACCIDENTAL BRIDE

Chaos reigns between the Scott and Barde clans in 14th century Scotland. To end the generation's long feud, King Robert II of Scotland decrees EADEN, LAIRD SCOTT, and Lady Miriam Barde wed with all haste. When marriage negotiations break down, King Robert threatens Eaden with the loss of his lands and title. Forced to take matters into his own hands, the laird kidnaps his bride, only to find the young woman he mistakenly drags to his marriage bed is not Laird Barde's daughter, but her lady's companion.

MARY MARSH fights for her freedom from the laird and the unwanted marriage, refusing to accept her new life as Lady Scott. Realizing his error, Laird Scott develops an attachment to the feisty young woman he has accidentally married. Can he win her heart and convince her she is more than just a *duty* to him? Or will the bond forged between the lady's companion and the laird be destroyed by secrets and the feud that will not be laid to rest?

Chapter One

1375, Scott Castle, the Scottish Highlands

She rolled her head slowly toward the brightness, the intensity of the light wringing a low moan from her as she opened her eyes. A shard of pain flashed through her skull as she lifted her head from her pillow. She gasped and a firm, capable hand pushed her gently back on the bed.

"Lie back, lass."

Soft words drifted to her ears. Her head spun. The voice wasn't one she recognized. She glanced around the room through narrowed eyes, moving as little as possible.

Tall ceilings and windows gave the room a spacious feel, and the heavy wall tapestries were of the finest quality. The woman at her side stared at her with a frown, touching her brow lightly with a cool hand.

Have I been sick?

"My name is Ina. I've the care of ye. Ye need a bit of broth to strengthen ye, lass. I'll help ye sit, but ye must speak up if ye feel sick to yer stomach," the older woman warned as she helped her to a seated position. With a final glance over her shoulder, the matron strode to the hearth and scooped a bowl of broth from the pot warming there.

"Here ye are, lass." Ina offered the bowl. "Drink this."

She did, and immediately felt better. The woman gave a nod of approval and rose to her feet, setting the dish aside.

"As soon as I'm back, we'll get ye fitted for yer wedding dress. Ye must look yer best for yer bridegroom tonight."

She bolted upright in bed, ignoring the warning pain shooting through her head. "*What* did you say?"

The woman hesitated in the doorway.

"Ye need a dress for yer wedding to the laird. Ye had nothing but yer nightclothes when ye came."

"But . . ." A thousand questions flooded her brain, and she choked on the words tumbling from her lips. "I didn't . . . Where . . .?" She raised a trembling hand to her forehead, stopping the flow of nonsense as she struggled to gather her thoughts. "Where am I?"

"Why, at Scott Castle," the woman replied. "'Tis where Laird Scott resides."

"Who is Laird Scott?"

The woman gave her a curious look. "Eaden, laird of clan Scott and earl of the lands of Craigievar. He's to be yer husband."

She turned wide, puzzled eyes on the older woman. "Who am I?"

* * *

Miriam paced the length of her room, then turned and paced the length again. Nothing made sense. What Ina told her wasn't true. Her mind was disturbingly fuzzy, as if they spoke of someone else. Why couldn't she remember? Why did her head still feel full of rocks and fire?

She touched the back of her head gingerly, probing the bump there, wincing when she pushed too hard. The only thing that made sense was she did not want to marry the laird. That much she understood. It resonated in the deepest part of her, dismay snaking through her at the thought.

A knock sounded and Miriam whirled, jolted from her musings. The door swung open and one of the largest men she had ever seen entered the room.

"Who are you?" Her hand flew to her throat in fear.

The man gave her a sardonic smile and paused inside the doorway. "I am Earl Scott. Ina tells me ye're having trouble with yer memory." His voice rumbled deep.

"I have a bump on my head," Miriam replied tartly. This was her husband-to-be? Her eyes drifted up the length of him, unnerved by the narrowed look he gave her. His nearly black eyes and soot-dark hair lent him a devilish air, more frightening than intriguing, and Miriam nearly swallowed her tongue as she imagined herself bound to this man.

"Doesnae matter. Ye'll marry me this day." He crossed the room to stand before the fireplace, holding out his hands to the one welcoming element in the room. After a moment, he turned to her, regarding her askance.

"Rest assured I am no more in favor of this marriage than are ye."

"Then why am I here?" Miriam persisted.

"To appease the king and end a feud between our clans."

"Ina said you kidnapped me last night and brought me here because you did not think my father would honor the king's edict." Miriam winced at the word *father*. It sounded foreign to her. Did she not get along with him?

"She told me ye've no memory of last night."

"I have no memory of anything before I woke this morning," Miriam replied with some asperity. The feeling of being trapped crept over her again, pairing with the inability to resign herself to marriage with this man.

"I apologize for the bump on yer head. It was quite unintentional, but ye slipped and conked yerself on the bedrail. I assure ye I meant ye nae harm. It seems we startled ye when we entered yer chamber."

She waved her hands dramatically in the air. "Ye kidnapped me! Was that necessary? Are you so certain we would have not married in a more normal fashion in time?"

The earl's face darkened. "Aye. Yer response to my proposal was somewhat less than enthusiastic, and yer sire has ignored the king's edict far too long."

Miriam paled at the harshness of his words. "You cannot be certain my words were more than simply talk. I cannot imagine feeling pleased to be forced to marry someone I don't know. Perhaps you are mistaken."

"Dinnae play coy with me, milady," Eaden snarled. "Ye know damn well ye wouldnae have married me now or a month from now. Everything I have is forfeit if this wedding doesnae take place. King Robert has placed his seal on the documents and we only await the priest. Ye will present yerself downstairs this evening, dressed and prepared to say yer vows!"

Without awaiting her response, the earl spun on his heel and strode from the room, slamming the door with a resounding crash, causing Miriam to jump at the sound.

"He will not intimidate me!" she swore aloud, but her words rang hollow. Her lower lip trembled, and she could do nothing more defiant than lift her chin. No matter what she said in defense of herself or her father, she would not be believed. Come morning, she would be forever bound to her father's sworn enemy.

* * *

People crowded about her in a blur of disapproving faces and a hushed murmur of sound. Unable to shake the disoriented feeling, Miriam felt caught in a dream. A very bad dream with no waking relief.

She dug her fingernails into her palms and winced. 'Twas no dream, but a nightmare of overwhelming proportions.

Her pale blue satin gown, alternately cool and warm against her skin, weighty with embroidery and jewels, did not make her feel special. The bodice laced tight about her and she found it difficult to draw a breath. The stone walls of the castle closed in around her, pressing upon her as heavily as the garment itself.

"Sign yer name, Lady Miriam."

Miriam stared at the priest as though he'd grown horns. He held the quill out to her and she took it, frowning at the dark blot on the parchment from her unsteady hand. Her head swam from the cup of wine she'd drunk earlier to fortify her, and she regretted accepting a second. Dizziness and the flickering light from hundreds of candles lighting the room compounded her sick headache.

She laid the quill on the table and returned to the earl's side. Furtively, she fingered the knot on the back of her head.

The earl, ramrod straight beside her, did not ease her feelings of dread, nor did the absence of tenderness on his scowling face. Eaden shifted his feet, his movement jerking her thoughts back to the proceedings.

"Lady Miriam," the priest said curtly, gaining her attention. "Ye must repeat the vows."

She glanced toward the priest who stared at her with a distinct lack of patience.

Miriam. She tilted her head, the name sounding foreign in her ears.

The earl threw her a disgusted look and she shot him a haughty glare. Forced to concede the edict of the king, she had reluctantly given her promise. Nothing and no one could change her fate. So, why such difficulty saying the words?

"Lady Miriam," the priest said once more, the warning clear in his voice, the sound a death knell to all her hopes of last-minute salvation. With great reluctance, she spoke the words of binding, her mouth moving in automatic response, her heart numb to their meaning.

All too soon, the ceremony ended, and she turned with her new husband to face the silent people crowding the great hall of Scott Castle. A narrow pathway opened through the throng, allowing them to pass, and Laird Scott at last deigned to touch her. Taking her arm in an iron-like grasp, he all but dragged her the length of the stone hall and toward the stairs as she hurried to keep up with him.

A murmur of low-pitched voices rose from the people as they pointed at her, some frowning openly. Embarrassed by her undignified exit from the room, she tried to pull her arm from the laird's grasp.

Laird Scott tightened his grip painfully. "Cease!" His angry stride carried them to the foot of the stairs. Only then did he pause long enough to sweep her into his arms, taking the steps to the second level two at a time.

Miriam's ears burned at the speculations from the people in the hall about Laird Scott's intentions as he carried her past the columns of the upstairs solar. Hot with humiliation, she tried to shut out the sounds of the crude suggestions and exhortations wafting after them.

"Put me down!" she hissed, squirming in his arms. His heavy muscles tightened their grip. She yelped in pained surprise but fell immediately silent at Eaden's countering glare. He shoved open a door at the end of the hallway and stepped inside. The freedom she'd sought moments before came without warning as he released her. She slid from his grasp as he spun her toward a chair.

He reached behind him, his eyes boring into hers as he slammed the door and threw the latch. Miriam rose slowly to her feet, straightening her skirts with trembling hands. She glanced about the room, noting the tall, narrow windows and the heavy wall hangings billowing slightly in the after-draft of the slammed door. A huge, curtained bed dominated the center of the room, its draperies drawn back to capture the warmth of the peat fire on the hearth. She brought her wary gaze back to the laird.

Her husband's face darkened and his jaw clenched. "We neither one want this marriage," he said, his voice harsh. "And now it's done, I've no doubt ye'd still flee if given the chance."

Miriam steeled herself against agreeing to the charge. It was true. She'd rather be anywhere than here, facing this man who frightened her so. But her scan of the room revealed no ready escape. A plunge from the window would mean instant death, and the only other doorway appeared to lead to a small dressing chamber.

"I brought ye here because the king threatened to take my lands unless I wed ye. I care naught for the ceremony or the revelry below. I care even less if ye share my bed beyond this night." Eaden narrowed his eyes as Miriam lost the battle to remain calm, slowly shaking her head in denial of his next words.

"We will do this." He spoke firmly, his voice losing its angry edge. "We could have waited until the guests accompanied us here, but I would rather no' have witnesses to this farce."

Miriam's eyes grew wide. "I am frightened," she admitted in a whisper.

He cursed under his breath and turned to a wooden cabinet. He opened the doors and she heard the clink of metal.

"Here." Eaden crossed back to her and held out a small goblet filled with an amber liquid. He handed it to her with a scowl.

Miriam ignored the proffered cup. "I know you hate me, but do I disgust you as well?"

"I dinnae know if *hate* is the right word, but the disgust is for the waste of good whisky to get a woman in my bed."

Curious in spite of herself, she asked, "And what do you normally use to get a woman in your bed?"

Eaden bared his teeth in a mirthless grin. "My winsome smile."

"And your overwhelming charm?" Miriam countered drolly. Eaden made no reply and Miriam took the goblet, sniffing the contents suspiciously.

"'Tis no' poison, and if it were, I'd no' make the mistake of showing ye the where of it," he noted wryly, motioning for her to drink. "'Twill warm ye and calm yer nerves."

Miriam took a hesitant sip and gasped as the liquid ignited a fiery path to her stomach. She thought Eaden's lips twitched, perhaps almost smiled, but her eyes swam with tears and she quickly discarded the absurd idea.

"Finished?"

Considering the alternative, she ventured another delicate sip, desperately needing more time to compose herself. Combined with the wine she'd drunk earlier, the whisky made pleasant headway toward slowing her wildly beating heart.

Eaden took the cup from her and drained the rest of the contents in a single gulp. "Take it off." He motioned at her dress with the empty goblet as he raked her from head to toe with an unreadable look.

Miriam raised a horrified eyebrow.

"Ye dinnae know the way of it?" Eaden sighed heavily.

"Of course I do," she lied, unwilling to show her ignorance. But undress before a man? Woodenly, she reached to undo the laces of her dress, her fingers clumsy with lingering fright and the unaccustomed alcohol blooming warmly in her veins. Her tingling fingers could not manage the task and she only created knots in the fine, silken threads.

With a curse, Eaden grabbed her shoulders and hauled her around. She jerked at the touch of his hands on her back as he tugged at the offending laces.

"Damn." With no care to the costliness of the fabric, he grasped the dress at the nape. With one wrench of his hands, he tore the gown and her chemise free to her waist. Released from their gossamer threads, pearls and silver beads tinkled across the bare wooden floor, loud in the charged silence of the room.

Miriam gasped and grabbed frantically at the front of her gown as it sagged forward. "You have ruined my dress!"

Eaden shrugged. "Do ye want to take it from here, or do ye still require assistance?"

Her jaw clenched in rebellion, but she dared not risk further help from him. His *help* had already cost her much, leaving her with no kin present to see her honorably wed, a ruined dress, and scant pride.

The last of the bejeweled fabric and silken chemise fell around her feet, leaving her naked before him. A small, gold filigree cross set with green stones settled cold against her skin. Her fingers lifted in an automatic gesture to cover the pendant as Eaden's gaze roamed over her.

His hands faltered in the midst of releasing his own clothing. Miriam thought his features softened, but the look fled before she could be certain.

Recovering quickly from whatever his thoughts had been, he finished removing his clothes and motioned her toward the bed, quirking an eyebrow as she hesitated.

Swallowing her fear of the unknown, she slid onto the bed, unwilling to turn her back on him. Eaden followed, stretching beside her on the mattress, and the heat of him warmed her skin. He touched her hair and she closed her eyes, intending to blot out whatever came next. Her scalp tingled as his fingers combed the tangled strands of her hair, igniting a reluctant fire in her belly.

"I dinnae want ye as a wife. I told ye I dinnae care if you hated me or no'. But we could make a marriage that would suit us both."

For a moment she softened at his words. Could they make something less disastrous of their marriage? Could they fashion threads of civility for their future? Respect?

Drunken laughter surged through the closed door and fists drummed an uneven tattoo on the wooden boards. Humiliation rushed over her and she stiffened to remember she was the unwilling captive of her father's enemy.

"Be done with it," she hissed through clenched teeth, her hands fisted tightly at her sides.

Eaden made no reply as he rose over her.

* * *

He rolled to his feet beside the bed. Miriam lay silent, eyes closed tight, determined he would not see her cry. Fabric rustled as he dressed, loud in the still room.

"'Tis done. Ye need not fear my attentions again." His voice was flat, emotionless.

His booted feet thudded dully on the wooden floor and a *snick* reached Miriam's ears as the bedroom door opened and closed. Tears seeped from beneath her lashes and she released the despair erupting from her soul. She'd dreamed of her wedding night as the first of years of bliss, her naïveté now lost amid the tangled bedclothes. She hadn't wanted to be married to Laird Scott. Silently she cursed her father. the king and the man they'd forced her to wed.

The ache in her heart eased and she slipped from the bed, moving gingerly to the wooden chest against the wall. Lifting the lid, she reached for her nightshift. The fine fabric grated like the coarsest wool on her sensitive skin and she shuddered as it settled over her body. Noise from the guests drifted from below, but Miriam had no intention of rejoining them. *Let the laird entertain them.*

She faltered, remembering the way he'd dragged her through the throng of gathered clansmen. They'd already been *entertained.*

Crossing back to the bed, she stripped away the bloodstained coverlet and climbed onto the soft mattress. She burrowed beneath the sheets and thin blanket, shedding more hot tears of anger and humiliation. He'd said she need not fear him again. Did he truly mean to leave her alone? Miriam glanced at the door and pulled the blanket tighter around her.

* * *

Eaden stormed into the upstairs hall, hardly sparing his brother a glance. Ranald shrugged and pushed away from his position against the wall.

"Thought ye'd be longer than this," he said to Eaden's back. "Of course, 'twas the shortest wedding in history," he added reprovingly.

Eaden did not respond, rounding the corner and hurrying down the back stairwell.

"Now ye've wedded and bedded the lass, ye're free to enjoy the rest of the evening." Ranald's voice mocked as he followed close on Eaden's heels.

Eaden whirled on him with a snarl. "Do ye have anything to say that doesnae involve my bride?"

Ranald pulled up short and gave him a wary look. "Nay."

Eaden grunted and turned away, taking the rest of the stairs in three bounding strides as he continued to the stables.

"So, ye'll no' spend the night with her?" Ranald leaned over the edge of the horse stall and petted the head of Eaden's deerhound who'd been confined to the stable for the evening.

Eaden scowled. "The subject is closed." He finished saddling his horse and tossed the reins over the stallion's neck. Grasping the plaited leather just below the shanks of the bit, he led Duff through the door. Duff, not at all inclined to leave his warm stall, stretched his neck reluctantly before he finally picked up his hooves and lurched forward. Ranald followed Eaden into the night, the deerhound, Sorcha, tagging along behind.

"I'll be back." Eaden mounted the stallion, leaning forward to check the fastenings of his saddle.

Ranald's eyebrows lifted at the sight of six other riders fanned out in the edge of the lantern light spilling from the stables. Slouched only a little in their saddles, they'd apparently not had time to partake fully of the wedding feast.

Ranald gave a short cry of protest. "Ye've guests and a new bride."

Eaden threw him a hooded look as he urged Duff forward. "Ye can handle things here. I've other men watching Barde. They'll alert us if he tries to raise an army or march in our direction."

"Where are ye going?"

"Troon."

"Why?"

"I've married the wench. Now I want my land back from the king."

Chapter Two

Morning sunlight fell in a brilliant puddle through the glass-paned window, painting the wooden floor with greenish-golden warmth. Groaning with reluctance to face the day, Miriam rolled over, shielding her eyes against the bright light. Unwelcome memories of the previous day flashed through her mind, and she winced against the harsh reality of marriage to the laird.

Then with a sudden, startled cry, she sat bolt upright in bed, her hand barely stifling the scream on her lips.

"My name isn't Miriam!"

She leapt out of bed, stumbling as her feet tangled in the thin blanket. Stomping the fabric into submission, she glanced wildly about the room, looking for the man who had dragged her into this nightmare.

Spying the door across the room, she rushed to the thick-hewn portal. After a moment of panic when the bolt resisted her efforts, she managed to drag the heavy door open. She ran into the hallway and stopped, unsure how to proceed. Voices rose from the great hall below, but she could not tell if her husband's was among them.

My husband! The words shot through her like a bolt of lightning, white-hot and frightening. Fresh panic sent her fleeing down the narrow hall, overwhelmed with the need to find some safe place. Catching the *clop* of footsteps coming up the back stairs, she whirled with the blind fear of a hunted rabbit, and ran hard against a solid wall of linen-covered flesh and muscle.

Her breath caught in her throat at the sight of the tall, dark-haired man looming over her. *Eaden*? She blinked. No, not Eaden, but his brother, Ranald, though the two were nearly alike enough to be twins.

"Easy, lass." His big hands grasped her upper arms, steadying her as she rocked back on her heels.

Her husband and Ranald were less alike than she'd thought. Eaden had scarcely said a single kind word to her since he'd dragged her here, and his grip on her arm the night before had been angry and impersonal.

Ranald's steadying hands and gentle words struck through the horror awakened in her only moments ago, and she blurted the terrifying words. "My name isn't Miriam!"

* * *

Ranald gave Eaden's new bride a puzzled look, noting the wildness in her eyes, tears sparkling in their emerald depths. "What?"

She blinked again, unshed tears magnifying her eyes, intensifying their color until he became mesmerized, wanting to protect her from whatever frightened her.

"My name is Mary." Her voice was an anguished whisper, the look on her face begging him to understand.

"Mary, Miriam." He shrugged, breaking free of his trance. "Whatever milady wishes."

The young woman stomped her foot impatiently. "No! You're not listening. My name is *not* Lady Miriam Barde. I am Mary Marsh, her companion."

Ranald's eyes widened as his breath left him in a loud *whoosh*. It was no secret Laird Barde's daughter had haughtily scorned marriage to her father's enemy. Now the marriage was done, how far would she go to be free? Perhaps she teetered on the verge of hysteria. But was she lying?

He motioned for her to return to her room. Whatever she was up to, it wouldn't do for the servants to overhear their conversation. She turned with obvious reluctance and did as he asked. Following her, he closed the door softly behind them.

She crossed the room and stood by the window, staring out at the late spring day. The morning light silhouetted her slender body through the thin night shift she wore. Ranald pulled himself together with a jerk, hoping she hadn't noticed his gaze. Turning away, he sought something suitable to wrap her in.

He spied the rumpled coverlet on the floor and snatched it up with relief. He shook it out, noticed the bloodstains on the silken surface, and halted mid-action. Wincing at the reminder the lass was now his brother's wife, he dropped the ruined coverlet back to the floor and crossed the room.

Disentangling the thin blanket from the sheets beside the bed, he draped the soft silk over her shoulders. "Here. 'Twill keep ye warm."

She absently accepted the fabric, cinching it tight around her, as though protecting herself from something. From him? He frowned and discarded the thought. More likely his angry brother, who had spent less than two minutes wooing his young bride the night before. Perhaps it would ease her mind to know Eaden was no longer at Scott Castle.

"Ye can rest easy, milady." Ranald took up his position beside the door. "Eaden left last night for Dundonald Castle."

The girl glanced at him over her shoulder. "Why would he go there?"

"To tell the king of yer marriage," Ranald replied matter-of-factly.

She blanched and faced him, wide-eyed. "But we can't be married . I'm not who he thinks I am."

Ranald sighed. "Perhaps ye'd better tell me what's going on, lass. I was with him when he, er, *fetched* ye from Bellecourt Castle. We watched yer father step inside the room to check on ye that night. We were no' wrong."

She slumped onto the lid of the chest beneath the window. "You had the right room. Just the wrong girl." She looked at him, pleading in her eyes. "You must believe me!"

"I dinnae know what to believe, lass, 'tis the truth. Eaden had seen ye a year or more ago at court. Do ye no' remember?"

She shook her head. "No. I didn't remember anything until I woke this morning."

"Aye, and ye hit yer head hard when Eaden and I woke ye." He gave her a rueful smile. "Ye were a bit fashed to find two strange men in yer bedroom."

Mary glared at Ranald as she rubbed the back of her head. "When I woke at Scott Castle yesterday morning, I had no memory before that moment. I did not know my name. Everyone told me I was Laird Barde's rebellious daughter. Why would I doubt them?"

Ranald stroked his chin thoughtfully. "But Eaden was satisfied ye were Lady Miriam."

Mary leaned her head tiredly against the windowsill. "Miriam and I look a lot alike. We have the same color hair and are about the same height. But I'm not Miriam. And I cannot be married to Laird Scott!"

Crossing his arms, Ranald sighed mightily. In Eaden's defense, he'd tried to arrange the wedding the proper way, but Laird Barde and his arrogant daughter had shown little interest in obeying their king's command. Not wanting the marriage any more than they did, it had taken the threat of the loss of his title and lands to force Eaden to act. In his haste to seal the marriage, he'd kidnapped his bride, married her, and consummated the marriage in less than a day's time.

His headstrong brother, who often served as herald to their king, and known as a shrewdly intelligent man, had quite possibly made a serious blunder. Ranald cringed to think he'd have to be the one to tell him.

* * *

At Dundonald Castle, Eaden stood before his king, head bowed, teeth clenched as he awaited permission to state his case. Guards lined the walls and colorful courtiers gathered in the corners of the room, eyeing him with interest. A buzz of conversation reached Eaden's ears, but he ignored it, awaiting the king's word. After several moments of silence from the king, he lifted his gaze.

With a languid wave of his arm, King Robert indicated the chair next to him, inviting Eaden to sit.

"What brings ye to Troon this day, Scott?" Formality between them was usually reserved for matters of the crown. The two men, though separated by age and their respective ranks, had long ago become friends as time and again Eaden proved his loyalty to his king. Whenever the two were not discussing the affairs of state, both were relieved to let down their guard.

This was not one of those times. Eaden shook his head and remained standing before the throne, his hands clasped behind his back, his feet planted firmly on the stone floor.

"The marriage is done, Sire," he said formally.

King Robert sighed. "And I suppose ye want yer lands back."

Eaden inclined his head in acknowledgement.

The frown on the king's face showed annoyance for the tactics employed to maintain peace in the Highlands. "Eaden, ye have yer lands and yer title. And now ye have a bride to bind together two prominent clans. 'Twas a simple solution to the interminable feud. Ye know it had to be done."

One corner of his mouth lifted in a smile. "Come, sit ye here and tell me about the wedding. And tell that dog of yers to stand down. She's bristling at me as though she'd like to take a bite out of me and I cannae help think she but reflects her master's thoughts."

Eaden sighed, his anger at last dissipating. He strode to the ample chair at the king's side and flopped tiredly onto its tufted cushions, motioning with a flick of his wrist for Sorcha to settle on the floor next to him.

"I will say ye managed to carry out our wishes rather quickly in the end," King Robert mused.

Eaden sent the king a lopsided grin. "Ye might no' like the way of it, but ye must admit the necessity demanded prompt action."

"Well, tell me the details," the king urged. "How did ye get Barde to agree?"

"'Tis well known he and his daughter fought the marriage. I, myself, wasnae in favor of it, either," Eaden pointed out, but King Robert merely nodded. Like it or not, Eaden knew marriages among nobles were things to be used for gain, not pleasure. He was not the first to marry thusly, nor would he be the last.

"'Twas one of the reasons I raised ye to the rank of earl," King Robert retorted.

Eaden shot him a dark look, knowing full well the rank had come with a price. "When ye declared my lands forfeit unless I came to heel and did as I was told, I decided no' to leave my fate in the hands of the bastard, Barde."

King Robert frowned fiercely. "What have ye done?" he asked, his voice hard.

"I'd tried speaking to Barde and doing things the traditional way. He was less than enthusiastic and mentioned hell freezing over as the only possible wedding date. His daughter was equally certain she'd no' marry into the Scott clan." Eaden shrugged. The feud between their families was generations old. He hadn't wanted a Barde bride, either. "So, I kidnapped her, carried her back to Scott Castle, and we married the same day."

King Robert jerked upright in his chair, shocked surprise clear on his slack-jawed face. "Ye kidnapped her?" He wheezed, unable to inhale a proper breath, and pointed an accusatory finger at Eaden. "Ye actually forced her to marry ye?"

"Nay, Sire. I simply saw 'twas done in a timely manner and without bloodshed. And Barde cannae cry abuse as the consummation was done *after* the vows."

"How certain are ye her father is not, this instant, standing before the walls of Scott Castle, demanding his daughter be returned to him? Are ye trying to promote peace or war between ye?"

Eaden gave an exasperated snort. "He cannae cry foul. I have the papers ye signed. And I have men keeping an eye on Barde." He shifted in his chair uncomfortably. "The marriage is irrevocable. She is now well and truly my wife."

King Robert collapsed back into his chair. "Do ye no' ken the ruinous upheaval yer actions could provoke? 'Tis true I commanded the marriage. I know ye dinnae favor the alliance. But kidnapping the lass is a far cry from having the marriage properly planned and executed!"

The king stewed for a moment, as if consumed in vigorous contemplation. At last he shrugged. "Scott." His voice invoked not Eaden's friend, but Robert II, King of Scotland. "Inasmuch as ye have followed my orders to the letter, if not their actual intent, I hereby commit yer title and land to ye and to yer descendants."

He leaned forward and clasped Eaden's shoulder. "I hope ye dinnae have cause to regret yer hastiness."

Eaden winced. He already did.

Chapter Three

Scott Castle

Mary paced the floor of her room. With her mood swinging alarmingly from horrified to angry and back again in the five days since her marriage, she found it impossible to think about anything other than the terrible deception played upon her.

Ranald said they thought she was Miriam. Mary waved her hands dramatically in the air as she whirled to pace in the opposite direction.

He thought? She snorted in derision at the concept. Nay, the man obviously had *not* thought! He had kidnapped her and she'd received a knot on her head in the process. *Just wait until the laird returns. I shall give him a piece of my mind, make no mistake about it!*

She came to an abrupt halt. With a shiver of apprehension, she remembered Laird Scott's barely leashed fury as he stood at her side before the priest, and the way he'd dragged her from the ceremony afterwards. Would he think her to blame for this? Would he free her from her vows? Or would he hold her responsible for this unintended deception?

The door creaked on its hinges and Mary spun to face the new threat.

"Milady?"

Concern laced the woman's voice and Mary inhaled a short breath of relief. Ina was one of the few people at Scott Castle who seemed to honestly like her. But it wasn't the promise of friendship from the castle's chatelaine that calmed her wildly beating heart. It was the fact Ina wasn't Eaden.

"Milady? The guests have all departed. Would ye come downstairs for yer supper?"

Mary considered the request. She would have to leave her rooms sometime. No one seemed to know how long Laird Scott would be gone and she couldn't very well cower in this chamber until then.

She offered a short nod. "Aye." Whatever lay in store for her, she'd face. Surely there wasn't much worse than what had already occurred.

Ina's face beamed with pleasure. "'Twill do the people good to see their mistress at the table this night." She turned to the two gowns hanging from pegs on the wall. "Would ye care to put on something fresh and pretty?"

Mary gave in to the carefully-worded opinion she appeared tired and rumpled in her present condition, and allowed Ina to help her change her gown. Though she did not want the title of Lady Scott, she'd heard enough of the gossip about her marriage to the laird to know his people already considered Barde's daughter insufferably arrogant.

She would not let them think her intimidated by their judgment.

Ina finished dressing Mary's hair and patted the gleaming chestnut curls as she stood back to survey her work. "Ye've lovely thick hair, milady. But 'tis a wee bit temperamental, aye?" She tweaked a fallen lock back in place, tightening the ribbon holding the mass in place.

Mary sighed. "'Twill be about my shoulders by the time I am halfway down the stairs." She rose from the stool and faced the older woman. "I thank you for your trouble, though."

Ina eyed Mary's dress critically. "Well, ye at least look fresh and bonny, though the dress doesnae do justice to the lady of the castle."

Glancing at the plain brown dress, Mary hastened to reassure her. "Please don't worry. I'm sure it is more than adequate."

Ina smiled at her. "Perhaps when Himself is home he'll find some lovely jewelry to place around yer pretty neck."

Mary winced. The only things Laird Scott would likely want around her neck were his hands. She responded with a faint smile and went downstairs. The murmur of voices in the great hall slowly faded as, one by one, people became aware of her presence.

Mary inclined her head slightly, acknowledging their stares. She strolled to the head table and chose the smaller chair obviously intended for the lady of the castle. If she must bear their scrutiny, she would do so as their mistress.

Ina leveled a cool gaze over the people gathered at the tables and instantly everyone's attention returned to their meal. Satisfied, she nodded to a nearby servant, sending the lass scurrying to the kitchen for fresh food and wine.

"They will get used to ye in the lady's chair." Ina busied herself with a platter of fruit and placed it before Mary. "It has been empty these past years, though many have wished to fill it. Here." She offered the fruit. "This should hold ye 'til the lass returns with yer dinner." Ina poured a goblet of wine, motioning for her to eat.

Mary took a bite of fruit, surprised at how quickly the servant girl returned with a platter of steaming meats and bread. Ina heaped food onto her plate and sat beside her while she ate, chattering about the life of the castle. Mary heard very little, too aware of the curious stares darting at her from all over the room, though they did not linger more than a moment under Ina's protective presence.

Finally, she set her plate back, indicating she had finished. "Ina, I do not wish to interfere with the obviously perfect way you've run Scott Castle." Her comment won the woman's approving smile. "I need some time to adjust. If you would continue with your good work for now, I'm sure we can combine our efforts in the future."

Ina beamed at her friendly words, obviously satisfied she'd not lost her position in the castle. She patted Mary's knee in a motherly fashion. "Ye leave it to me, milady. I'll keep things running smoothly."

Mary nodded, thankful to have Ina's support while she figured a way out of her marriage to Laird Scott. She glanced around the great hall, wishing for something to do to keep her mind from her present troubles. "I'd like to take a walk around the castle, if you don't mind."

Ina stood, a pleased smile on her face. "Of course, milady. There's still some time before dark. I'll have someone show ye aboot." She pursed her lips. "And ye'll need a lady's maid, too." She nodded her head decisively. "Kirsty will do fine."

Mary caught herself before she could protest the need of a maid. Ina called and waved to a young, red-haired girl who stopped her work and hurried over. She gave a hasty curtsy and a swift glance at Mary before turning her attention to Ina.

"Ye'll accompany Lady Scott aboot the castle, lass, then see to her as lady's maid," Ina instructed. Kirsty nodded, but Mary could not tell if her new duties pleased the girl.

Mary rose to her feet. "Thank you, Ina. I'm certain your choice is a good one." She eyed Kirsty, who didn't appear much younger than herself. "What can you tell me about Scott Castle?"

* * *

Mary's soft slippers slid on the bare stone steps worn smooth with the passage of time and the tread of many feet. Following Kirsty through the great hall, she found herself greeted along the way by the cool nods from the castle staff. She sensed their veiled animosity and understood she was an intruder, one of the hated Bardes.

"'Tis the laird's dining room, milady," Kirsty said, bringing Mary's thoughts back to the present. "The laird and his family can eat in private here."

Mary glanced around the room. Weapons and heraldic symbols hung against the stone walls. An enormous fireplace nearly engulfed one end of the room, and numerous candles set in wrought iron holders hung suspended from the high ceiling.

"This is lovely," Mary murmured politely. In truth, though Scott Castle was impressively large and obviously well-fortified, she found herself comparing its almost militant starkness to the elegant courtyards and gardens of Bellecourt Castle. Remembering the comfort the open air had always brought her, she suddenly yearned to be outside and feel the wind on her face.

"Is there a garden in the courtyard here?"

"There's no' a ladies' garden, only one for the kitchen with vegetables and herbs and such. But there is a view of the surrounding hills ye may like."

Mary brightened. "I love being outside. Will you take me there?"

Kirsty nodded. "Aye." She led the way from the laird's private dining room and skirted the great hall where tables were being dismantled and stacked along one wall for the night. Once through the far doorway, she pushed open a wooden door and peered into the stairwell.

She canted a look over her shoulder. "Here, milady. We can go up."

Mary hurried after the maid, at last coming out into the fading light. Overhead, shades of vivid pink splashed across the evening sky, taking her breath away. Pearly gray clouds slipped past on the evening breeze. Kirsty motioned for Mary to follow her and they strode to the chest-high crenellated walls. "'Tis the most beautiful view, milady. But ye must be careful no' to lean over the walls."

Mary flattened her palms on the warm stone and pressed her body as close to the rock as possible in order to see beyond the thick wall. "Why?"

Kirsty shook her head. "'Tis no' safe, milady," she said, her voice tight and apprehensive.

Mary noted the distress etched on the young girl's face, and took a step back from the wall. Kirsty visibly relaxed.

More than worry for safety lay behind Kirsty's unease. "Tell me what bothers you so," Mary addressed her sternly. "I have no wish to jump, if that's what you're afraid of, and the wall is much too high to accidentally fall."

"Oh, milady, 'tis the ghost of Lady Fenella who walks these stairs at night." Kirsty's eyes had widened, her voice now an excited whisper. "She fled her cruel husband, and came to be with her lover, Laird Magnus Scott, many years ago. But her husband followed her here, and though Laird Scott challenged him for the beautiful Lady Fenella, the laird was killed."

She paused for breath. "When Lady Fenella heard her lover was dead, she flew up these stairs, gazed over the parapet and saw him sprawled at the feet of her evil husband. Some say she flung herself over the edge, others say she leaned too far and fainted at the sight of her dead lover. Either way, she died on the bloodstained ground beside him."

Kirsty sighed and pointed past the chapel where a worn stone cast a solitary shadow against the castle wall.

"They were buried in the same grave, milady, there, beneath the stone. Ye can hear her cry of dismay on the stairs late at night, and once I saw something white fluttering off the edge of the wall." Her voice dropped even lower. "Like the fabric of her dress as she fell to her death."

A ragged thrill raced down Mary's spine. Her gaze slid from the maid to the edge of the stone wall. "Truly?"

Privately, she thought the height of the parapet and the thickness of the wall seemed safe enough as long as she did not try climbing on top of the wall — which she certainly had no intention of doing. But the little maid was clearly enthralled by the tale.

Kirsty nodded her head wisely. "Aye. 'Tis said any lass who hears the lady's cry is compelled to follow her to her death."

Mary blinked. "I shall endeavor to not be near the stairs after dark, then."

A cloud passed over the remnants of the sun, absorbing its warmth, and they both shivered at the sudden chill. As quickly as it began, the cloud was gone and the mood lifted.

Kirsty took a cautious step forward and pointed over the wall. "Ye can see the sheep on the hills. There, on the grass, heading toward safety for the night."

Glad for the change in subject, Mary peered at the flocks moving across the fields.

"Why, they look like clouds!" she exclaimed, moving closer to the wall. "And look at the little ones, scampering about!"

"The lambs are born out in the hills, but any who are sickly or injured are cared for in the sheds near the stables. 'Tis noisy, it is, when the lambs are born."

"I suppose so. Oh, they look so soft and white!"

Kirsty shook her head. "They are greasy and full of grass and twigs," she informed Mary. "'Tis glad I am I dinnae shear or card the wool."

They lingered a moment longer as the sun dropped below the hills and the white lambs became dull gray spots against the grass. Finally, Mary turned to her maid. "All right, show me the rest of the castle."

As Kirsty led her from the parapet, Mary's ears couldn't help but strain her ears for a ghostly cry of lost love.

Chapter Four

Scott Castle

He'd only been gone a fortnight, but Eaden knew her. Even in a gown as dusty and drab as those of the work staff, there was no doubting her identity. Though the scarf tied over her hair made her almost as anonymous as the other women around her, there was no mistaking the fact that his bride, the new lady of Scott Castle, was busy cleaning the tapestries in the great hall.

Eaden scowled. But before he could decide if he was more annoyed to see her dressed like a servant or to find her cleaning like one, Ranald captured his attention.

"It appears the immediate danger is past." Ranald motioned to the inner stairway leading to the battlements.

In silence, Eaden followed his brother and climbed the narrow stone steps to the southward vantage point facing the border between the Scott and Bard lands. The mountains sloped in the distance to green hills dotted with clusters of white sheep. Nothing appeared amiss as sheep grazed unconcernedly on the early spring grass.

"Barde has turned back?"

"'Twould seem he has. He raised an army, such as it was, then halted slightly north of Bellecourt where he apparently awaited reinforcements. Other hot-headed soldiers joined him and they headed toward our border where they again stopped for the night." Ranald made a gesture of disgust and Eaden hid a slight smile. He knew his brother's opinion of those who would allow such a minor inconvenience as darkness to hinder their progress.

"Word of Lady Miriam's disappearance is rife all over the Highlands. Ian left to warn ye at the first indication Barde headed this way. We had no way of knowing the spineless bastard would turn tail and return home before he got here."

"Does anyone know why he turned back?" Eaden rubbed at his tense neck muscles.

"Nay. I'm still waiting to hear."

"I had fully expected him to camp outside my walls and protest loudly because I'd kidnapped his daughter, though I dinnae actually imagine he would be so foolish as to attack." Eaden frowned. "He spent time and effort gathering a force, traveled this far, and then turned back. Why?"

"He's less stupid than we'd thought?" Ranald offered with a shrug.

"We'll have to wait and see. Perhaps my *wife* would have an idea about her father's actions." Eaden pushed away from the wall and headed for the stairs. Ranald started visibly at Eaden's statement and raised a hand to check him, but Eaden strode past his brother without stopping. Just the mention of his new wife put him in a decidedly bad mood.

"Ah, Eaden." Ranald's raised voice brought him to a halt.

He turned. "What?"

"There may be a problem with your, er, *wife*."

"I saw her with the servants." Eaden scowled at the memory. "I'll speak to her about her duties."

"Och, 'tis no' the problem."

"Then what is?"

"She's no' yer wife."

"What do ye mean?" Eaden bit out the words. Damn the Barde wench! What kind of trouble had she stirred up in the two weeks he'd been gone?

Ranald squared his shoulders. "I mean, ye married her, but she isnae the woman we thought she was."

"What!"

"The day after ye left for Troon, yer bride came running from yer bedroom all in a panic." He tossed Eaden a wry look. "I wasnae too surprised about that."

The edge to Ranald's voice reminded Eaden of his less-than-sympathetic actions on his wedding night.

"She kept insisting she wasnae Miriam."

"What are ye talking about?" Eaden ground out, his voice thin with impatience.

"She swears she isnae Miriam Barde, but Mary Marsh, Lady Miriam's companion."

Eaden's face flushed hot as he digested the news and considered the ramifications. "The woman is lying. She has fought me tooth and nail from the beginning. The treacherous wench is trying one last time to put an end to this marriage." He glared at Ranald, daring him to disagree.

"You dinnae see or hear her that day," Ranald replied evenly. "She was pale and trembling. I dinnae think she was lying."

Eaden didn't bother answering. He spun on his heel and strode down the stairs and into the castle, looking for the woman turning his life upside down.

* * *

Mary absently tucked a loose curl beneath the scarf she'd donned to keep the dust from her hair, and stared at the tapestry on the wall. Running a hand appreciatively across its surface, she fingered the mingled textures of different threads and stitches used to create such a masterpiece.

A whispered commotion rose behind her and irritation burned her cheeks. If she turned, the stares of the castle servants would dart away as they did every time she entered a room. She'd caught the murmurs of disapproval when she'd appeared dressed in servants' clothing, but she was heartily bored with the insignificant jobs Ina appointed her. Besides, she grew impatient to confront the laird and convince him to send her home, and cleaning tapestries was a fine way to use her time and energy until such a time as he returned to Craigievar.

Heavy footsteps pounded the floor behind her and Mary dragged her gaze from the tapestry as a strong hand clamped down on her shoulder. Startled by the touch, she spun around, her eyes wide as she came face-to-face with Laird Scott himself. Or, rather, face-to-chest, for she'd forgotten what a very large man he was, and she craned her head backward in order to see his face.

Eaden released his grip on her shoulder and folded his arms across his broad chest. "Ranald tells me ye are no' Miriam," he stated bluntly. "Is this the truth?"

This was not how Mary envisioned this conversation with the laird. She'd imagined herself properly dressed, composed and clean, and with a clear sense of what she needed to say. She brushed the loose strand of hair from her face again and struggled to gather her thoughts, which foolishly fled at his unexpected appearance.

"No. I mean, *yes*."

His gaze narrowed and she hastily amended her answer. "*No*, I am not Miriam. *Yes*, it is the truth."

Eaden grabbed her wrist and Mary stumbled as he dragged her behind him. Her anger flared and, planting her feet, gave her arm a twist and a jerk, neatly freeing herself from his grasp. Eaden whirled. He'd clearly not expected her to resist.

The astonishment on his face almost made her smile. Instead, she bit her lip and stood before him, her hands clasped demurely. Her gaze met his with challenge.

Eaden quirked one eyebrow.

"I will not be dragged anywhere in this castle ever again." Her voice held deceptive calm and she was secretly proud it did not tremble. "I am capable of following both verbal and written directions." She lifted her chin. "Choose."

With each servant's ear turned in their direction and all eyes marking their every move, surely he could not fault her for maintaining what dignity she had under the circumstances. A slight grin played about his lips as he inclined his head toward her and motioned for her to precede him. Giving him a wary look at his unexpected capitulation, mocking though it was, Mary swept from the room and up the stairs to the bedroom she'd inhabited for the past two weeks.

She'd obviously made a point with the laird, and she was about to congratulate herself on her small victory when the closing thud of the door behind them triggered her doubts and fears all over again. She took a deep breath and faced him, her thoughts going from uncertain to resolute in the moments it took her to compose herself.

Ranald said the king named Eaden's lands forfeit if he did not wed Miriam, and she was not Miriam. How could things possibly be any worse?

"So, which is it?" His deep voice dragged her from her dire thoughts.

"Which is what?" she stammered, her throat suddenly dry.

"The look on yer face, lass. Ye're either about to faint dead away from fright or preparing yerself to meet yer doom. Which is it?"

She blinked at him, completely taken aback. Scared to death she might be, but she wouldn't disgrace herself no matter what he said about the matter.

Just then, an enormous canine ambled from behind the laird and Mary's mouth fell open in astonishment at the sheer size of the hound. It approached her with a swaying tail and ears perked forward in interest. Mary cautiously held out a hand for the dog to sniff.

Her husband's jaw dropped as the hound leaned forward to inspect Mary's proffered limb. She sniffed every inch of Mary's hand and even a portion of her arm before allowing Mary to rub her chiseled head.

Eaden grunted, his eyebrows raised in surprise. "She doesnae often take to strangers," he admitted gruffly. "Her name is Sorcha. She is usually not far from me."

"*Sor* uh kha," Mary repeated softly as she stroked the dog's fur, marveling at the coarse hair that was crisp, yet surprisingly silky to the touch. "She's beautiful."

Eaden cleared his throat. "Tell me exactly what ye told Ranald."

Mary glanced apprehensively at him, taking note of his forbidding face and piercing dark eyes. Sorcha leaned against her legs, offering unlooked-for strength.

She inhaled sharply. "Miriam and I grew up almost as sisters. She asked me to sleep in her bed that night. I don't know what mischief she was about, but she said she would explain the next morning. We look enough alike, especially in the dark and tucked under the covers, and she'd told her father she wasn't feeling well. I was supposed to be there in case he decided to look in on her."

"And who would ye have me believe ye are?"

Mary flushed. Obviously, he didn't trust her and she was growing weary of explaining herself over and over again. "I am Mary Marsh, Miriam's companion. You can ask Laird Barde. Miriam is still there."

Eaden moved a step away. "Actually, Lady Miriam isnae at Bellecourt." He slowly faced Mary, his eyes searching her face. "Word is she left Bellecourt to be married. But no one can say where, or to whom."

He advanced on her. Mary's heart leapt in her chest as she took a hasty step backward.

Sorcha whined and Eaden's face darkened. "Two weeks ago I brought ye here and married ye at the insistence of the king," he growled. "Three days later Barde mustered his soldiers and advanced on the border, where he waited for reinforcements to join him. As my men remained on alert for them to cross the border, he abruptly changed his mind and went home. Now my men tell me he is upset with his daughter's marriage. Can ye tell me why?"

"I have no idea," Mary whispered. "Truly I don't."

"If ye are no' Miriam, why did Barde ride on the border?"

Mary stared helplessly into his furious eyes and wracked her brain for any clue to Miriam's or her father's actions. "Though we were close, it is true Miriam had been secretive lately. I can only assume she's met someone Laird Barde wouldn't approve of and decided to marry him."

"Someone less desirable than myself?" Eaden's voice dripped sarcasm.

Mary tossed her head, her patience with this interrogation growing thin. "Laird Barde thought Miriam was perfect. There would not be many men he would approve of as a husband for her. Miriam had her own standards as well." She lifted her chin. "Neither approved of you."

Eaden sighed. "Is there any way ye can prove who ye are?"

"Without returning to Bellecourt?" Mary shook her head. "No one here knows me, Laird," she reminded him with a frown. "They all believe I am Miriam. You'll have to accept my word."

He eyed her narrowly. "And if I decide to believe ye, what d' ye expect to happen?"

Mary's heart raced, but she replied bravely, "I expect you to have our marriage annulled and send me home."

"Annul the marriage and send ye home? To Bellecourt?" Eaden repeated, surprise coloring his voice.

She nodded emphatically. "Of course."

"If ye are Miriam's companion, then Barde, by turning back from the border, has indicated ye're no' worth coming after. Think ye have a home there still?"

"I believe so, yes." Mary willed her voice to remain firm. But to know she meant nothing to Laird Barde and hear it told to her as fact was disheartening. What *would* be her place at Bellecourt if she returned?

"If ye are Miriam, yer father has gone home to sulk, leaving ye here with me."

"You have given me an impossible task." Mary stomped her foot, frustrated and dismayed in equal measure. "I cannot prove anything from here. I am trying to be honest with you and you are being so difficult!"

Eaden shrugged. "Ye have every reason to lie to me. 'Tis well known ye swore ye wouldnae be forced into marriage with me. And now ye are, forbye, and I know ye will try to find a way out of it. 'Twas a good effort. Ranald is all but convinced of yer story. But until I have proof, ye are my wife and will behave as such."

Mary bristled. "What do you mean by that?"

"Ye willnae dress as a servant and become one of them." His derisive glance raked her dusty, threadbare clothing.

She lifted her chin mutinously. "I will not sit around all day and do nothing!"

"Then have Ina give ye duties befitting the lady of the castle."

"You've married me!" Mary raged, furious about many things, and now being criticized for her hard work. "You'll simply have to put up with me!"

*　*　*

Eaden eyed his wife, astounded and somewhat impressed despite himself that she hadn't backed down. Her eyes flashed and her chest heaved with anger and he felt an unexpected stirring for this woman who'd caused him such trouble.

"You have other wifely duties, too," Eaden reminded her as his body responded to her nearness. He flicked his glance to the sturdy bed a few feet behind her.

Mary drew back, her eyes wide. "No!" Her voice filled with more than a little dread.

Eaden raised an eyebrow at her. "Ye think to defy me?"

She fanned her hands out behind her and carefully backed away from the bed's proximity. "No. We cannot get an annulment from the church if we . . ." Her gaze slid to the bed before snapping back to him.

"But we already have," Eaden pointed out. He advanced until he stood mere inches from her, and breathed deeply. The scent of flowers filled his senses, and he ached to feel the warmth of her skin. But she dropped her gaze and refused to meet his look.

"That doesn't count," she replied, stubbornly studying the stone floor at her feet.

Eaden laughed aloud. "It doesnae? Explain this to me."

Mary cut her gaze to his. "You didn't know who I was. You can still request an annulment for being tricked into marriage with me."

"So now *I* was tricked into marrying *ye*?"

"You can view it that way. I'm sure it was an accident."

A pulse beat frantically in her throat. He wondered what would happen if he touched her. Would she swoon, repulsed? Or would he feel the fine response her body promised? He sidled closer and she quickly retreated.

"What if ye carry my child?" he murmured, noting the way her breathing quickened, her breasts rising and falling beneath the thin fabric of her gown.

"No! I want an annulment. You cannot be so cruel as to force me to bear your child just to keep me here."

"Well, ye can try telling the priest who married us ye'll no' have me. He'll be shocked and completely unsympathetic to ye. We are married, lass, whether ye are Miriam or no.'"

"You cannot want me," she stormed. "You didn't want Miriam, so how could you want me?"

Eaden lifted his gaze to the window, staring blindly at the twist of light on the river beyond the castle walls. With no answer to her question, he searched for a compromise to gain some time until he could decide the matter.

If she was not Miriam, it was possible King Robert would be unhappy with the results of taking matters into his own hands. Perhaps if he left her alone until her fate was decided, it would be easier to appease the king. Accident or not, they now faced a long life together.

Mary or Miriam? Whoever she was, what could be the harm in giving her a little time to come to terms with her new life? He hadn't wanted her before and he certainly couldn't explain why he wanted her now.

He brought his attention back to the woman before him. "How long until ye know if ye are with child?"

She turned a startled gaze on him. "I don't know, m'laird." Mary seemed clearly puzzled by his question.

Eaden found he liked the pure green color of her eyes that reminded him of the mountains in spring. He frowned at the thought. He was a practical man, not one given to comparing women's eyes to lush, grass-covered hills.

With difficulty, he dragged his attention to her answer and sighed, posing his next question bluntly, anticipating her maidenly reaction. "How long until yer next woman's bleed?"

Mary's mouth dropped open, clearly shocked. "I cannot . . ."

"Days? Weeks?"

A fiery blush now stained her cheeks. "A week, or less."

Eaden nodded. "I can wait that long."

Chapter Five

Eaden perused the great hall but did not see his wife. On his first night home in nearly two weeks, he had worked at settling what business was required of him. Yet he'd been hard-pressed to think much beyond the fact he didn't know his wife's name. Damn the wench! He had enough problems without fighting with her about her identity.

Stretching his arms above his head, he sighed deeply. If the state of the damped fireplace indicated the late hour, he could probably safely assume his bride, whoever she was, had already gone to bed.

A lazy smile curved his lips. Now, there was something to think about. Would she still be in his rooms? Or had she insisted on her own? His tiredness slid away and he pushed himself from the table with a squeak of wood on the stone floor.

"Off to bed?" Ranald glanced up, his arm draped loosely about the shoulders of a young widow who had taken his fancy a few weeks earlier.

Eaden nodded and idly wondered if the attachment between Ranald and the widow would last. He could certainly think of worse arrangements. His own, for instance.

His steps dragged as he ascended the stairs. Prepared for a life of contempt and outright loathing from the wife he'd been forced to wed, he'd not considered a pleasurable alternative. Though he hadn't expected smiles and kisses on his return today, neither could he have imagined this new twist. He'd been surprised by her counterattack to the marriage, though he admitted it was brilliant.

Coming to a stop at the closed door to his rooms, he tested the latch, relieved to find it unsecured. Despite his current, dangerous mood regarding the possible treachery of his new wife, kicking in the door would have been difficult. *Damned if I'll let her run me out of my own bedroom!*

Nor was he about to have where he or his wife slept gossiped about by the servants. He gritted his teeth and shoved the door open. With only the slightest moan of protest, the heavy panel swung open and he eased inside.

The banked embers on the hearth cast a warm glow around the room, illuminating the bed and his wife's small form tucked beneath the covers. Her skin glowed like porcelain lit from within and her silky hair spilled into the shadows. He frowned. He had promised he would not touch her until she knew if she carried his child. It gave him a week to determine if she was in fact Miriam, and what to do with her if her identity proved otherwise.

Eaden turned abruptly from the bed and strode to the bathing chamber, stripping away his clothes with more force than necessary. He splashed cold water on his face and reached for a piece of linen to wipe the moisture away.

With the cloth at his nose, he stopped, sniffing experimentally. He drew back in surprise. It smelled like flowers! Flicking his gaze across the table, he noticed the bar of soap in a dish beside the basin. He picked it up, noting the soft texture, and sniffed again. Flowers!

The scent was subtle, but warm and enticing. And it belonged to his wife. Absently, he used the damp cloth to wipe the travel dust and grime from the rest of his body as he remembered his conversation with Ranald earlier in the day.

"How certain are ye the lass ye married is Lady Miriam?" his brother had asked.

It hadn't been a difficult question. As a herald for the king, it was very important for Eaden to pay attention to people, the details of their lives and actions. The futures of kings could depend on his observations. He had seen Lady Miriam once before; not an introduction, but he'd had reason to ask who she was.

Miriam herself was the difficult part of the question.

"I remember the lass. How could I no' notice her?" he'd retorted.

Even now he recalled the shine of gold-shot chestnut hair, the slender form that had garnered his initial admiration.

Ranald had grinned. "What did ye think of her, then?"

"I dinnae like her."

"Ye dinnae?" Ranald had scratched his head, his raised eyebrows indicating his surprise.

"Och, she was lovely, to be sure. Quite a feast for the eyes. But she made no attempt to hide her dislike of me." He'd shrugged. "Lovely as the lass was, she had a mean spirit that dinnae suit her fair form."

"Was there a companion with her? Is it possible your lady wife is speaking the truth?"

Eaden had frowned at his brother's query. Anything was possible. He'd stayed at Edinburgh Castle for three days awaiting King Robert's pleasure, with ample time to observe the people gathered there. The king had hunted each day and Eaden had ridden out with him and his retinue, returning in the evenings to find Lady Miriam surrounded by more than her share of eager young swains. Try as he might, he could not say whether another lass amid the young ladies could have been Lady Miriam's companion.

He mentally compared his memory of Lady Miriam with the young woman he'd married. Her looks were as striking as the girl he remembered, but he could not imagine Lady Miriam toiling amongst his servants, as he'd seen his wife doing earlier today. He could not align the new Lady Scott with the shallow, haughty young woman who'd turned his head and his stomach at court that day.

Eaden snorted. His king couldn't have done him a greater disservice than to demand he wed the conceited witch, no matter how beautiful. Peace between the clans be damned. He wanted peace in his own house.

With a muttered curse, Eaden shook himself from his reverie and opened the chamber door. He stared across the room where his wife lay peacefully sleeping, and strode to the bed for a closer look.

She faced him, and stretched against the back of her legs lay Sorcha, contentedly snoozing amid the soft bedding. Eaden sighed in irritation. With the long-legged deerhound sprawled across the mattress, the pair left precious little space for him to sleep.

"Move, Sorcha." He snapped his fingers in command at the hound. Sorcha cracked one eye open in disgruntled response before returning to her slumber. Eaden shoved at the dog's haunch and Sorcha twitched the leg once in response. With a scowl, he grabbed the hound by her collar and attempted to drag her from the bed. She was a large beast and her uncooperative weight impressive, but Eaden would not countenance her usurping his place on his own bed.

"Damn it, Sorcha! Move yer carcass!"

He tugged at the beast. She groaned and lurched to her feet. Giving her master a long-suffering glare, Sorcha slipped to the floor and padded to her rug beside the fireplace.

Disturbed by the commotion on the bed, Mary rolled onto her back, flinging one arm across the mattress, but did not wake.

Another sigh of frustration hissed through his lips. As wide as the bed was, Mary now managed to take up more than her fair share, leaving only a sliver of mattress available to him. When had retiring for the night become such a difficult task?

Eaden stalked to the far side of the bed. Leaning over, he grasped Mary's arm, intending to move it enough to allow him to take his share of the bed. A whiff of flowers drifted up, teasing his senses, and his resolve took a direct hit. What a fine thing it would be, to simply hold her against him during the night. Her scent intrigued him and he rather fancied falling asleep, breathing in the heady aroma.

Surely he could just hold her. His promise was only to not make love to her, after all. Easing into the bed, he grabbed the blanket, pulling it to his waist before reaching for Mary. But Sorcha would not be denied her new infatuation. As Eaden hesitated, she leapt back onto the bed, burrowing herself between her master and her new mistress.

Reluctantly conceding defeat, Eaden at last fell asleep with the scent of hound in his nostrils.

Chapter Six

Ranald tapped lightly on Eaden's bedroom door and strolled in without waiting for an answer, as was his wont. It was a rare enough day he caught his brother still abed, but the sight that met his eyes this morning stopped him dead in his tracks. He hovered between outright laughter and leaving the room immediately. The absurdity of it all won, and he laughed.

"Wha . . .?" Mary's eyes flew open at the sound. Blinking owlishly in sleepy surprise, she sat upright, clutching the thin blanket to her chest. On the other side of the bed, Eaden came awake with a jerk and a muttered curse. Sorcha snored gently, sprawled between them, undisturbed by the tableau around her.

Mary tried to scramble to her feet, but the hem of her night shift caught beneath more than a hundred pounds of slumbering dog, and she sat abruptly, unable to rise further. Ranald's first instinct was to rush to her to keep her from falling off the bed, but before he could take more than a single step, Mary slid off the edge and onto the floor. Her shift rode high beneath her arms as it refused to pull free from beneath Sorcha's weight. Ranald turned on his heel and seated himself a safe distance away in the chair beside the fireplace.

Eaden cursed loudly as he rolled to his feet. He usually slept naked, and last night was no exception. Mary averted her eyes, her pale skin flaming pink to the very tips of her ears.

Unable to completely stifle another laugh, Ranald snorted as his brother stomped across the floor to the private bathing chamber. As soon as he disappeared through the portal, Mary struggled to her feet, tugging the hem of her night shift from beneath the slumbering hound.

Ranald waited until Mary straightened her clothing before he spoke, a broad grin on his face and good-natured humor in his voice. "Should I assume the two of ye have made amends?"

Mary's look of horror sobered him, and he leaned forward, his forearms braced on his knees. "I'm sorry, lass. I dinnae mean to intrude. But seeing the two of ye together this morning was no' what I expected." His lips curved wryly. "I would have waited until Eaden bid me enter had I thought ye'd be in here with him."

"I've slept here every night for the past two weeks. I didn't give it a thought when I went to bed last night." With her brow wrinkled and her lips in a downward curve, Mary looked decidedly unhappy. "Laird Scott was much later than I getting to bed."

"Och, the two of ye'll work it out," Ranald offered kindly, relaxing in his chair. "Ye'll see."

Mary slumped on the edge of the mattress. "But I don't want to work it out, Ranald. I want to go home."

"I'd prefer it if ye dinnae voice yer displeasure outside this room." Eaden's voice rumbled with annoyance as he paced into the room, settling his breeches about his hips. He shot his bride a glare that made her flush. But her eyes narrowed with visible defiance.

"You agreed to wait." Mary reminded him.

Eaden came to a halt and regarded her with a blank stare. "Wait for what?"

Mary huffed and frowned at Eaden. Intrigued, Ranald leaned forward in his chair, unwilling to miss a word.

"You agreed to . . . to not sleep with me," she blurted. Her face flushed anew.

"I dinnae touch ye last night!" Eaden growled.

"But what will the servants say if they know you slept in here with me?"

"I dinnae give a damn what the servants say!" Eaden turned an even darker shade of red than his bride, obviously out of sorts with whatever agreement they'd reached between them.

"Of course ye do," Ranald interjected from the relative safety of his chair. "'Tis why ye slept in here with her and no' in one of the empty rooms down the hall."

Eaden rounded on Ranald, waving furiously at the door. "Get out!" he bellowed.

With a shrug, Ranald rose to his feet and left the room, closing the door softly behind him.

* * *

"If you sleep in here with me, the servants will assume . . ." Mary continued as soon as Ranald was out of the room. Her gaze dropped. "We cannot get an annulment if everyone thinks we've . . ." She glanced back at Eaden, a defiant look on her face. "Then I'll move out!"

"Ye'll do no such thing!" Eaden thundered, his face taut with the strain of keeping his anger in check. "I'll no' be dictated to by a hysterical wife or a castle full of servants!"

"You promised!"

Eaden's eyes darkened as he slowly advanced on his wife. Mary held her ground, clenching her hands into fists.

"'Tis not the sleeping ye're afraid of," he retorted scornfully. He stopped before her, his chest nearly touching hers. "This is what frightens ye."

Before she could take a step away, his lips swooped down and claimed hers. His hand caught her waist, and he pulled her against him, ignoring her half-smothered gasp, determined to kiss her thoroughly.

But as her hand braced against him in protest, he changed his intent. He'd meant the kiss as a demonstration of his frustration, and in denial of his growing attraction for the woman he'd been forced to marry. Instead, he gentled the kiss, coaxing her to participate as he nipped gently at her bottom lip. From her response to their marriage, he realized she'd likely never been kissed before, and the barrier she'd naturally formed against him after their wedding night would be difficult to overcome. Yet, tension ebbed from her body as Mary began to respond, her hands sliding up his chest to grip the front of his shirt.

For a moment, Eaden savored the weight of her against his chest. He lifted his head, reluctantly ending the kiss, and gazed at her face, sliding one hand gently across her cheek. She blinked at him, and before he could banish his satisfied grin, her muscles tensed as strength flowed through her. She shoved hard against him and he released her, though he didn't let her retreat further than an arm's length from him.

"That, milady, is what ye fear." His voice rumbled deep, the vibration sliding demandingly through his belly.

Mary's eyes flashed. "That, Laird, is what you promised to keep in check!"

"Aye," he agreed. "But only for a week or so."

"I'll not stay here a moment longer. I will not stay if I am not with child." Mary's cheeks flamed.

Eaden twitched his gaze to the bed and back at her. "Would ye care to increase the odds?"

This time Mary jerked from his grasp. "No!" she shouted, her frightened look destroying his hope she'd trust him.

His lips curled in self-disgust. "I said ye had no more to fear from me," he flared. "I willnae force ye."

Mary's look of disbelief broke the last vestiges of his control and he pushed past her without another glance. He threw open the door and kept going, not pausing as the door slammed back into its frame with a resounding crash.

Chapter Seven

Gusting wind whipped Mary's hair from her braid as she leaned against the parapet, gazing silently at the clouds roiling darkly in the distance. Her hand absently stroked the silken head on level with her waist, and Sorcha whimpered softly at her side.

"Oh, Sorcha." Mary sank to her knees and hugged the dog tightly, feeling the strong, muscled body wriggle against her. The dog's pink tongue licked her cheek and Mary gave a slight laugh as she averted her face. Sitting on the rough stone floor, she leaned against the big hound, her arms wrapped firmly around Sorcha's warm, furry body.

"You're the only one here who likes me." She sighed. "Well, Ranald isn't too bad, and Ina thinks, since the laird married me, I must be acceptable." She gave another sigh. "I wish I could fly away from here like a bird. No barriers to keep me so far from home." She stared across the hills, imagining the distant walls of Bellecourt Castle. Sorcha sat perfectly still beside her, poised as though listening to her mistress's unhappy words.

"Ye are the most fascinating young woman I have ever encountered."

Mary gasped and snapped her head around at the unexpected sound. Sorcha crooned softly, looking anxiously between her master and her new mistress. Laird Scott leaned a shoulder negligently against the doorway at the head of the stairs, his arms crossed over his chest, an inscrutable look on his face.

"What do you mean?" Mary inadvertently tightened her grip on Sorcha who licked her arm in response. She relaxed her hand and stroked the dog's head, grateful to have a reason to turn from Eaden's gaze.

"Ye argued with me this morning like a fallen angel, and this afternoon I find ye looking like a homeless waif with yer arms wrapped around *my* dog."

Sorcha thumped her tail on the ground. Mary buried her face against the dog's furry neck.

He sighed. "At least ye don't appear ready to leap from the parapet."

Intrigued, she glanced back at Eaden. "Do many Scott brides jump?"

"Och, so ye've heard the ghost stories?"

Mary nodded. "The castle seems to have a rather sinister reputation."

"Aye. The worst."

"And what of its laird?" she dared to ask. "What is his reputation?"

Eaden appeared surprised, but not angry at her question. "Until ye, lass? Sterling."

She stiffened. "What have I done?"

"Och, not specifically ye, lass. Presumptuous arrogance and bitter impatience would appear to be my downfall."

"I'd have thought a king's herald . . ." She paused, biting back the retort.

"Ye thought I'd have the patience of a saint?" He gave a short, mirthless laugh. "Even a saint grows weary if the provocation is great enough."

"So, why did the king think marrying you to Laird Barde's daughter would bring peace between the clans?"

"Apparently King Robert has a malicious sense of humor," Eaden quipped. He sighed and pushed away from the wall, rubbing the back of his neck wearily. "There was one too many complaints from Laird Barde against Clan Scott. All untrue, unless ye count defending yer people a crime. The king decided an alliance between the clans was long overdue, so he bade me wed Barde's daughter."

"That isn't me," Mary said quietly.

"So ye've stressed."

They were silent for a few moments. Mary could plainly tell Laird Scott was not ready to believe she was not Miriam, and she grew weary of trying to convince him otherwise. She bit her lip, refusing to re-enter the argument.

"Does the view please ye?"

"Yes," Mary replied, glad for the change in conversation. She rose to her feet and leaned over the chest-high stone wall. "It is beautiful from up here. It's as though I can see forever, almost all the way to Bellecourt."

Eaden didn't respond to the jibe and left the doorway to join her at the wall. "What did ye see from the parapet at Bellecourt?"

"Miriam and I were not allowed on the walls. 'Twas for our safety. We spent our time in the beautiful gardens beyond the kitchen. I've never seen a view like this before."

"If ye promise to no' jump, I'll instruct the men to allow ye up here whenever ye wish—provided we aren't at war, of course," he added dryly.

A sense of dread crept over Mary, capturing her as fully as the walls of a cage. "You'd prevent me from coming here?"

Eaden shrugged. "As Lady Scott, ye have the complete run of the place. But I'll no' have ye taking advantage of my men and trying to slip past them. 'Twould put them in a verra bad light."

Mary dropped her gaze. "As I do not know where Bellecourt lies, beyond somewhere south of here, I have nowhere to go until you release me." She spoke with quiet dignity.

"Ah, Mairi, lass, yer home is here, now."

Mary shivered when he called her *Mairi*. It seemed a softened version of her name, a Scottish compromise between *Mary* and *Miriam*, full of secret longing the way it fell from his lips.

She gulped a breath against the unexpected heat sliding through her and considered a more pressing problem: her unwillingness to admit no one from Bellecourt seemed to care what had happened to her. It had to have occurred to someone—Miriam, at least—that something dreadful had befallen her. How was it possible she could disappear without someone noticing?

Her heart had leapt to hear Laird Barde had ridden toward Craigievar, and it had eaten at her ever since to know he'd turned back. What had happened? Where was Miriam? Surely her friend missed her.

Mary settled a direct gaze on Eaden. "I don't want to live here."

"I know ye dinnae," he replied evenly. "But we've a good bit to sort out before we decide what's to be done. I'd ask yer promise to no' leave the castle without an escort."

Mary thought about his request. Not knowing Scott Castle's location meant she would have difficulty simply starting down the road for Bellecourt. Add her fear of horses and the fact she'd never learned to ride, and thoughts of escape were hopelessly impossible.

Surely the wait wouldn't be so bad if he allowed her up here. The high stone walls of the castle closed in like a prison, the parapet her only chance to breathe the crisp, clean air. It wasn't as though she would be here forever.

She nodded. "I promise to keep to the castle grounds except with an escort." And the agreement did not sound like a death-knell.

* * *

For the next few days, Mary managed to keep out of Eaden's way during her waking hours. She maintained at least the appearance of domestic civility by joining him at mealtimes. But she didn't act like a new wife, or a wife of any kind, for that matter, and the servants' quick eyes missed nothing.

Mary's cheeks heated to see furtive looks as she seated herself at the table. She watched other men and women greet each other with quick kisses or a touch of easy familiarity. She shared no visible warmth with Laird Scott, but a part of her longed for the little intimacies. Yet she refused to consider such with the formidable man who bided his time until it was clear if she carried his child or not.

Uneasy in this limbo, Mary endured his presence in her bed at night, Sorcha between them, and tried not to flinch when his hand touched hers as he passed her a dish at the table.

A stir rose among the diners as the door to the hall opened and Ian and two other soldiers hurried in. Sending his two companions to the far table with a nod, Ian approached the head table. Ranald, seated at Eaden's right, scooted his chair enough for Ian to sidle close to his laird. Mary, on Eaden's other side, strained to hear the low-pitched voice of the laird's trusted soldier.

"'Tis said Laird Barde's daughter has married du Melville's youngest son. Barde realized the morning after your, er, wedding, his daughter went missing." Ian cut his eyes to Mary, who placed a piece of meat into her mouth with a calmness she certainly did not feel. "He assumed you had kidnapped her, and mustered his soldiers to ride on Scott Castle. But before he crossed the border, he received word his daughter was no' here, but at Melville Manor, and he withdrew to Bellecourt."

Eaden said nothing. He listened to Ian's report and finally nodded his head. Ian took his leave and settled at the table with his men as dinner concluded in a leisurely fashion, but Mary's hands trembled as she set her goblet down, her appetite a thing of the past. Her eyes met her husband's steady gaze, wondering how this would end. She had news of her own she'd yet to share with him, and she quaked with anticipation.

"Take my hand." He spoke quietly as he rose to his feet. Caught unawares, Mary lifted her hand, but stopped, afraid to touch him, remembering only too clearly how she'd succumbed to his kiss just days before. Noticing her hesitation, Eaden smoothly covered her lapse by catching her fingers and bringing them to his lips before tucking her cold hand into the bend of his elbow. He laid one of his own hands over hers, trapping it firmly when she would have pulled away.

With a hooded look he urged, "Please, come with me." He stepped away, all but pulling Mary to her feet. Aghast to realize she'd almost refused his politely worded invitation in front of everyone in the room, Mary rose and followed him to a small room upstairs with Ranald and Ian close on their heels.

* * *

The men entered the room, Mary in their midst. Ranald closed the door behind them with a soft snick of the latch. With exaggerated politeness, Eaden motioned for his wife to be seated in one of the chairs. He took his place next to the window, his face in shadows, his expression carefully blank.

He wondered what Mary would say about Ian's information. Since she'd first denied being Lady Miriam, she'd surprised him with the strength she'd shown these past few days. He doubted a lady's companion had much reason to use her brain or backbone, and even less opportunity to form her own opinions. Mairi was proving to be an enigma.

He'd been fully prepared for daily fights and tearful accusations from Lady Miriam after the wedding. Not a life he'd looked forward to, and an expectation that had unfortunately colored his treatment of his wife immediately after the ceremony.

Marriage to a lady's companion didn't appeal to him, either, for he couldn't imagine himself bound for life with what he'd always considered to be such a mousy creature. But Mary's bouts of spirit intrigued and pleased him. He almost looked forward to this.

As the silence lengthened, Mary glanced at each of his men in turn, but he knew they waited for him to speak. He observed how his wife studiously avoided his eyes, her bottom perched on the edge of the chair as if ready to flee.

"So." Eaden spoke conversationally, noting the way Mary jumped at the sound of his voice. "Miriam Barde has married du Melville's youngest son." He shifted his weight and crossed his arms. "What do ye suppose her da thinks of the union?"

"I'm guessing he'd rather she'd married ye," Ranald offered. The men in the room nodded, knowing only too well what the prospects were for du Melville's fourth son. The boy and his lavishly spoiled new wife would be hard-pressed for money unless Barde took pity on them and offered his home or at least a generous dowry for his daughter.

Eaden shot his brother a quelling glare. "How do ye think Lady Miriam managed to marry a penniless younger son?" He turned back to his wife, noting her pale face. Her green eyes shone with apprehension, and he almost reached to smooth the worry lines from her forehead, stopping himself just in time.

"I would suppose," Mary began, taking a deep breath. "I would suppose she met him about six months ago when she and Laird Barde visited with the king at Edinburgh. I did not attend, so I cannot be sure."

"Ye cannae be sure?" Eaden mocked. Mary scowled and he quickly hid a grin at her show of temper.

"Several months ago Miriam and her father attended King Robert at Edinburgh." Mary's words slowed as realization dawned. Her mouth opened in an 'O' of surprise. Eaden tore his gaze from his wife's soft lips and spotted the look of astonishment on Ian's face.

"And when you kidnapped me from Miriam's bed — she must have planned to run away with him that night! There is the proof you require, am I correct?"

"*If* Lady Miriam is where Ian says she is, and *if* she has married du Melville's youngest son, then, perhaps there is some proof to what ye say," Eaden allowed.

Mary bounced on her seat, clenching her hands in her lap. "You know there is!"

Eaden shrugged and turned to Ian. "Well," he drawled, "what d' ye think? If yer information is true, it seems my lady wife is no' Lady Miriam Barde, but Mary Marsh, milady's companion."

With a glance from Eaden to his anxious bride, then to Ranald who merely raised his eyebrows and offered no help, Ian's face flushed. "What is it ye ask, Laird? My information is accurate."

Eaden pushed away from his stance by the window and crossed to Mary's chair, casually resting a hand along the wooden back. "My king bade me marry Lady Miriam in order to keep my lands." He stared at his captain, not bothering to hide the sour look on his face. "What would ye say aboot it?"

Ian struggled for the right words, but his innate honesty won out. He blurted, "I think I'd say ye've married the wrong lass."

Chapter Eight

They were alone in the room. Mary watched uneasily as Eaden paced the floor. Ian's words, true though they were, had echoed endlessly in the room until she wanted to scream. The tension nearly unbearable, it had taken a mere nod of his head to send both Ranald and Ian bolting for the door. His frown kept Mary rooted to her seat.

She fidgeted as the walls closed in on her. Eaden's slow, booted footsteps echoed on the stone floor, the only sound in the room except for the dizzying tattoo of her racing heart. Fear and relief washed headily through her. She wanted the man to stop his pacing and tell her he would put the actions in motion for a divorce, but the scowl on his face dried her mouth and she could not speak.

"So, what do ye propose I do with ye now?" Eaden asked, his voice deceptively soft. With a start, Mary realized he stared broodingly at her. Which was better than snarling at her in anger, but it gave her little insight into his thinking.

"Allow me to return to Bellecourt." Thankfully, her voice held only a faint tremble.

Eaden snorted his opinion on her suggested course of action, and Mary bristled. "I am of no further use to you." Growing anger gave her strength. "You brought me here under false pretenses, and now you've been found out. You should have the grace to at least admit you were wrong and send me home!"

"Send ye home? Any man would argue ye are home now, milady." Mockery colored his voice. "What would yer prospects be at Bellecourt? Is there some smitten young swain who would take ye now, another man's woman?"

"You twice-cursed idiot!" Mary raged, bolting from her chair. "'Tis not as if I had willingly taken a lover! I know other men have divorced their wives! And it's not as though I carry your child . . ."

"Ye are no' with child?" Eaden demanded, speaking over her indignation.

"No," she replied shortly, her cheeks burning to share the intimate detail with him. "I have not had time to speak privately with you yet. I knew this morning I . . ." Her voice trailed off in embarrassment. She looked away, but not before she thought she saw a look of disappointment cross his face. *How could that be?*

She dared to turn back. "Were you hoping I was?"

Eaden did not answer, but his glower told her she hit closer to the truth than he would admit. When had she become adept at reading his scowls?

"Why?" she asked. "Why would you want a child from me?"

Eaden looked away. "I need a son," he stated bluntly.

"Would it be so hard to find someone else who would make you a good wife—a good mother for your child?"

"What qualities would that be?" Eaden took a step toward her, but Mary swallowed hard and held her ground. "Tell me, lass. What makes a good wife?"

She grabbed at the first thing that came to her mind. "You need someone of your social status. And someone who knows how to run the castle and deal with the servants." She stared boldly at him. "What will the king say about me?"

"King Robert will be fashed," Eaden admitted with a tight shrug. "But we are wed now and so is Miriam." He frowned. "Ye were raised with her. Surely ye know about running a household."

"You know nothing of me." Quiet dignity colored her reply. "Nothing at all."

Eaden advanced on her, step by slow step. Mary's breathing quickened but she dared not flinch or back away. She couldn't bear to show her cowardice, not when she stood to gain her release from this marriage if she remained strong. She would let nothing stop her bid for freedom from a life she'd never asked for. Nothing.

He touched an errant curl against her cheek, cupping it in his hand as though weighing the silken heaviness. Warring with her intent to stand and force the issue, every instinct now screamed at her to run. But a strange lassitude came over her, holding her in place, and she swayed slightly into his caress.

"Ye are beautiful," he breathed into her ear as he stroked her hair. His other hand cupped her chin and he eased her face up.

Mary blinked. "I am not beautiful," she corrected him with firm assurance.

"Ye need look in the mirror, milady. Ye have the greenest eyes I've ever seen, and yer hair has strands of gold running through it."

"I do?" she stammered. "It does?"

Eaden's lips curved and a slow smile creased his face. "Aye. And there's this intriguing little cleft in yer chin." He ran a thumb across the spot under discussion. Her head jerked as she tried to see what he was talking about. "And yer lips are soft and full," he whispered, moving his thumb to rub gently across her mouth.

Heat slid through her body. Her lips parted, tingled with sensation. She found herself mesmerized by the expression on his face, so close to hers, the way his eyes darkened and his nostrils flared as though drinking in her scent. The instinct, which a moment earlier urged her to flee, now kept her rooted to the spot.

To her surprise, she found she wanted to touch him, wanted him to touch her. The muscles in her arms trembled as she fought the unfamiliar desire to twine herself around him. The same instinct urged her to press against him, to open her mouth further, to receive his kiss . . .

No! Her mind protested as his lips touched hers and stole the very breath from her. She did not want to fall under his spell, for she knew full well where his kisses could lead, and the memory of her wedding night echoed ever fresh in her mind. Though she'd become used to his presence and his occasional, casual touch, this was so much more dangerous.

His hands slid around her to pull her close against him, and she gasped as she made contact with the length of his hard body. He deepened the kiss, urging her to respond to him, and for a moment she did. Her hands slid between them, over his shoulders, slipping her fingers through the soft hair at the nape of his neck. But as he splayed his palms over her bottom, pulling her tightly against him, she stiffened at the intimate touch and pushed away.

"No!" Her eyes widened as she dodged his grasp. "I cannot do this again!"

"Do what?" Eaden clutched her arm as she tried to break away.

"I cannot wait another month to see if I am with child."

"Then, stand still for a moment, damn it!" he growled between clenched teeth.

Still reeling from the shock of her response to his caresses, Mary ceased her struggling and stood quietly. She released a shuddering breath as she mustered her flagging resources and stepped back. Glancing up, she caught Eaden staring at her heaving bosom.

"Stop looking at me like that!" she snapped in irritation. Eaden ignored her and closed the gap between them, sweeping a tumbled lock of her hair from her shoulder with a brush of his hand. Mary jerked sideways at the unexpected contact and his fingers trailed across the tops of her breasts. He caught the delicate links of the chain she wore around her neck and tugged on the necklace, pulling a pendant from the depths of her gown. He sent her a wry look as the piece of jewelry cleared the top of her bodice.

"I dinnae know 'twas such a long chain," he quipped, a brief smile touching his lips. He held the pendant aloft, turning it this way and that. It caught the light with a warmth having nothing to do with heat and everything to do with mystery.

Four green stones, smooth to the touch, were each set in gold filigree to form the shape of a cross. A modest, but still impressive diamond, mounted at the juncture of the four stones, sparkled cold and brilliant in the light.

"I am no' familiar with this green stone. Do ye know what it is?"

"The necklace belonged to my mother," Mary replied in a hushed voice. "The stone is called *jade*. She told me it is found only in the courts of emperors."

"And how would ye come to have a stone of the emperors?"

Mary snatched the pendant from his grasp, plucked at the front of her bodice, and dropped it back inside. "As I said, it was my mother's. It became mine after she died."

"I thought ye said yer ma was the chatelaine at Bellecourt."

"And *I* told *you*, you know nothing about me."

"Then, who was yer father?" he countered.

"I did not know him."

"Dinnae know him, or dinnae know who he was?"

"My mother would not speak of him."

"Was he from Bellecourt?"

"No. My mother and I arrived at Bellecourt when I was less than a babe. Lady Barde was confined to her bed after a difficult birth. Mother took her duties as chatelaine and when Lady Barde died, she also took over the rearing of Lady Barde's daughter."

"Miriam."

"Yes. Miriam."

"So yer past is as mysterious as this stone cross ye wear," Eaden stated, not making it a question.

"It makes no difference to me, but if you'd rather not be wed to someone who is possibly illegitimate . . ."

Eaden frowned. "Half the English court is illegitimate," he scoffed. He waved away her protest and gave her a thoughtful look. "Did yer ma always keep the cross hidden away on such a long chain?"

"Yes, though she laid it on her dressing table when she bathed." Mary's lips curved in a slight smile. "I can remember playing with it when I was quite small. The chain hung almost to my knees."

"Do ye suppose 'twas a gift to her from yer da?" Eaden asked.

"Yes. But 'twas all she would say on the subject. She threatened to forbid me to play with it should I ask more questions. For a child growing up amid wealthy splendor, and none of it mine, it was an effective threat. It was the only thing I did not have to share with Miriam."

"Did the two of ye no' get along?"

"Oh, we were raised as sisters, and acted like sisters as well," Mary replied. "But she was the heiress and I the unfavored one, except when I was alone with my mother in the evenings. She told me stories of court, and hugged me tightly and cautioned never to take my circumstances for granted." Mary shrugged. "I assumed she meant we were fortunate to have a protector such as Laird Barde."

"I'm sure 'tis what she meant." Eaden absently fingered the chain at her neck. He smoothed the thin metal over her skin, and heat rose in her again.

"Don't do that," she whispered through lips growing soft, begging for his touch.

Eaden sent her an unreadable look. For a moment Mary thought he would kiss her again. But he slowly drew his hand away as though uncertain what to do, then turned on his heel and left the room.

Mary sank slowly onto the chair. How could her body betray her so? Why did she wish to leave this man, yet melt at his touch?

She shuddered to remember the one occasion Eaden had lain with her. Since her mother died, she had longed for a family of her own with children to love. But if repetition of her wedding night was the price she'd pay to get them, perhaps she was better off without children.

But what of the kisses that stirred her so? Were they merely a ploy to sway her into letting the man have his way? Eaden's kisses certainly made her lose her senses and self-control. She sighed. Since she was about to be divorced, she'd see to it he didn't kiss her again.

Now that she knew what to do, she felt better, and rose to her feet. Walking to the fireplace and the oval mirror hanging above it, Mary stared at herself with Eaden's words in her head. Were her eyes a pretty green? She studied them, opening her lids wide to judge their true color. They were nice enough, she supposed, a bright, clear green rimmed in black.

She tossed her head, watching as her hair bounced about her shoulders. The color seemed pretty, and if the sun struck it just right, a bit of gold did flash within it. Her curls, however, had always been a trial. If she wore her hair up, it quickly worked its way loose. And if she left it unbound, it tangled and snarled in a most aggravating manner. She'd kept it braided for the past few days, covering it with a scarf or veil, the unruly strands somewhat under control. With a shudder, she remembered the way sparks had shot along her scalp when Eaden ran his fingers through her loose tresses. Perhaps she should keep it better confined.

Her eyes filled with tears. *I want to go home.*

Chapter Nine

Eaden strode through the great hall and out to the stables. Although intent on cleaning his horse's tack, Ranald glanced up as his brother passed. Eaden held out a restraining hand to ward off his brother's questions and saddled Duff with quick efficiency. With a look of concern, Ranald rose to saddle his own horse.

"I need to clear my head," Eaden muttered by way of explanation as he swung up onto his horse.

"Aye. And ye need someone to watch yer back," Ranald replied grimly. Eaden bit back a rebuff, knowing the dangers of riding the mountain trails alone. Too impatient to summon further retainers or soldiers for his protection, he scowled but accepted Ranald's company.

Eaden rode from the stable, spurring the horse into a dead run before they cleared the castle gate, leaving his most immediate troubles far behind.

After riding the trail for several minutes, he reined the stallion toward the river, though the horse was far from winded and pulled at the bit in protest. Ranald drew his horse to a walk beside him.

"Leave me," Eaden snapped, in no mood for company or conversation. Ranald withdrew to a promontory near the river with a view of the trail and surrounding hills. Eaden threw himself from the saddle as soon as the horse slowed to a walk, and set off across the ground in long, pounding strides.

How dare she demand a divorce! His thoughts infuriated him even as he ignored the pride he felt whenever Mary stood up for herself. He couldn't explain why he'd teased her and then kissed her a few minutes ago, but he'd been unable to stop himself and his blood still ran hot from their encounter.

He wheeled abruptly, heading for the cooling embrace of the river. Duff followed close on his heels, trailing his reins in the grass. As soon as Eaden spotted the sparkling waters, he wrenched away his clothes, flinging them to the ground. Two steps later he launched himself into a faultless shallow dive and sliced into the cold water, certain he heard it sizzle against his heated skin.

It took several moments for his blood to cool, even in the cold river water, but soon his head cleared and he stroked to a pool eddying gently against the bank, away from the main current. Rolling onto his back, he floated there, staring at the clouds churning lazily across the sky.

He still could not understand how the lass had gotten under his skin. He was known in two countries as a man long on patience and courage and with the good of his country at heart. In less than two weeks he'd all but forfeited the backing of his king, routinely lost his patience with the woman he'd married, and succumbed to her tears and pleading with a complete lack of courage.

Eaden doubted he would be granted a divorce simply because he'd been stupid. Marrying another to enhance a political advantage might garner approval from the king, but no other prospects for marriage came to mind. If Mary failed to provide him an heir, he could perhaps divorce her, though many men simply adopted an illegitimate son and avoided the trouble of remarrying.

The problem remained. Eaden had no real reason to pursue divorce, beyond the fact Mary wanted to go home. He'd lost interest in the other women he'd taken to bed over the years. He couldn't say if it was due to the overwhelming duties as laird of Craigievar and King Robert's herald, or the green eyes and outspoken boldness of a certain lass he'd married.

A splash reached his ears and he quickly righted himself. For the first time he could remember, he wasn't pleased to see the fan of night-dark hair or the slender arms pulling the body he knew only too well across the water toward him.

He waited as Isobel stopped before him and rested her feet on the bottom of the pool. They were currently eye-to-eye, but Eaden knew if he stood upright, the top of her head would reach no higher than his chin. He also knew if he touched her, she would allow him to do anything he wanted. Anything at all.

Isobel's slender fingers smoothed her hair back from her face, letting it pool in a shining curtain around her. She glanced down, and Eaden's gaze followed hers to her breasts, tantalizingly visible just beneath the surface of the water. He lifted his gaze to meet hers and she tossed him a mocking smile.

"I understand ye have married," she finally purred when Eaden made no move to speak or touch her. Her full lips pursed in a seductive pout.

"As have ye, now," he reminded her bluntly.

Isobel flushed and looked away. "I'd not known ye would wed so quickly." She dragged one arm back and forth across the surface of the water. Eaden caught himself staring at the smooth perfection of her skin. "And not knowing if I carried yer child or no' . . ."

His eyes narrowed. "What game is this ye're playing, Isobel? We'd no' been together for more than two months before my wedding. The whole castle, and likely the village, too, had been abuzz with the news I would wed Barde's daughter. I'd sent for ye to explain, but yer maid said ye were *indisposed.* A common response if ye were either bleeding or put out with me."

Isobel sighed prettily. "Of course I was put out with ye, my love. I'd no idea ye were finished with me."

"Dinnae make it sound more than two people using each other." Isobel stiffened at his brusque dismissal of their previous intimacy. "Ye knew I wouldnae marry for love, but to serve the king. I was honest with ye from the beginning."

"So ye admit ye are no' in love with yer wife." She targeted quickly on his words.

"Are ye in love with yer new husband?" Eaden countered.

Isobel glided closer, the water swaying in seductive eddies between their bodies. "How could ye believe I would love anyone but ye?"

Eaden stared at the woman before him. Only a few weeks ago, he'd have readily sampled all she offered, and more. Only a few weeks ago, he would have enjoyed their banter, knowing what would come of it. Now something held him back, kept him from reaching for the delights brazenly displayed before him, what his body remembered so eagerly.

He watched her face, the pretty pout to her lips, the seductive tilt of her head, her incredible green eyes . . . *Damn!* Isobel's eyes were brown, not green! He blinked and the vision faded as Isobel's eyes returned to their proper color. He scowled and drew back, realizing he had been close to kissing her.

Isobel flushed darkly. "'Tis plain to see the little whore is on yer mind," she snarled.

"Mind who ye name *whore*, Isobel," Eaden warned, an iron edge to his voice. "'Tis past time ye should return to yer husband."

Isobel tossed her head. "I've heard the gossip at the castle. The poor thing is too young for ye, my love. She most likely doesnae know the difference between a man and his expectations."

Eaden scowled. "What are ye talking about?"

She reached unerringly for him under the water and he sucked in his breath at the tug of her hand as it found its goal. "The *man*." She stressed the word with a devastating twist of her hand. "And his expectations." She tapped the side of his head with her other hand. "What do ye expect from yer mousy wife?"

Eaden tried hard to ignore the pressure of Isobel's hand on him but found it impossible. He gritted his teeth, meeting her look of defiance with an even stare as he reached for her hand to stop her bold grip. He swallowed a moan as she released him, avoiding his grasp, sliding her hand further between his legs.

"Cease, Isobel," he grumbled, his voice gruff with repressed emotion. "Enough."

Isobel drew back. "I hope yer wife can finish satisfying ye," she spat. Her eyes flared as anger twisted her lovely face. "Though I dinnae suppose ye will get too much from an inexperienced child such as her." She took a deep breath and leaned forward, her breasts firm against his chest.

"I would have loved ye forever," she whispered achingly in his ear, her mood again changing with alarming abruptness.

Without another word, she turned and swam away. Grateful for the cold water, a long time passed before Eaden summoned enough control to follow her out of the water. He yanked on his clothes, snatching at the trailing reins of his horse's bridle. Passing Ranald, who scrambled to collect his own steed, Eaden rode back to the castle at a gallop, his thoughts in turmoil, his body reminding him hungrily of Isobel's offer.

* * *

Mary lay awake far into the night, waiting for Eaden to come to bed, uneasy to think what would happen if he chose to continue their earlier conversation. Or worse, if he decided to act before talking. She wasn't sure she would be able to withstand another devastating kiss in the privacy of their bedroom. She gulped. *Or in our bed.*

What would she do if he came to her? His kisses ignited something inside her she did not want to contemplate, yet the memory stirred just beneath her skin.

Heated tendrils curled inside her and a mild panic rose in her breast. If he touched her again she was not certain she could fight the attraction between them. She grasped frantically for reassurance he would maintain his distance. Surely he would not come to her during the next few days, until her cycle was complete. Or would he?

Sorcha lay on the floor at the threshold of the room, not her usual sleeping arrangement. For a long time Mary tossed and turned, the emptiness of the bed unfamiliar around her, until she finally gave into sleep and restless dreams of the man who confounded her days and haunted her nights.

Eaden met her at the top of the stairs the next morning. He appeared fresh and clean. *And handsome*, her traitorous mind told her. He glanced at her in a distant fashion as he took in her appearance.

"I will be leaving this morning. King Robert will be in Edinburgh tomorrow. I will tell him of yer desire to return to Bellecourt."

"And will you also tell him of my desire for a divorce?" she countered. "I want to be free to marry whom I choose."

Laird Scott bowed low before her. "As milady wishes." He turned away, descending the stairs two at a time, as if he couldn't wait to be rid of her.

Chapter Ten

Eaden's furrowed brow was enough to cause King Robert to clear the room with an abrupt wave of his hand. Courtiers lingered at the edge, curiosity almost overcoming their monarch's command. It was unheard of for King Robert and the loyal earl to be at cross purposes, but this was the second time in a month such strife had been witnessed. And it was rumored a private wager awaited the outcome of this night's accounting by the earl.

King Robert slouched on his throne, lips thinned into a forbidding frown, his chin resting in his hand as he surveyed the man before him. Eaden waited at the base of the shallow steps before the dais, his back rigid, his hands clasped together beneath his cloak. He had not been offered refreshment, a testament to the king's disapproval, though he chose to ignore the obvious concern among those who still believed in the earl's ability to retain the king's favor.

Eaden remained unmoved by King Robert's scowl after he spoke, knowing his liege was less than amused by his accounting. Of course, Eaden's delivery had been abrupt and unapologetic, further adding to the king's obvious lack of sympathy with the tale.

King Robert sighed. "So ye married the wrong lass and she wants to go home," he summarized with a frown.

"Aye."

"And the Lady Miriam has run off and married Du Melville's youngest son, leaving us without an alliance between yer clans?"

"Aye."

"I thought ye had this well in hand," King Robert groused.

Eaden, fully aware the king was no more pleased to sort this mess out than he was, silently cursed all stubborn men and women who couldn't simply do as they were told. Of course, he had to admit his assessment likely included the majority of King Robert's subjects.

"So. Will ye let her go back to Bellecourt?"

"Nay," Eaden replied evenly.

King Robert straightened from his resigned slouch in his chair and stared at Eaden, amusement lighting his eyes.

"If I remember correctly, ye were no' happy with the marriage to begin with. I am to assume ye've changed yer mind, then?"

Eaden narrowed his eyes but did not answer.

"She's uncommonly beautiful, perhaps?" King Robert prompted.

Eaden refused to respond.

"Passably good-looking, then?"

Eaden took a deep, fortifying breath. "She's quite lovely," he allowed.

"She's knocked ye on yer arse!" King Robert exclaimed with accuracy and triumphant humor.

The look Eaden gave his king was anything but humorous, but the king continued, undeterred. "So ye mean to keep her." He stroked his chin thoughtfully. "And she wants to leave." He cocked his head to one side. "And yer well-known charm that had ladies vying for the title of *wife* of this handsome, wealthy earl, who may or may no' have his lands at the end of this day, isnae working?"

Eaden ignored the threat, but his scowl must have given the king the answer he sought. "So, if the lass doesnae want wealth, or prestige, or the much-touted delights of yer bed—what does she want?"

Eaden's face turned dark and forbidding as he gritted out the truth. "A divorce."

King Robert's laughter roared loudly and the courtiers at the far end of the room glanced up in surprise. His advisor gave the earl a dour look before turning back to his work. Eaden did not laugh.

"Tell me, Laird Scott," King Robert said in a softer voice, though his eyes still danced merrily. "Tell me what you plan to do? Your position as my herald . . ."

"I resign," Eaden interrupted firmly.

The king raised his eyebrows in surprise. "Now, why would ye resign yer post?"

"It appears the affairs of the king pale in comparison with the affairs at Scott Castle."

King Robert nodded, a thoughtful look on his face. "So, that's the way of it, then?"

"Aye."

"Ye're a man of few words when it comes to yer wife, Laird." With a rueful grin, King Robert motioned for refreshments to be served. Eaden shrugged, relieving the tension from his neck and shoulders before he acceded to the king's invitation to sit in the chair next to him.

A young serving girl appeared with goblets of wine. King Robert nodded absently to her, but Eaden was struck by the sight of a pendant around her neck. It was a simple thing, nothing as elaborate as the one Mary wore, but it reminded him of it nonetheless, and he turned back to the king.

"Sire?"

The king raised his eyebrows in response.

"Sire, I've seen an abundance of jewels and precious stones on the ladies at court, but I saw a pendant the other day, a cross, with unusual green stones set in it."

King Robert turned to him with vague interest. "Ye'd ask me to identify a stone for ye?"

Eaden shook his head impatiently. "Nay, Sire. I was told the stones were *jade*, a precious stone from the courts of the emperors. I'd no' seen these stones before, but I seem to remember a tale, long ago, about a fantastic jade cross given by a king to his lover, and it's been hanging at the back of my mind ever since." He tilted his head. "Do ye recall the tale?"

King Robert sat straighter in his chair, eyeing Eaden thoughtfully. "Perhaps ye'd be better off asking one of the court minstrels. I'm sure he could invent a tale for ye fit for our court if he doesnae know one already."

The king drew himself to his feet, forcing Eaden to do the same, and motioned for his advisor to come to him. "Bring yer pretty wife to court, Laird," he said by way of dismissal. "We would like to be introduced to her."

Eaden bowed low. "As ye wish, Sire." Taking care on the shallow steps, he relinquished his seat, backing with servility from the king before he turned and strode from the room.

Chapter Eleven

From her seat at the window, Mary's thoughts were a hundred desolate miles away. She almost missed the faint squeak of the bedroom door as it opened and closed. Expecting either Ina or Kirsty, she was startled to see a stranger enter. Though she'd been at Scott Castle for more than three weeks, she'd made no close friends amongst the wives and daughters who lived within its walls. They were unfailingly polite to her, though obviously leery of *The Barde's daughter*, as she'd heard herself called more than once.

The castle servants seldom had reason to speak to her since Ina still maintained her position of authority as castle chatelaine. Intent on her desire to leave Scott Castle, Mary saw little need to take Lady Scott's rightful place in the daily life of the clan's people. And the lack of friends was her forfeit.

The tall, dark-haired beauty entered the room. "Good morning, milady!"

"Good morning," Mary replied politely. "Who are you?"

"My name is Isobel. Yer maid, Kirsty, isnae feeling well this day, so I am here to help." The woman stopped beside Mary and gazed out the window.

"I used to live here," she murmured in a voice so soft Mary wasn't at first sure if the woman spoke to her or not. Isobel gave her a crooked smile. "I meant in the castle. But I married my husband, Peadrus, a few weeks past and moved to his home just outside the village. I came in this morning to visit a friend, discovered Kirsty wasnae well, and so here I am to help."

Somewhat overwhelmed by the woman's chatty manner, Mary was unsure which statement to reply to first. She smiled bravely. After weeks of near-solitude, she supposed a new friend might be a nice change.

Isobel turned from the window, her long, dark hair sliding across her shoulders. She placed her hands on her hips as she surveyed the room. "Let's get ye dressed." She crossed the room to a row of pegs on the wall where Mary's dresses hung. "What would milady like to wear today?"

Gathering her robe around her, Mary slid from her seat and padded on bare feet in the other woman's wake. "It doesn't matter. They're much the same," she said with an apologetic note to her voice.

Isobel pulled a gown from its peg and held it up. "Hmm. `Tis well-made." Her shrug expressed little hope for the garment's other attributes as she held it against Mary. "But the color simply does nothing for ye."

Taken aback by the woman's condescending attitude, Mary gave Isobel a quelling glare she'd seen Miriam use on more than one occasion. Isobel flushed at the silent reprimand, her lips thinning in an offended line.

Instantly contrite, Mary amended, "You have a lovely gown." Aiming to soothe any hurt she'd caused, she tilted her head in a friendlier gesture. "What would you suggest?"

Isobel's response was stiff and formal. "I am sorry, Lady Scott. I dinnae mean to overstep my bounds."

Mary gave her a faint smile. "In view of my rather plain gowns, perhaps it was for the best."

For a moment, Mary thought the woman would refuse her overture. Suddenly, Isobel flashed a conspiring smile and motioned for Mary to remove her night shift, waving the plain, dark brown dress before her to hurry her along.

"Here. Put this on for now. We're going to the wardroom!"

* * *

"Milady would like fabric for a new dress," Isobel announced. Ina cast a dubious glance at Mary's serviceable gown.

Mary was sure her own surprise at Isobel's words showed on her face. "Oh, but. . ."

Ina shook her head. "I'll let the two of ye in the wardroom, but I've no time for the sewing, myself. Agnes will do a fine job, as will ye, Isobel." Ina tossed the dark-haired woman a sharp look as she gathered her skirts and began climbing the stairs.

Mary followed the two women to the room where the clothing items were stored. Unlocking the door with one of the many keys hanging from her girdle, Ina pushed the heavy wood panel open. Mary's eyes watered, her senses instantly overwhelmed with the pungent smell of dyes and newly tanned leather. They entered the room, past the folded linen and coarse wools and the piles of cured leather, to a series of large chests arranged against the far wall.

With another, smaller key, Ina unlocked each chest and flung open the lids to reveal costly velvets, shimmering silks and glowing satins in a dazzling rainbow of colors. Another chest contained furs of every kind, and the final chest overflowed with both sewing and embroidery threads and other adornments in a surprising array of hues.

"Oh, my," Mary breathed. Even helping Miriam prepare for visits to neighboring castles or to attend the king, she'd never had access to such finery. She ran a finger lightly across the velvets in the chest nearest her, feeling the deep nap of the cloth. Turning to the chest containing the rich furs, she plunged one hand within the luxurious depths. Her fingers sank into the silken pelts and she marveled at their obvious quality.

Ina smiled. "Almost makes ye wish for cooler weather, doesn't it, milady? But these are more appropriate for now."

Reluctantly, Mary turned from the furs as the other women perused the silks and soft linens. Ina reached inside the chest and pulled out an armful of fabric, setting it on the top of a nearby table. She placed another stack next to the first.

Mary stared at the lavish display, all of which was meant for her, and suddenly realized what she was about to do. The thought of being clothed in the costly fabrics was exhilarating, a privilege easily belonging to Lady Scott. But she was not Lady Scott. *Not really. Or, at least not for much longer.*

She watched with growing dismay as the other two women rifled quickly through the piles of fabrics, disregarding some, pulling others out and placing them aside in an ever-growing pile.

"Wait!" She raised her hands to halt their work. Both women turned to her with question in their eyes.

"Yes, milady?"

Mary hesitated. There simply was no way to explain to Isobel or Ina she was an imposter and would not need the sumptuous clothing once she became plain Mary Marsh again. As much as she counted on being released from her marriage any day now, she couldn't bring herself to expose Eaden and the horrible mistake he'd made. She wracked her brain for a way to explain her sudden change of heart.

Finally, she gestured toward the trunks. "This is all so grand." She steeled her heart against the shimmering silks within reach. "I'm sure it would be more practical to use durable fabric in serviceable colors." There. At least the clothing could be given to someone else once she left.

Isobel tossed her head. "Ye are wearing *serviceable*," she reminded Mary. "'Tis why we came here."

"But, I shouldn't . . ."

Isobel walked to another pile of fabric and pulled out a length of silk the soft color of moss. She held it beneath Mary's chin and nodded with satisfaction.

"The color matches yer eyes, milady." Isobel carried the fabric with her to the chest of threads, running an expert hand over the wooden spools until she found what she wanted.

"There! A cream underskirt, face the sleeves with that gold fabric. Use this gold thread for embroidery at the neck and sleeves. Scatter a few stones — topaz would be nice, I should think."

"No!" Mary cried in frustration. "I need nothing so grand."

Isobel shrugged. "No jewels, then." Turning to Ina, she dropped the fabrics and thread she'd collected into a pile on an empty table. "Perhaps another in brown. Shot with gold threads, it will show off that lovely hair of hers. I'm sure ye have Lady Scott's measurements, and ye can set Agnes to the task immediately. I'll do the embroidery myself."

Mary's head spun with the complete authority falling from Isobel's lips, shocked and a little envious of the ease with which she ordered the new dresses.

Isobel turned back to Mary, a superior look on her face. "There. That's settled. What shall we do with the rest of our day?"

Chapter Twelve

Mid-morning sun slid lazily down the castle walls and warmed the bailey. The open area bustled with people carrying out their daily chores. With satisfaction, Eaden noted the relaxed atmosphere among those gathered here, indicative of their faith in him to protect them from the troubles among the clans. He cast a critical eye over the guards standing at attention on the wall. Everything appeared to be in order. If only his personal life could be so neatly arranged.

He left Duff in the care of a stable lad, feeling Sorcha's desertion. He supposed there were worse things than watching his hound become a besotted bodyguard to his wife. Though the dog kept him faithful company on his journey, as soon as he'd halted to speak to Ranald and others he'd left in charge during his absence, Sorcha had bolted into the great hall in search of Mary.

With a purposeful stride, he crossed the bailey. No sense putting off the inevitable. He had to tell Mary she would remain his wife. Surely she'd come around in time. So why could he imagine the slow *tap, tap, tap* of the executioner's drum in his blood?

There was no sign of Mary in the hall. She could be anywhere in the castle. He stopped a serving lass who hurried by with a jerk of his head. "Where is Lady Scott?"

"In the bower, Laird."

With a nod of thanks, Eaden headed for the spiral stairs winding upwards. He followed the hallway to the sun-filled room where generations of castle ladies spent their time—a room he'd not visited since a lad at his mother's knee. As he poked his head inside the doorway, the sight of the women seated there, Sorcha lying placidly at Mary's feet, flooded him with locked-away memories of his mother and her ladies in years past.

But his recollections were brought to a screeching halt as his mind registered who sat in the bower with his wife, chattering away, an embroidery hoop in her busy hands. His heart slammed in his chest as Isobel glanced up, her sloe eyes lighting with pleasure at the sight of him, her sensuous mouth curving upward in a sly smile at his obvious discomfiture.

"Laird," she said smoothly, inclining her head in a submissive manner.

He narrowed his eyes as he came fully into the room. He didn't know whether to question her or threaten her, and finally gave a curt nod. It was only an instant in time, but the air charged with their animosity.

Eaden swept his gaze over the other women, coming to rest on Mary who, much to his surprise, appeared excited to see him. Her green eyes glowed and her tentative smile slowly filled her sweet face. His pulse quickened in response to her look of joy before he released a quiet sigh. Mary's happiness wouldn't last long. She anticipated her long-awaited freedom, not him or the decision he'd made.

But he was prepared to reap the benefits of her sunny mood before sharing his quelling news. "Milady." With a short bow to the ladies, he offered Mary his hand. She quickly set aside her sewing and placed her hand in his, rising to her feet. Something wicked in Eaden reared itself and he pulled her against him, claiming a bold kiss from his wife in full view of the others.

"Welcome home," he coached her softly, his eyes on hers as he released her. Breathless at his unexpected embrace, Mary's free hand touched her flaming cheeks. The look on her face slid from shock to secretive delight as she pulled her composure back together.

"Welcome home, indeed, Laird," she replied, her voice low, a tiny smile lingering on her lips.

Eaden tucked her hand in the crook of his elbow and tried to control the satisfied look on his face. He found it impossible to deny himself something that pleased him so well, knowing he'd face certain tears and recriminations in the very near future.

He led Mary from the bower and to the stairs, though he was forced to follow her down the narrow, winding steps. The view from behind was compensation enough, and he quickly reclaimed her hand once they reached the great hall. Wishing to delay the inevitable fight between them, he guided his wife through the castle gates and over the dusty trail toward the village.

He nodded to people in passing who acknowledged them with respectfully inclined heads or a murmured *Laird* or *Lady*. Mary strode quietly beside him, and Eaden sought a way to begin a conversation.

"Tell me news of the castle since I've been gone," he began casually.

Mary gave him a puzzled look. "But you've only been gone a few days. I know of nothing out of the ordinary that has occurred."

He patted her hand to distract her from the intent behind his next words. "But ye seemed to be quite relaxed today in yer bower with the other women. There were a couple of new faces there, no?"

"If you're asking if I've made friends, well, I suppose I have. Though I haven't much reason to form close ties here," she reminded him pointedly.

Eaden ignored the jab. "Who are yer new friends, Mairi?"

Mary sighed. "One is a clothier, a young woman named Agnes who is adding embroidery to a new pair of shoes for me . . ." She paused abruptly, and Eaden turned to her in surprise at her sudden halt. "I didn't mean for it to go so far!" Guilt spilled across her stricken face. Eaden braced himself for whatever came next, alarmed to see her so distressed.

"But Isobel insisted my clothes were dull and unfashionable and not befitting the lady of the castle, and she took me to the wardroom and she and Ina picked out the most beautiful fabrics . . . I know I shouldn't take advantage of your wardroom when it isn't mine to use — not really, that is. I told them only one dress, since I didn't want to explain the situation between me and you, but then they added a bliaud and shoes, and a veil . . ." Her voice trailed off.

Eaden huffed impatiently to hear the rest. It took a moment of silence for him to realize Mary had stopped speaking. Fearing the worst kind of behavior from his former mistress, he managed to control his ire. "Tell me again what Isobel has done," he demanded.

"'Tis not her fault, Laird, but mine. She only wanted me to have something nice to wear."

Eaden was silent for a full minute before he finally understood Mary's words. "Ye are upset because the woman is making ye a dress?" he asked in disbelief. He'd not heard a word other than Isobel's name nor seen past the distress on Mary's face a moment earlier. He had been sure the other woman had been up to no good. This was about a *dress*?

"I have no right to the wardroom as I am not really Lady Scott." Mary's eyes searched Eaden's face as she spoke quietly. "The fabric is quite costly and I have no way to repay you." She paused. "You did talk to King Robert, didn't you?"

Eaden cursed softly. He hadn't thought this through very well. He'd all but convinced himself Mary would take his news better if he showed her all he had to offer her. But now they were in full view of a number of people, and their curiosity in his and Mary's conversation was well-evident. He pulled her to him and gave her a quick kiss. There, let that settle some questions of the people watching them and perhaps turn the gossip in his favor. 'Twas best the people of Craigievar thought their laird and lady to be in accord. It wasn't going to last long.

* * *

Mary was again thrown off balance by Laird Scott's actions. First, he showed up unannounced and scowled at the ladies in the bower room. Then he kissed her as only a husband should, and in front of the others! He didn't seem to be at all upset she used items from the wardroom as only the lady of the castle had the right to do. From his forbidding frown, she had thought he would dismiss her new friend, Isobel, from the castle for instigating such use of his property.

A few moments ago, he'd kissed her in front of the people near the village, and now he led her down a narrow trail winding through the blooming yellow broom shrubs and up the slope rising slowly away from the castle.

They came to a stop in a grove of trees at the top of a rocky hill. Mary sensed the change in the breeze and knew they stood near the river even if she could no longer see the water. Eaden released her hand and strode to the edge of the grove where it appeared the land simply disappeared from sight.

He stared into the distance and Mary's spirits plummeted. Had the news been good he would not now be struggling for a way to tell her.

Eaden motioned for her to come forward and she crossed to him with reluctant tread, only to stop in fearful surprise when the ground seemed to drop from beneath her feet. She scrambled backward, intent on self-preservation, but Eaden grabbed her arm and pulled her against his side, not heeding her distress.

"'Tis one of my favorite views," he said.

Mary swallowed and nodded, closing her eyes against the dizzying drop to the river waters below them.

"Ye can see the village, castle and river all from here."

Holding her breath against the panic rising within, Mary did not reply.

"I thought ye'd like it here. Ye liked the view from the parapet well enough."

Mary ventured to open one eye and caught him staring at her, his lips quirked in something resembling a smile.

"Yes, but there was a sturdy wall between me and falling!"

Eaden chuckled and leaned against the tree at his back, spreading his feet to brace himself. Pulling Mary around in front of him, he turned her toward the river and wrapped his arms firmly about her, holding her close.

"There, lass," he murmured in her ear. "Take a look at the beauty of Craigievar. I willnae let ye fall."

Broom spilled its yellow flowers across the mountains, and white, fleecy sheep dotted the landscape. Scott Castle loomed nearby, its stone tower house rising above the curtain wall, looking both timeless and invincible. Now intrigued by her surroundings, Mary leaned cautiously forward and peered over the edge of the cliff. Sunlight danced on the water below and she spied children playing on the broad banks of the river. Shrieks of laughter rose on the currents of air as the children ran and dodged each other in their game.

"It *is* beautiful," she sighed.

"Then, Mairi, lass, learn to love it well, for the king will grant us no divorce."

Chapter Thirteen

Eaden felt Mary's body stiffen an instant before she tore from his arms. For a moment, he was too stunned to move, and Mary stumbled as she pulled free of his grasp, windmilling her arms to catch her balance.

Muttering a curse under his breath, Eaden shoved away from the tree to chase after her. He'd expected her to dissolve into tears, not run away. Once again, she'd caught him off guard, and he found himself several strides behind her, alarmed at how close she raced along the edge of the cliff. It would only take a single misstep or a loose rock . . .

Eaden redoubled his efforts. "Mary, *stop!*" But his words had no effect on his young bride. She did not hesitate, did not slow her headlong bid for freedom.

Eaden lunged for her. Grabbing one arm, he planted his feet firmly in the rocky soil and brought them both to a sudden halt. The force swung Mary around, and she cried out. The despair in her eyes as she rounded on him stabbed straight to his heart. He pulled her close, wanting only to soothe the hurt he'd caused her.

"No!" She slapped at him with her free hand as she tried to escape his grasp, but Eaden held on, letting her fight him, making no move to shield himself from the fist pounding him with furious intent. Finally, drained but unvanquished, Mary stood before him, breathing heavily, eyeing him with loathing.

Eaden's heart swelled with admiration at her spirit, even as exasperation filled him for the way she refused to listen.

"Why?" she choked, breathless. "You promised!"

"Aye. I promised I would wait until ye knew if ye were with child or no'. And I promised I would then make yer request known to the king." He faced the fire in her eyes. "But I dinnae promise ye a divorce."

"But you couldn't wait to go to the king!" she protested. "You were so angry when you left!"

"Aye, I was angry. But I was angry ye insisted I ask King Robert for a divorce, no' because ye were no' with child. Nor because I dinnae want ye."

Mary chewed her bottom lip in a thoughtful manner. Suddenly she reached out and pinched his arm, hard.

Eaden flinched away with an oath of surprised pain. "What the . . .!"

Mary sighed, the anger at last fading from her face. "I wanted to make certain this wasn't a bad dream."

"By pinching me?"

"You can't feel pain in a dream," she pointed out.

Eaden rubbed his arm over the still-red mark. "Then pinch yerself," he growled.

Mary blinked in wide-eyed surprise. "It would have hurt."

He stared at her in disbelief. "'Tis no' a dream, lass."

"But you know you don't want me! And this is not what *I* wanted . . ."

Eaden's lips quirked ruefully. As disillusioned as he knew her to be, his wife still believed in her girlish dreams. "What do ye want of marriage, Mairi?" he asked, recapturing one of her hands.

Mary tugged uselessly against his grip. Giving him a sidelong glance, she hesitated as though weighing his interest. He returned her look evenly and ran his thumb slowly across the palm of her hand, but he did not release her.

Her shoulders slumped as though in defeat. "I wanted to marry for love. Though someone in my position would have little chance of marrying for wealth or status, there was always a chance I would be able to marry someone of my choosing."

"Is there a lad who has yer heart, lass?"

To his relief, Mary replied, "No. There is no one. Only the dream."

In spite of his good intention to listen seriously, Eaden uttered a short laugh.

Mary glared at him. "I suppose you have a different outlook on marriage, don't you?" she mocked bitterly.

"I am more practical, aye," he admitted. "I have always known I would most likely marry to suit my clan or my king. I gave no thought to seeking a wife who would suit *me*."

"And what if you were forced to marry someone you didn't like?" Mary challenged him, jutting her chin defiantly. "Like me?"

He shrugged. "I can adopt any son as my heir. It doesnae matter if he is legitimate."

Mary bristled. "You can please yourself, then? Love the woman you chose, and ignore the wife bound to you by your vows? Does that mean your wife is free take a lover, too?" She flung the words at him, surprising him with the anger and hurt in her voice.

She apparently did not understand he was not taunting her, merely stating a fact. He knew her own parentage to be a matter of some concern to her. But the thought of her in another man's arms instantly set his blood to boil. His eyebrows met with a snap as he scowled at her, and Mary drew back, eyes wide.

"Discreetly?" she offered in a small voice, though it sounded to him more like an appeasement than an apology.

Eaden couldn't believe his ears. Surely, she knew such an action on her part was unthinkable. Surely, she was not so naïve!

He advanced on her again, holding her wrist against her retreat, until he stood mere inches from her. "Nay," he whispered, the menace in his voice daring her to pursue the argument.

"Because women live by different rules than men?" she taunted.

"Nay. Because I would kill the man who dared lay a finger on ye."

Mary glanced up, clearly confused. "Why do you want me?"

Eaden reined in his anger, realizing his ire only alienated her further. Using his free hand, he stroked the satin skin of her cheek, gratified to see the stiff lines soften at his attempt to calm them both.

His temper abated, and he could at last speak without heat. "Because ye belong to me and no other. Because ye are beautiful to me and I would not have ye in another man's arms."

As her eyes changed from a hard, brittle green to the soft color of the leaves in the spring, desire rose in him, and he slowly lowered his head. "And because of this," he murmured as his lips touched hers.

To his surprise, Mary did not pull away, or attempt to slap him. Her body stiffened, but she also quivered beneath his hands. His breathing grew ragged as he fought to contain the passion exploding in him, damning himself to remember that beyond a kiss, she feared him.

He wanted to show her how to love him, how to respond to him. He wanted to learn how to love her, to know what pleased her. But there was little or no privacy beyond the height of this cliff and a few well-placed rocks and trees. Releasing her wrist, he wrapped his arms around her, pulling her against him, letting her sense the strength of his embrace and the wonder of what she aroused in him.

A small cry escaped her as her weight shifted against him. Desire slammed through him, almost overriding his sense of caution. A nearby shout broke them apart.

Eaden set Mary back on her feet, holding her until she caught her breath. He glanced at her flushed face and tucked her against his chest, angling her away from Ian's direct gaze as he climbed the path toward them.

"Ye told us to begin work on the second moat, and there are some questions only ye can answer, Laird." Ian checked his gait, ducking his head in apology.

Eaden weighed the man's words, then grunted in acknowledgement and nodded once in Ian's direction. "I'll be there shortly," he said, holding Mary's suddenly stiff body against him. Ian bobbed his head once more and hurried back down the trail. Mary's breathing quickened, her muscles tighten beneath his hands. She pushed against him, struggling to break his embrace.

He kissed the top of her head. "Hold," he murmured, tightening his arms enough to let her know he was not ready to release her. She struggled harder.

"Don't fight this." He kept her close, minimizing the damage her hands and feet could inflict.

Trembling, Mary at last gave in and Eaden relaxed his grip, stroking his hands up and down her back in a soothing gesture.

"Hush now, lass. We'll finish this later."

Mary shook her head in denial, and Eaden sighed deeply.

"Ye cannae fight me on this. Ye cannae change the way things are. It willnae be a bad life here, I promise ye. We need to begin again, ye and I, and we need to set things straight between us." He set her back from him just far enough to read the mutiny in her eyes. And the hurt still lingering there.

"I'll arrange for ye to get a message to Miriam. And I'd like to see ye in yer new gown," he teased her lightly, hoping to bring a smile to her face.

Mary's gaze cut away from his. Finally, she nodded and Eaden had to accept her silent agreement. Taking one of her hands tightly in his, he led her over the trail to the castle where the decisions she made would affect the rest of her life.

Chapter Fourteen

The faint slap of leather slippers on the stone floor caught Isobel's attention. Intrigued to see Lady Scott enter the great hall alone, she noted the look of dismay the woman wore as she passed Isobel's hiding place.

Easing out of the shadow of a recessed doorway, she followed Mary as she fled up the stairwell. Moments later the laird's bedroom door slammed shut. Isobel approached the closed portal and leaned her ear against the door, trying to gauge the activity beyond. A curious, muffled sound drifted through the thick wood.

Waiting several minutes in silence, Isobel was undecided what to do next. If those were sobs she heard — and she sincerely hoped they were — could there be a way to turn this to her advantage?

Her burning curiosity to see the woman who stole Laird Scott had brought her to the castle in the first place. Knowing she had no business there, she'd nevertheless lingered in the great hall and listened to the servants' chatter. When she heard Lady Scott's maid had fallen ill, Isobel had seized the obvious opportunity. Ina had to appoint someone to attend The Barde's daughter, didn't she?

"I'll do it," Isobel had said, startling everyone around her, including Ina, who had been too busy to question Isobel's willingness to serve.

When she'd viewed Eaden's young wife for the first time, Isobel's heart had lurched painfully. The new Lady Scott was young, very beautiful, and most assuredly competition for Eaden's affections. It would not take him long to sire a brat on this child-bride of his, but would she be obliging enough to die birthing it?

From the beginning, Isobel knew the risk of Eaden's growing attachment to the girl. Surely there was something she could do to make Eaden send his bride away. She'd use her time in Lady Scott's bower to her advantage and search for any insecurities the young woman might reveal. So far, Isobel's efforts to ingratiate herself had fared well.

Now, she disengaged the latch and eased the door open enough to see inside the room. Sunlight streamed through the narrow window on the far wall, but it took Isobel a few moments to discern the outline of the woman curled in the middle of the bed, crying brokenly. Her arms were wrapped around a pillow, her face buried in its softness.

For several minutes, Isobel savored the muffled sound of Mary's distress. Finally, she smoothed the smile on her face to a more appropriate expression of dismayed commiseration and entered the room.

She crossed to the bed and settled on the edge, ignoring the embarrassed look on the younger woman's tear-stained face as Mary scrambled to a sitting position, clutching the pillow protectively against her stomach.

Isobel picked up the corner of the coverlet and wiped the girl's tears away. "There, milady," she crooned. "Whatever 'tis, it cannae be so bad as all that."

"N-no," Mary replied, a wary edge to her voice.

"I can see ye dinnae want to share yer troubles," Isobel said gently. "But I'd be honored if I could help in any way."

While Mary silently twisted the pillow in her hands, Isobel studied her closely. To her knowledge, Mary had formed no close friendships in the castle, and Isobel waited impatiently to see if Mary would confide in her.

"I don't know what to do," Mary finally admitted in an anguished whisper.

Isobel's heart leapt with expectancy. "Perhaps if ye told me a bit of what's botherin' ye, I could try to help."

Indecision showed plainly on Mary's face. Isobel swallowed the hateful words she wanted to snarl at the young woman. She'd seen Eaden's dangerous expression this morning when he realized she'd insinuated herself with his young wife. Stunned, she'd managed to contain her fury when he'd taken Mary in his arms and kissed her soundly in front of her.

She burned for the feel his hands on *her* body, yearned for the hunger of his kisses on *her* lips, and had astonished herself with the depth of her hatred for Eaden's wife.

There had to be a way to win Eaden back. Her new husband was too easy to manipulate, too amazed she'd said *aye* to his proposal of marriage to naysay her in any matter, and she'd grown completely bored with him already. She wanted raw power and unleashed passion. She wanted Eaden. Badly.

"I don't want to stay here," Mary whispered.

Startled to hear Mary speak, Isobel dragged her attention back to the miserable girl on the bed. Her breath caught in her throat as she considered Mary's statement. Short of murder, there were few ways to rid herself of Laird Scott's young wife. She wasn't willing to wait and hope the twit would die someday in childbed or through some fortuitous accident, though the urge to form such a plan had crossed her mind on more than one occasion. But there was too much at stake, including Eaden's love, should he suspect Isobel's involvement in his wife's death.

But Isobel wanted him back *now*, not some time in the distant future.

Slowly, an idea began to take shape and Isobel tilted her head to the side as if in sweet empathy for the young, heart-sore woman beside her. "Och, milady," she crooned softly. "'Tis homesick ye are."

Mary blinked back tears, her shoulders stiffening, her hands trembling in her lap.

Isobel missed nothing. She reached a hand to tuck a strand of fallen hair behind Mary's ear in a motherly gesture. "Tell me what it is, lass," she whispered. "Ye can trust me."

"I'm afraid. I don't know what to do."

What could Eaden's wife possibly be afraid of? As Lady Scott, she had the protection of the entire clan. It had to be something much more personal, and Isobel recalled the gossip around the castle. The Laird and his Lady were not in accord. Though they slept together every night, they showed no outward signs of affection when away from their bedroom. She thought back to the way Eaden had greeted his wife that morning, and wondered about the truth of their relationship.

"What frightens ye, milady?" Isobel asked carefully.

"I'm not used to this." Mary waved a hand vaguely around in a circular motion. "All of this. And, please call me *Mary*. It's what I *am* used to."

Isobel nodded. "All right then, Mary," she said with deceptive calmness, even as her heart raced in her chest. "Now, tell me what it is ye need to know."

"Everything!" Mary wailed. The familiar use of her name seemed to break her inhibitions free, and she turned eagerly to Isobel. "I don't know how to be Lady Scott. I don't know how to run a castle." She hesitated, staring at her hands, white-knuckled as they gripped the pillow. "I don't know how to be a wife."

Isobel struggled to keep the skepticism from her face. Though she knew Mary was young, and most likely completely inexperienced in the ways of men when she arrived at Scott Castle, from her own personal experience, Isobel couldn't believe Eaden would have not completely initiated his young wife in such intimate pleasures. Could Mary be completely immune or indifferent to Eaden's skills as a lover?

"Your duties as Laird Scott's wife? In his bed?"

Mary swallowed and nodded, the mortification of the personal subject evident in the flush spreading across her pale cheeks.

"Lass, ye need to know what he expects from ye, 'tis all," Isobel soothed. "I know how intimidating he can be. He's so large, so frightening." Isobel patted Mary's hands. "Can I tell ye, from my own experience, what a man wants from his wife?"

Relief and gratitude spilled across Mary's pretty face and Isobel suffered an instant twinge of guilt at what she was about to do. But she wasted less than a second on the unappealing emotion and squelched it easily as she took Mary's hands in hers in friendly reassurance.

"Listen to me, Mary," she said firmly. "I'll tell ye everything ye need to know."

Chapter Fifteen

Eaden did not appear at the noon meal. Mary listened with poorly-concealed irritation to the young man he'd sent with his message of regret. With a sigh, she toyed half-heartedly with the food on her plate. Unable to create an appetite, she crept back up the stairs to her room. Slipping out of her gown, she slid beneath the covers of the bed Kirsty had straightened earlier and closed her eyes. Drained from the morning's events, the burgeoning throb in her head was the last straw.

The mattress dipped and swayed as Sorcha lurched up beside her, settling to join Mary in an afternoon nap. Within minutes Sorcha's light snores filled the room. Mary's mind raced as sleep eluded her. How could she have come to this end? Wrestling uselessly with unanswerable questions, she finally faded away into exhaustion and disappointment.

Mary's nap did little to alleviate her unease and she remained fretful and out of sorts later, as Kirsty brushed the wrinkles from her gown.

"Stop!" she cried, throwing her hands into the air in emphasis, seeking to be free of the girl's well-intentioned help. "I can't stand here any longer. I have to be outside!"

Not waiting to comb the sleep-wrought tangles from her hair, Mary jerked her skirts from Kirsty's hands and fled the room. Taking a scant moment to compose herself, she glanced about the hall before striding purposefully through the main doors and out into the bailey. The cool air fanned her hot cheeks, refreshing and instantly calming. Taking a deep draught of the misty air, the last of the tension drained away.

Her anxiety at a more manageable level, Mary searched the area, seeing the stables and armorer's building, clamoring with the noises of men at their tasks. The shrill whinny of a horse split the air, and she jerked as a chill passed over her. She turned from the stables and saw Ranald entering a smaller building with half-walls and a gate for a door. Her interest piqued, Mary followed him.

Taking two steps inside the stone building, she paused, letting her eyes adjust to the dim light. The interior of the building divided into several pens with a wide aisle down the middle running the full length of the single room. The half-walls allowed air to flow through the building, but the sun only cast dust-filled streamers around the edge of the room.

Sounds of scuffling in the pens caused Mary to draw back in alarm. Her fright giving way to excitement, she realized this was a kennel where the sounds were not rats among the rushes as she'd feared, but chubby puppies pushing past each other to get to their dams who shifted on their beds to accommodate their greedy babies.

"Oh!" she cried in delight as she moved to lean over the gate of the first kennel.

"Hold, lass!" The voice in her ear held an urgent warning and the hand encircling her arm stopped her from getting any closer to the hounds. Mary whipped her head around in alarm, relieved to see Ranald at her side.

Ignoring his warning, she pulled from his grasp and leaned over the gate. "They're adorable!" She rested her chin on her forearms as she propped them along the top of the low door, watching the wriggling mass of puppies.

Ranald paused beside her. "Aye, but ye need be careful. These dogs are bred to hunt wolves and deer and are no' so friendly as Sorcha."

Mary tilted her gaze to Ranald. "Is it all right if I come and watch the puppies?" she asked.

"Ye need to be sure ye stay out here and dinnae open the gate. These bitches can be aye protective of their bairns and Eaden'd no' forgive me for letting ye get yer pretty self bit."

Heat rose in Mary's cheeks at the oblique compliment and she ducked her head so Ranald wouldn't notice. "I promise. Though I doubt he'd care," she added under her breath. But she underestimated Ranald's hearing as well as his ability to keep his own counsel.

"What d'ye mean, lass? Eaden'd have my head and my teeth to play with if anything happened to ye."

Mary continued to watch the fuzzy puppies as one rooted in to his dam's belly from beneath one of its siblings, causing it to roll away, bleating in protest.

Ranald touched her arm lightly. "Why d'ye no' think Eaden cares about ye?"

Mary sighed heavily. "Oh, he does care. But I'm just a mistake he's trying to make right. He doesn't want me."

"I think ye're being too hard on him, lass."

"Hard on him!" Mary cried, rounding on the hapless man. "I slept in the wrong bed one night and woke to find myself being married to a stranger!" Her eyes pooled with tears and she brushed them impatiently away. "He spent less than two minutes with me after the wedding then took himself off to prattle to the king about his *duty*! That's all I am to him, Ranald. His *duty*. And the king won't grant me a divorce."

Ranald drew back with a frown. "Divorce, lass? Ye still think ye cannae live with this marriage?"

Mary turned around to prop her back on the kennel gate, crossing her arms over her chest in frustration. "I don't see how it could. I'm not even the person he was supposed to marry and no one here likes me, anyway."

"Och, lass, ye haven't given it enough time. I know Eaden is just as frustrated with the way things have turned out. He isnae usually so hot-headed. But 'tis over and done, and time to start fresh." Ranald bumped his shoulder against Mary's. "Besides, I like ye," he teased her.

"Argh!" Mary groaned as she tilted her head back, closing her eyes against the reality of Ranald's words. "I don't know how to start."

Ranald nudged her again. "Look over there."

Mary opened her eyes as he pointed to one of the puppies, turning to see what caught his interest.

"He's been pushed away," she noted with dismay. The chubby puppy had rolled clumsily to his side and away from his dam's belly.

"But watch. He'll no' give up." The puppy flailed with his rubbery legs, trying to find footing amid his siblings' round bodies. His head bobbled as he searched sightlessly for his dam.

"He's lost!" Mary exclaimed in worry. "Can't we help him?"

"He's no' lost, lass. But he is a fighter. See?"

As they watched, the puppy strained forward until he was once again in position. Rooting vigorously, the puppy shoved himself between two of his littermates and at last found what he sought.

"He's no' a quitter, Mary," Ranald said. "He knows what he wants and willnae let anything stop him. No' without a fight. Find what ye want and dinnae let anything stand in yer way. I want ye to be happy, but fighting against the truth willnae help."

"In other words, take what I have and make it work for me?"

Ranald sent her a huge grin of relief. "Exactly! There are plenty of folk here at Scott Castle who like ye. Just be yerself and let people get to know ye."

Mary sighed. "I understand here," she said, touching her head. "But it's taking time to reach here," she added, moving her hand to point to her heart.

Just then the puppy rolled down the furry backs of his littermates as he was once again rousted from his spot. His feet pawed the air as he tried to right himself, and in moments he rejoined the fray.

"Never give up, lass," Ranald said. "Never give up."

Chapter Sixteen

Eaden viewed his sleeping wife once again protected by Sorcha's slumbering body. He'd sent word to her after the noon meal with his regrets at being detained and he hoped to join her at supper. Deep in the mud of the second moat, he hadn't made it in time for the evening meal, either, and she'd obviously not waited long afterward to retire.

He hunkered beside the bed, brushing a lock of her hair from her face. Mary sighed and stirred, her lashes quivering against her cheek. Her eyes fluttered open and she stared at him, the relaxed question in her eyes telling him she was still mostly asleep.

"Ye dinnae wait up for me, Mairi," he scolded softly.

"I didn't know you were coming," Mary replied grumpily.

Eaden patted her knees and gave her a little shove to get her to move over. But with Sorcha against her back, all Mary could do was straighten her legs, affording Eaden a few scant inches of mattress to claim for his own. He frowned. This would never work.

"Sorcha!"

The hound moaned and snuggled deeper into the coverlet. Eaden reached over Mary and swatted the dog on her flank.

"Get by, dog!"

With a groan of protest, Sorcha rolled onto her chest. Eaden waved a hand at her and pointed to the floor. "Off, Sorcha!"

The dog scrambled to her feet and bounded from the bed in a graceful arc, crossing to her blanket by the hearth. Turning around on it three times, she sank down with a grunt of discontent and laid her head on her enormous paws, gazing balefully at the two humans across the room.

Eaden yanked the coverlet from the bed and quarter turned it before smoothing the material with a flick of his wrist.

"I dinnae want to sleep with the smell of hound in my nose," he replied in answer to Mary's questioning look. "I've slept all I will with the dog between me and ye. 'Tis yer scent I want, no' some hairy beast."

"What about me?" Mary asked.

"Have it washed on the morrow," Eaden said carelessly, sliding into bed beside her.

"No. I mean, you're a fairly hairy beast yourself."

Eaden stopped, stumped for a moment by her unprecedented statement. He grinned at her, liking the way sleep loosened her tongue. "That well may be. But at least I've bathed this night." He carefully touched her shoulder, sliding his hand down the length of her arm, his work-roughened hands catching on the delicate nap of her silken night shift.

"I'm sorry I've no' been able to be with ye this day," he said, his voice a husky rumble. "I promised ye we'd fix things between us, and I mean to do it."

Mary stiffened beneath the slow stroking of his hand and did not reply. Eaden sighed. His anger at the king's command to wed Barde's daughter had cost him much. He knew he was wrong for using her as he had and was still paying dearly for a moment of ill-advised pique.

"I dinnae want ye to fear me, Mairi. I want ye to like me to touch ye. Can ye at least let me hold ye and no' be afraid?"

Her breathing quicken and he bit back an oath. "Come here, Mairi," he said firmly as he rolled onto his back, pulling her close. "Put yer head on my shoulder."

Hesitantly, Mary scooted against him and laid her head on his shoulder. Eaden sighed and cuddled her against his side. "Lay ye here," he murmured. "And learn to sleep next to this hairy beast. That must, then, be the first step."

* * *

Mary was gone when Eaden woke the next morning. He cursed roundly as he rolled from the bed. It was early, the sun barely up, and he'd thought he'd have a chance to take things further with his wife before they left their bedroom for the day. Her soft body, tucked warmly against his, had played havoc with his senses long into the night. But he'd held himself and his desires in check, hoping to give Mary time to accept their intimacy. She might have played the compliant wife in her own mind, but he'd not felt her body ease until she'd at last fallen asleep.

It took only a moment to rinse the grit from his eyes and don his clothing. Since Sorcha was also missing, Eaden assumed Mary had taken the dog out for her morning walk. He stomped down the stairs, past the tables in the great hall holding mugs and pitchers of water, bread and freshly carved cheese. Everyone awake at this hour already bustled at their work and gave their laird no more than a respectful nod as they went about their chores.

Eaden climbed the stairs to the parapet, exchanging greetings with the men-at-arms he passed as he strolled along the wall, searching the bailey below for a sight of his wife. At last he spied her, Sorcha at her side, as she crossed the courtyard and entered the kennel where the hounds were kept.

"Damn!" he muttered as he whirled and bounded down the stairs. Those hounds were bred to hunt, not to be pets, and she could be seriously injured if she bothered one of the nursing bitches, or thoughtlessly intimidated one of the large males. He crossed the courtyard in long, purposeful strides, reaching the kennel mere minutes behind Mary.

Pausing in the doorway to let his eyes adjust to the dim light, he saw Mary nod a silent greeting to Auld Fionn, the grizzled kennel master. The normally crusty old Scot merely grunted in answer as Mary slowly approached a bitch who had whelped her puppies only a few days earlier.

Before he could shout a warning, the dog lowered her ears against her skull and thumped her tail on the floor in greeting. Eaden wasn't sure if he was more surprised at Fionn's or the dog's acceptance of Mary.

"Oh, what beautiful babies you have!" Mary crooned softly. She squatted on the floor, drawing herself into a small, non-threatening position, her hands dangling loosely in her lap. Again, the bitch thumped her tail on the floor and Sorcha whined in answer.

Mary crept forward and stroked one of the furry morsels of puppy as it nursed its dam vigorously, the wet sounds noisy in the quiet kennel. It wriggled beneath her hand and she laughed softly as she moved to pet each puppy in turn. Eaden's heart leapt into his throat as the bitch swung her head around, but the dog merely licked Mary's hand once and then turned away.

He battled his heart rate back to a manageable pace and strolled into the kennel. His shadow fell over Mary's shoulder and onto the dog and her litter. Caught unaware, Mary's surprise at seeing him turned quickly to a dismay she tried to hide, though the blush on her cheeks betrayed her thoughts.

Eaden frowned. Who had she been expecting? "Careful, Mairi," he warned her, his voice soft, not wanting to alarm the mother dog. "She is verra protective of her bairns."

Nodding, Mary rose to her feet and stepped out into the aisle, closing the gate to the kennel behind her. "I know. But that littlest one isn't doing very well." She turned to look back into the pen. "I wish I could help, but Ranald says he must stay with his mother." A slight smile played on her lips. "She likes me."

Eaden couldn't argue. In fact, it seemed everyone was beginning to like Mary. Amazingly, she'd charmed the fiercest of his dogs as well as garnered grudging respect from even the most irascible of the Scots who would normally have never spoken to The Barde's daughter, much less accepted her as their laird's wife.

"Ye're charming all of us here at Scott Castle."

She hunched her shoulders as she dusted her skirt with her hands. "No. I'm not welcome here. Not truly."

Eaden's eyes narrowed in astonished anger. "Who has told ye so?" he thundered, though he knew full well there were those who still resented the new Lady Scott.

"No one." Mary sighed. "But it's so difficult. I don't fit in because I'm a Barde, and no one is anything but scrupulously respectful because I'm Lady Scott." She gestured with her slender hands. "Well, Ina and Isobel both talk to me as if I'm a person, not a *thing*. And Kirsty is very nice as well." She tried a brief smile. "I'm sure it will get better." There didn't seem to be much hope in her voice.

His fingers itched and he wasn't sure if he wanted to stroke the misery from her eyes or punch whoever made her sad. Unfortunately, he could probably attest to being the biggest cause of her unhappiness, and so he merely nodded.

"Aye, it will." But after last night, he wasn't sure he spoke the truth.

* * *

"The king has invited us to visit," Eaden commented as they headed inside. Mary glanced up, alarm on her face, and almost missed her step. "Wheesht, lass," he admonished, catching her by her elbow to help her regain her balance. "'Tis no' a death sentence to see the king. Even if ye once were a Barde, he willnae hold it against ye now ye are properly married to a Scott."

Mary stared at him through narrowed eyes. "I didn't think the king would likely to have me drawn and quartered simply for being raised a Barde. But why has he invited us to court?"

"When I last saw King Robert he asked I bring you to visit him, but I wanted to wait until he returned to Troon. 'Tis a nice ride from here and a grand view of the ocean once we're there. I think ye'll like it."

"I've never seen the ocean," Mary said. "But I don't like long coach rides. Miriam and I never traveled far from home."

"I've no coach for ye to ride in." Eaden handed her to her seat at the table. "We'll go a' horseback."

Eaden sat and motioned for the platter of bread next to her hand. When she did not respond, he spared her a curious look, noting the pallor of her skin.

"What is the matter, Mairi?" he asked her. "D' ye no' ken how to ride?"

Mary shook her head and opened her mouth, but no words came.

"Mary?" Eaden's voice was sharp, his teasing gone. Mary acted as though she scarcely heard him. He reached to grasp her arm and she bolted out of her seat, her eyes unfocused and wide with alarm.

"Mary," he called to her in a low voice, struggling to calm her before she caused a scene he knew she'd regret. She blinked once then slowly looked around her. Heads turned in her direction and she gave a stiff nod as she slowly settled back into her chair.

"I'm sorry," she whispered, bold splashes of color tinting her pale cheeks. Eaden slid his grasp down her arm to catch one of her hands and squeezed it reassuringly.

"D' ye no' like horses?" he asked with a wry smile.

"I never learned to ride," Mary replied. "Miriam was thrown from her pony as a child and we were never afterward allowed to ride."

"A bad memory, then?"

She tilted her head as if unsure, then shrugged and turned her attention to her plate. So, she feared more than a bad memory. He vowed to seek the root of the problem, but this was clearly not the time or place to push her further. He filled his plate with food, then laid a hunk of bread and a meat pasty on Mary's plate.

From the corner of his eye he watched as she prodded the crumbly pastry with her knife. When she made no move to feed herself, Eaden cut a bite-sized piece of meat from the pie with his own knife, spearing it to wave beneath her nose.

"Eat up, Mairi," he told her. "We've a minstrel to entertain us this day."

Carefully, Mary plucked the offered piece from his knife and put it in her mouth. She chewed the morsel thoroughly before swallowing and Eaden smothered a sigh as he finished his own meal. He turned and spoke to Ranald and a few others who came to the table with comments and questions for him.

At last, the meal drew to an end and the minstrel rose from his seat, tuning his lute with nimble fingers. The room quieted as everyone's attention turned to the performer in their midst. After a moment, he began to sing, and even Mary seemed to have forgotten her earlier moment of panic. The young man's voice rang clear, his poignant ballad of love the only sound in the otherwise silent room.

Eaden watched his wife's face as they listened. A blush rose to her cheeks as the melodic words described the lovers' plight. He now knew Laird Barde had not allowed his daughter or her companion to stride the parapets of Bellecourt Castle, nor had he allowed them to learn to ride. 'Twas obvious no one had prepared Mary for marriage. What else had Laird Barde kept from the two young women in his care?

Recalling the fabulous green cross hidden beneath the bodice of Mary's dress, he had to wonder what other secrets he would find locked in Mary's past.

Chapter Seventeen

People milled about the great hall, putting off the end of the day for as long as possible. Mary and Eaden sat beside the enormous fireplace, its banked coals glowing hotly. Desultory conversation mixed with yawns while others congratulated the minstrel whose voice was near to cracking from the strain of his lengthy performance. He'd been invited to stay and entertain them again at supper, and after a wry glance at the driving rain outside, he'd needed no prodding to linger the night.

Try as she might, Mary couldn't push aside the alarm surging in her breast each time she recalled Miriam and her ill-fated pony. Concentrating on the night to come was also less than soothing. With no alternative but to remain at Scott Castle, she would soon have no choice but to allow Eaden past the defenses she'd built between them. One night soon, he would not be content with just a kiss.

Isobel's counsel had certainly changed the way Mary imagined a husband and wife should behave toward each other, and she found it nearly impossible to remain impassive in his arms as she now knew she should. His warm hands and heady kisses were not making things easy for her, and she grew increasingly ashamed of her body's response to him.

Once again, the memory of Miriam's pony slipped through her mind. Caught off-guard, Mary closed her eyes as she fought the unwelcome snatches of memory.

A scream of fright and pain.
Miriam sprawled lifeless on the ground.
The smell of fresh blood and bowels released in sudden death.

Mary recoiled from the recollection as she jerked back to reality. She sought out Eaden, relieved to see him facing away, his attention on the man beside him, chatting lazily. As she struggled to recover her poise, conversations and activities swirled senselessly around her. Hands fidgeting in her lap, twisting the heavy silk of her gown, she betrayed the disquiet of her mind.

Something cold and wet shoved beneath her fingers and into her lap. Mary gasped at the feel of icy, water-soaked fur against her skin. Wrenched from her unpleasant thoughts, she looked down to see the tiny body of the puppy she'd worried over earlier. Sorcha nudged the puppy deeper into Mary's lap.

"Oh, Sorcha!" she murmured in dismay. "What have you done?"

The puppy mewled pitifully and turned its blind head back and forth, seeking warmth and nourishment. Gently Mary picked the puppy up and held it tightly against her chest, the unnatural cold of the tiny body seeping through the fabric of her dress.

"Eaden!" she cried, looking to him for help as the puppy soundlessly opened its mouth, too weak to do anything more.

Eaden turned to her and his face fell as he noticed the puppy in her hands. "Where did ye get him, Mairi?"

Mary nodded at the hound at her side. "Sorcha brought him to me," she said. The deerhound whined, her attention pinned on the puppy.

Eaden touched its chilled pelt. "He's no' a thriver, Mairi. He's smaller than the others by a good bit. I'm afraid his ma pushed him away, knowing he wouldnae last the night."

"I can't let him die." Mary lifted a hand to brush a tear from her cheek. She flung him a pleading look, her eyes wide, brow furrowed, begging him to help her.

Eaden sighed and motioned to a servant. "Bring me a mug of warm milk. And a clean cloth."

With a nod, the girl hurried to do his bidding. Eaden turned back to Mary. "Come to the fire, then. We need to get him warm."

Mary inched her chair closer to the hearth and laid the puppy in her lap. She picked up a corner of her gown and rubbed him vigorously, drying his coat, helping warmth seep into his tiny body. Her fingers kneaded the short, dense fur, fluffing the coat as it began to dry.

"Here, Laird."

Eaden took the napkin from the serving lass, and, twisting a knot in its corner, dipped it in the warm milk.

With a nudge, Eaden handed Mary the dampened cloth and she touched it gently to the puppy's nose, experiencing a twinge of relief as his mouth opened in response.

"Here, now, little one," she crooned, placing the false teat on the puppy's tongue. He mouthed it twice then stopped, letting the milk leak out the sides of his mouth.

Eaden cautioned, "Wheesht, Mairi. He cannae eat too fast. He needs to take his time, build his strength." His voice sounded strained, his attempt at bravado evident, but Mary ignored all but the encouragement. She nodded her head jerkily, striving to keep the tears at bay. She stroked the soft fur with one hand as the puppy rested quietly in her lap.

"Come," Eaden urged. "We'll fix him a basket and put him near the hearth in our room. He'll stay warm there."

Mary flashed him a tremulous smile, grateful for his understanding. She knew the puppy might not survive the night, but it made her feel better to try.

* * *

Mary settled the puppy in the basket on the hearth, but Eaden wasn't looking at the pitiful scrap of fur. The flames of the fire lit against Mary's night shift, revealing her body through the thin fabric in dark, voluptuous silhouette. He shifted in his seat against the tightening of his breeches and gripped the arms of his chair until his knuckles whitened.

"Is this good?" Mary turned from the basket to face him.

With a start, Eaden jerked his gaze to Mary's eager face. "Er, aye," he managed, clearing his throat. *And were it any better, we wouldnae be discussing a fading puppy.*

"I was afraid he might be too close to the fire." Mary pushed the basket an inch or two further from the warmth of the flames.

Too late. I am already burned. He wanted to cross the short distance to her, take her in his arms and kiss her until she could no longer hold herself from him. But he knew she was not trying to entice him, and he balked at taking her as he'd done once before, no matter the provocation this night.

"How often should I feed him?" Mary turned her innocent gaze back to Eaden.

I need ye more than food. Eaden swallowed hard. "I suppose whenever he cries." He stared into her soft green eyes, aware of the way the fire caught the golden strands in her hair and turned them into a halo of amber light. Mary tilted her head quizzically, and the movement plunged her face into shadow. Eaden caught his breath.

"M'laird?"

Eaden shot to his feet. "'Tis nothing, Mairi," he lied. "Come. Let us be abed."

She hesitated, the fabric of her night shift billowed in a draft from the chimney. He held out a hand, and slowly Mary laid her hand in his. Her fingers trembled.

* * *

Eaden leaned over the parapet, his hands dangling into the darkness below. It had taken little more than Mary's quick breath of stifled protest to unman him. He knew he pushed her to be his wife. He knew she wanted more from her husband than protection and children. Mary wanted love. He could give her protection, and, hopefully, children. Could he give her his heart? Would she then come to him willingly? Or would her distrust of him ever be their undoing?

Faint footsteps on the stone interrupted his dismal thoughts and Eaden turned to see his brother approach. Ranald stopped several feet away and leaned over the parapet in mirror-image of his brother's actions.

"Have ye anything to say that doesnae concern my bride?" Eaden drawled, forestalling Ranald's words.

Ranald cocked his head in consideration. "Unless ye have some new reason to be stalking the parapet at night, then nay." He leaned an elbow against the stone. "I've forsaken coming to yer room of a morning to rouse ye." He hesitated, looking at his hands for a moment before he continued. "Do ye now have a reason to forsake yer own rooms at night?"

Eaden flashed his brother a dangerous look. But Ranald had been on the receiving end of his brother's glares often enough, and this one elicited no real concern.

"My wife still remembers her wedding night, it seems."

Ranald's eyebrows shot up for an instant before he managed to return them to their normal position. "Perhaps there no' has been time for the memory to fade."

"Och, there has been plenty of time. Time filled with hopes of divorce—which I am no' inclined to give her."

This time Ranald's eyebrows would not be gainsaid. "She doesnae want to be married." His voice fell matter-of-fact, making a statement, not asking a question.

"Och, she wants to marry," Eaden replied, waving one had in a dismissing gesture. "Just no' to me."

"Well, the king hasnae offered to help ye with a divorce, has he? I'm thinking he doesnae have another daughter of a feuding clan waiting to take Mary's place." Ranald shrugged. "And though I'm sure he felt inclined to have yer ballocks for the way ye mucked this up, I believe ye've gotten the best of the deal after all."

"I know what I have, now. And I want more from her than a shadow of that night forever between us." Eaden clenched his fists, the line of tension visible up his arms and into his shoulders. "I dinnae know what I must do."

"She'll no' make it easy for ye, aye?"

"I want her willing."

"Other than the obvious–that she is beautiful–why?"

Eaden pushed restlessly away from the parapet. "She has no training to run the castle. She defies me. And she closes her eyes and draws away at my touch."

He faced Ranald, frowning in frustration. "And yet I see in her strength, and kindness, and a passion she has yet to discover."

"And ye feel guilty for the way ye've treated her."

"Damn it! Aye."

One side of Ranald's mouth twitched upwards. "Then why do ye stand here talkin' to me? The lass has a right to know ye're properly fashed."

Eaden spared one more look of disgust for his younger brother before he turned on his heel and disappeared down the dark stairway.

Chapter Eighteen

"Himself would like ye to join him for supper."

Mary looked up from the puppy on her lap as Ina delivered Laird Scott's request. Eaden had not returned to their room after their disastrous attempt at lovemaking the night before. Mary's cheeks burned at the memory and she resolutely turned to the matter at hand. At least he wanted to see her, although she quailed to consider why.

She knew he was busy with the construction of a second moat around the castle, as well as other duties, and could not be expected to dance attendance on her every moment. Instead of his absence giving her breathing space, the uncertainty of how to face him again made her worry far too much. She'd spent a sleepless night wondering when he would come to her again.

Or even if he would.

Ina touched Mary's arm lightly. "Ye should wear yer new gown, milady," she wheedled, the mention of the green gown with the beautiful gold embroidery an obvious ploy to lighten her spirits.

Unwilling to cast further aspersions on her marriage by refusing to accede to his summons, Mary nodded to Ina. "Tell him I will be there."

She saw Ina scowl lightly at Isobel, but could understand no reason for it.

"I will have a bath drawn for ye, milady," Isobel said as she turned and left the room.

Ina lingered until Isobel was gone, then inclined her head to Mary. "Have a care, milady," she cautioned. "Isobel can be ambitious."

"What are you saying?" Mary asked.

Ina sighed. "I dinnae like gossip, milady, but it has been said the woman cares a wee bit much for the laird."

"But, he's married now. And so is she."

Ina pursed her lips and set about straightening the room, refusing to say anything further.

Mary finished feeding the puppy and settled him in his basket on the hearth, his breathing slowing as he drifted off to sleep. Her brow furrowed in confusion as she considered Ina's words. Isobel had offered to help her, not hurt her. She'd even given candid insight as to what her husband wanted from her. And, though it didn't make Mary anxious for his attentions, she at least now had a guideline for how to behave with him.

Mary frowned to remember Eaden's abrupt departure from their room the night before. He hadn't seemed very pleased with her attempt to submit to him. Was he too used to the attentions of *im*proper women? Would he ever want his proper wife?

Perhaps Isobel had once been close to Eaden. But surely the infatuation, or whatever it had been, was over. Both she and Eaden had married other people, and while Mary could say with fair certainty she was not Eaden's first choice for a wife, she sincerely hoped Isobel had been able to marry her choice of husband.

Isobel returned, Mary's new green dress draped over her arm. Two strong lads followed, each toting a brace of buckets, steam rising from the gently sloshing water. They emptied the buckets into the tub, hot water mingling with the cold. Mary would have liked the tub to be closer to the hearth and the warm coals banked there, but she'd been pleased with the small, private bathing room adjacent to the bedroom, a luxury she'd not had at Bellecourt.

She closed the bedroom door securely as they left, then crossed to the bathing chamber, where Isobel added a few drops of oil to the water. The resulting aroma filled the room with the scent of roses. Still unused to the attention, Mary tried to hide her embarrassment at her nakedness as Isobel helped her undress, and quickly slipped into the tub. Isobel seemed to understand Mary's reticence, for she bustled about the room laying out drying cloths and soaps, paying little heed to Mary as she bathed.

The water cooled, reminding her of the passage of time and that Eaden would soon be waiting for her. Reluctantly, Mary eased from the tub and wrapped herself in a soft robe, belting it snugly about her waist. Walking into the bedroom, she sat before the dressing table, moved to the room for her use several days earlier. She picked up a hairbrush, preparing to set her hair in order.

"Here, let me do that." Isobel took the brush from Mary's hand. "I can fix yer hair for ye."

"Thank you," Mary said. "But it's so difficult to manage. It's always falling down when I try to put it up."

"Perhaps ye should wear it down, then," Isobel replied, brushing Mary's hair with brisk motions.

"Eaden said he liked the color," Mary admitted shyly, unable to prevent a slight smile from lifting the corners of her lips. The hairbrush hit a snarl in Mary's curls and jerked her head painfully. "Oh!"

"I'm sorry, milady. I'll dress yer hair. It won't fall when I'm through with it," Isobel vowed.

Mary endured the twisting and pinning of her hair as Isobel worked her skills on the shining, gold-streaked tresses. When finished, Mary had to admit her hair would probably not fall for any reason, save a prolonged high wind. Pulled sharply away from her face and tightly braided, it twisted back on itself in a manner deceptively intricate and severe. Mary didn't particularly care for the style, but she hesitated to criticize Isobel's hard work. At least the dress looked beautiful, and she had to admit Isobel had a deft hand with embroidery.

With a smile of thanks, Mary slipped out of her robe and into the cream-colored underskirt. The sumptuous green silk gown followed, settling over her with a slim, flattering style. She preened before the mirror, steeling herself against the moment she would face Laird Scott.

* * *

Eaden glanced up for the tenth time since he'd entered the great hall. He'd instructed the servants to set a table for himself and Mary outside in the late sunlight, hoping she would enjoy the beautiful afternoon and a little privacy away from the crowded hall. After inspecting their efforts, he strode into the great hall to look for his wife, trying to suppress his impatience.

A stir on the stairs caught his eye and Eaden stopped his pacing as his wife glided down the steps, her skirts trailing behind her. He stared at her, wondering how he'd kept his hands off her the past three weeks.

Her hair, pulled severely back, revealed glowing skin stretched across the elegant planes of her face. The gown she'd felt so guilty about having made hugged her slim form perfectly, and the color, he knew, matched her eyes.

Mary stopped at the last rung, unable to move past the spot where Eaden blocked her descent. Taking her hand, he tucked it in the crook of his arm and led her through the hall, past the eyes of the people gathered for supper and out into the evening sunshine. Mary lifted her face to the sky, a rare smile curving her lips. Pleasure boomed in Eaden's heart at the sight. He'd been right to bring her out here.

"I'm sorry I havenae seen ye today," he offered.

"I understand," Mary murmured. "I'm sure many things required your attention."

Unable to keep from touching her, he guided her into her chair, one palm resting lightly on her waist. He slid his hand up her back and down her arm as she sat, twining his fingers with hers before releasing her. Dropping a quick kiss on her knuckles, he considered his seating options and chose to look at her rather than sit next to her.

"I'm afraid a certain lack of attention has made my day longer than it should," he said.

Mary raised her eyebrows.

"My thoughts kept turning back to ye, Mairi. I couldnae keep my mind on my work."

Mary blushed and parted her lips to speak, but they were interrupted as a servant arrived, setting food on the table. Eaden quickly filled his plate, passing each platter to Mary. He watched her slowly spoon some marinated vegetables onto her plate.

"Ye dinnae like the salmon?" He nodded to the bowl of creamed fish at Mary's elbow.

She jumped at the sound of his voice, setting her spoon back on the table with a loud clatter. "I'm sorry." She grabbed the bowl and began ladling the fish onto her plate.

Eaden covered her hand with his, stilling her actions. "Wheesht, Mairi. Ye're no' required to eat everything on the table."

Mary glanced up and he detected the uncertainty lurking in the soft green depths of her eyes. "I'm not very hungry," she admitted.

Making an abrupt decision, Eaden spread his napkin across the table and tossed bread and cheeses onto it. He pulled the corners together to make a neat packet, then rose to his feet, motioning her to stand as well.

A wary look on her face, Mary took the goblet he offered her. As she sipped the wine, he teased, "Only the best for the laird's lady." She flushed becomingly.

Eaden motioned toward the path out of the courtyard. "Come. I know of a better place." He nudged her with his elbow, shrugging to show her his hands were full, and once again, Mary smiled. Encouraged, Eaden grinned and together they walked through the bailey and down the winding path to the river.

Mary cast a glance over her shoulder as they passed people hurrying toward the castle in the afternoon's fading light. "Shouldn't we be in the gates before dark?"

"I know the warden," Eaden replied carelessly. "I suspect he'll let us in."

A note of mirth escaped her and Eaden looked at her in surprise. "Still not used to being Lady Scott and doing as ye please?"

Mary instantly sobered. "No."

Understanding her predicament, Eaden abandoned the difficult subject and gestured toward the bend in the river. Ahead of them were the wide, flat banks where the children were wont to play. Above loomed the overhanging cliff where he had taken Mary to survey the lands of Craigievar.

Beneath the edge of the rocks, the evening shadows lengthened. Clumps of yellow broom swept to the foot of the cliff, reflecting the last of the sunlight and charging the air with a clear, golden quality, mingling eerily with the mists rising from the water.

"It's beautiful," Mary breathed, turning slowly to take in the scene. Eaden caught his breath at the sight of his wife, her arms outstretched, her head tilted back to inhale the soft evening air. His hands itched to release her hair from its tight coils and send it cascading over her shoulders. As if reading his thoughts, Mary pulled the pins from her hair, using her fingers to comb apart the strands of her braids. She let the mass fall down her back where streaks of it blended with the golden embroidery of her gown.

Eaden dropped the food package and the wine flask on a nearby rock. With a moment of reverent hesitation, he moved slowly to the vision before him. The last of the sunlight glinted off Mary's unbound hair and surrounded her in a halo of pure gold as she turned to him.

* * *

Power and restraint showed in the way Eaden's muscles bunched beneath the thin shirt he wore. Opened in a deep 'v' on his chest, the single lace at the neck dangled untied. Mary could only stare as he moved closer. She took in his raven-dark hair and the way his sun-bronzed skin gleamed in the evening light. His eyes met hers, as if questioning her mood.

Over the past sleepless nights, she'd had more than enough time to examine her plight from every imaginable angle. It bothered her greatly no one from Bellecourt had searched for her, and she fretted to have received no response to the missive she'd sent to Miriam several days earlier. For all she'd considered Bellecourt Castle her home, she'd been made uncomfortably aware since her mother's death she was no longer of much, if any, interest to Laird Barde.

If she stayed at Scott Castle, she'd have the protection of Eaden's name and all who swore fealty to him. And she'd have the man himself.

Again, she looked from her thoughts to her husband. Though his size and aura of utter confidence stole her breath, she was beginning to learn he possessed a gentler side. Stern and unyielding though he could be, he'd offered her more than a chance to come to terms with her new life, and even now wooed her in the bargain. Mary blinked in surprise at the thought. *Laird Scott wooing me, Mary Marsh?* It sent an unaccustomed thrill down her spine and she twitched at the sensation.

"Cold?" he asked, his voice pitched low.

Mary shook her head. "No, just unsure. I mean, after last night . . ."

"Could ye come over here and let me settle the question, then, lass?"

Did he offer to let her chose to come to him? Or did he use his infamous diplomacy to hide a well-phrased command? Mary took a deep breath and made her decision. With Isobel's advice running through her mind, Mary stepped into her husband's arms.

Chapter Nineteen

"Ye smell like heaven," Eaden murmured as he held her close, his face buried in her soft hair. Her form and scent fueled his pounding heart. He could scarce believe she'd walked willingly into his arms. After her withdrawal from him the night before, he had been unsure if he could mend things between them. His relief at her apparent concession, if not actual surrender, gave him hope, and he nuzzled her neck.

Tilting her head, Mary exposed her throat to his kisses, and he greedily nibbled the creamy skin within his reach. He lifted a hand to cup her breast, and felt her stiffen in response.

"Settle, Mairi. I willnae hurt ye." Willing himself to slow down, he gently stroked his hand up and down her side, accustoming her to his touch. He wanted her, but on his terms, not resentful cooperation wrung from her in tearful submission.

As Mary released a pent-up breath, easing the tension from her body, Eaden turned his attention to her lips, remembering how she responded to his kisses. She arched into his caress, wrapping her arms about his neck, and he needed no further encouragement. He scooped her off her feet and strode near the base of the cliff where the yellow broom bushes stopped and the soft moss grew in the cool shadows. So far, his efforts at wooing her had ended dismally in their bed. Mayhap a change of scenery would soften her mood. He let her slide slowly to the ground, feeling her slender length press against him.

"Turn around so I can unlace ye," he whispered against her ear, his voice husky with passion. For an instant, Eaden wasn't sure if she would comply, but Mary slid her arms from his neck and turned, presenting her back to him.

"Yer hair feels like silk, Mairi." He filled his hands with burnished curls before brushing the mass over her shoulder. He nuzzled the back of her neck, trailing slow kisses over her bare skin, delighting in her delicate shivers. With minimal trouble, he freed the laces of her dress and slid it from her shoulders, steadying her with a hand beneath her elbow as she stepped out of the gown. He turned her to face him, staring hungrily at her slender form in the thin, creamy underskirt only a shade darker than her pale skin.

He plunged both hands into her hair and pulled her to him, drinking in the honey of her lips. He slid his fingers down her neck and across her shoulders, trembling with need as he fumbled for the single tie at the top of her shift. Mary flinched as he tugged the lacing impatiently. Belatedly, he realized she likely remembered the way he'd torn her dress in frustration with the tangled laces the night of their wedding. *Damn*. With a muttered curse, he carefully opened the neck of her dress, which only needed a nudge of his fingers to slide it off her shoulders to pool, soft as a sigh, on the ground at her feet.

He stared at her. He had no breath, no ability to move or even think. Only one part of him was doing any thinking and it strained against his breeches, demanding immediate attention.

"Ye're so beautiful, Mairi." Clumsy in a way he couldn't understand, he knelt at her feet and picked up the thin cotton shift. He shook it out and spread it over the moss at the base of the cliff. Removing his own clothes, he slung them impatiently to the side before he turned back to Mary.

She stood motionless, her body a study of moonlight and shadows. Her hands fisted at her side and Eaden covered the distance between them in two long strides, refusing to give her time to fear him all over again. He gathered her against him, feathering his hands down her arms.

"Come with me," he said as he grasped her hand in his and led her to the soft bed he'd prepared for them.

* * *

The cool night air enveloped Mary's skin like a soft glove and she caught her breath only with effort as Eaden's heated gaze drifted over her. "Are ye well, Mairi?"

Even as she considered his words, she marveled at the frisson of something strange and new coursing deep within her. Would things be different this time? They had to be, for there could be no turning back. After this, her decision would be made, and she would belong to Eaden forever.

With Isobel's warning running through her head, Mary nodded, swallowing hard against her nervousness and the urge to touch him as he followed her down to the shift he'd spread on the moss. She felt the soft bumps and hollows of the ground beneath her in sharp contrast to the powerful arms pinning her on either side. The heat from his body poured over her, banishing the chill of the earth and the apprehension she couldn't entirely keep at bay.

His hands roamed her skin, touching her in ways no one ever had before. She trembled, biting her lip to stifle the cries fluttering at the back of her throat. The bold feel of him, naked against her, was exciting beyond anything she could imagine. Knowing what would come next did not change her determination to let him do as he wished. Isobel had promised her he would finish quickly, and she wanted nothing more than to please him as his wife should.

As Eaden continued his determined assault on her senses, she began to wonder if enduring would be as easy as she'd thought. Each touch of his hands, each caress of his mouth caused her breath to quicken, and her skin burned as though on fire. His fingers sought out the most intimate part of her and she tensed, dreading what was to come.

"I'll no' hurt ye again, Mairi," he vowed hoarsely. "Let me love ye."

With a great force of will, Mary relaxed and discovered he did not lie when he loved her gently in the moonlight.

* * *

His breath harsh and deep, Eaden almost missed the sounds she made. Fighting back the rapid echoes of his thudding heart, he listened again for the unmistakable sound of Mary crying. And heard it.

Caught between frustration and anxiety, Eaden rolled to his side, pulling her head onto his shoulder, stroking her hair in an effort to calm her agitation. "What's wrong, Mairi?"

She remained silent, a mute denial anything was amiss.

He tried again. "'Tis no' wrong for a husband to love his wife. Even here beneath the stars, 'tis a fine thing."

"I know," Mary quietly replied. Too quietly.

Eaden sighed. "Did ye no' like it, then?"

Mary stiffened and he knew he'd hit the mark. But it was downright embarrassing for a man of his experience and reputation to have left his wife feeling so, so . . .

Damn.

He eased his arm from beneath Mary's head and started to rise, but couldn't resist one last kiss. "Come, Mairi," he said as he released her. "Let us see if the warden will let us in this night."

He helped her to her feet. She gathered her clothes and pulled them on, turning so he could tighten the laces on her gown. Eaden caught her sidelong glance at him as he dressed and hid a relieved grin. *At least she's curious.*

As soon as they both were ready, he led her back along the river to the path leading to the castle gates, his fingers twined with hers. He followed her through the narrow door beside the main gate and heard the heavy thud of the latch as the warden fastened it securely behind them.

Sorcha bounded across the floor as soon as the bedroom door opened, flinging herself with a happy *woof* at her mistress, nearly knocking her down in her excitement.

"Wheesht, now, Sorcha," Eaden admonished the big hound. "Stand on yer own feet." He gave the dog a good-natured swat and Sorcha responded with a bounce of pure delight. With a leap defying the sheer size of the dog, she landed in the middle of the bed and whirled to watch the pair who halted inside the door.

"No' tonight, lass." He strode to the bed and took the dog by her collar. He dragged her onto the floor and after a glance at Eaden's unyielding face, Sorcha padded to her blanket beside the fireplace. Turning around and around to bunch the blanket into an acceptable jumble, the dog flopped down with a sigh and closed her eyes.

"Ye look ready to collapse," Eaden said as he turned back to Mary. "Slip into bed and relax."

She eyed the bed, then firmed her chin and once again stripped out of her clothes. Eaden saw her hand falter as she reached for her night shift. With a quick look over her shoulder at him, she abandoned the shift and slid naked between the sheets.

He didn't know what to think about Mary's actions, but matters would surely change between himself and his lamentably naïve wife. He pulled off his own clothes and slipped into bed next to her. Wrapping his arms around her, he brought her close against him and nuzzled her ear, letting one hand slide over her shoulder and down to cup her breast.

"Och, Mairi," he murmured as he felt her body tense. "Ye've got to forget what yer ma told ye about making love."

"My mother died more than four years ago," Mary said quietly. "I was only thirteen."

"Then dinnae be afraid of me, Mairi. I cannae bear it. I'm paying dearly for the way I treated ye on our wedding night. I'll never harm ye again. I swear it."

He held her against him for a time, unable to tell from her uneven breathing if she believed him or not. Just as he made up his mind to drag the problem out into the open again, Mary turned in his arms. Now facing him, she pulled his face to hers, molding her lips to his, drinking him in hungrily.

Her daring resulted in Eaden's undoing and he could hold himself back no longer. He buried himself in her with a shudder and gave himself up to the best way he knew to please her.

* * *

The heat of him, the restrained power shifting beneath her hands, made Mary gasp with a pleasure so fierce it shook her to her core. She stiffened the instant the sound left her lips, afraid, so afraid to let him see what he did to her.

She couldn't hide the fierce pounding of her heart or the way her breathing labored as he stroked her intimately, and she gritted her teeth against the flames streaking through her. He slid inside her, stretching and filling her. She wanted to shout at him, use her hands to urge him on, unsure if she rushed him to finish quickly or to meet with the frantic demands of her body.

Her hands clenched on his shoulders and she choked back a sob. Isobel had told her he would take great pleasure with her, but only low-bred women with insatiable appetites would derive pleasure from the act. Such men as Laird Scott did not want a wanton woman for a wife. A hint of enjoyment from her would lead only to his disgust.

Determined to be the wife she'd been told was acceptable to the laird, she fought her body's responses to him, and this time, when Eaden buried his face in her hair, his heartbeat pounding in her ears, she carefully hid her tears.

Chapter Twenty

Mary followed the shrill sounds of children's laughter out to the bailey. In the streamers of sunlight slanting through the early morning mists, several of the castle children ran screaming with delight as one small boy aimed a ball in their midst. Mary laughed wistfully at their antics, but her soft sound of mirth was not what stopped their play. It was the sight of Sorcha who ambled out into the yard beside her.

A red-haired boy spotted the deerhound first, and, with a shout, he left the group and loped over to Mary, the rest following with more caution.

"M' name's Geordie, milady." He gave a quick bob of his head for courtesy's sake, his eyes on Sorcha. "Ist that yer dog?"

"Well, she belongs to Laird Scott, but she is with me a lot." Mary tilted her head at the lad. "And how did you know who I am?"

"Beggin' yer pardon, milady, but there's none who can own these dogs and they're no' an earl at least." His lips lifted in an impish grin. "And everyone kens the laird's new lady is a Barde."

Mary frowned. "But . . ."

"An' his dog is guarding ye."

Before Mary could question him further, the girl at Geordie's side jerked hard on his sleeve. "Wheesht, Geordie! Ye'll be getting us into trouble, now." She peered from beneath lowered lashes at Lady Scott. "I apologize for my brother, milady." She cut her gaze to Geordie, giving him a frown and another jerk on his sleeve as he opened his mouth. "He's a bit forward. Our own ma says he is."

Mary tightened her lips to keep from laughing. It was obvious though Geordie was unapologetically interested in both her and Sorcha, his sister either did not like having a Barde clanswoman as Lady Scott, or perhaps sincerely feared for her brother and his brash ways.

She composed herself and let a slight smile touch her lips. "No disrespect noted," Mary reassured the pair. "What is your name?"

Geordie's sister gave Mary a short bob. "Cathella, milady. Though most call me Ella."

"I'm Ailie," the littlest girl piped up, bobbing her knees in an attempt at a curtsy.

Ella pointed to the other two children, as alike as down on a thistle. "An' yon's Hamish and Kyle." She pointed unerringly from one brother to the other, and Mary had to take her word for she could see no difference between the pair.

With a solemn nod, Mary accepted the introductions. "I am Mary, Lady Scott." She rested her hand on Sorcha's head. "And this is Sorcha."

"May we pet her?"

"Ist she friendly?"

"Wheesht, ye maunt get yer fingers bit off!"

Mary held her hand up for silence. Five expectant faces turned to her. "You must be very still and hold out your hands, each of you. Don't approach her. Let her come to you."

With great solemnity, each child did as Mary said.

Apparently willing to humor the children, Sorcha strolled among them, sniffing each outstretched hand and offering a lick here and there. At last she returned to Mary and sat her furry rump on the ground at her side, tail swishing gently in the dust.

"D'ye suppose she'll play ball w' us?" one of the twins asked.

"Dinnae be daft," Geordie scoffed. "Th' dog is a hunter, no' a pet," he informed the others loftily, willing to share his obviously superior knowledge. "She's also here to guard milady."

"Ist she mean?" Ailie turned solemn eyes to Mary for reassurance.

"No, Sorcha is not mean. But she *is* a hunter, as Geordie said. And she *does* protect me." Mary leaned forward to Ailie's level. "I don't think she plays ball."

"Will she guard us if we go to the river?"

"Yes! We'll go to the river!"

"Come on, Kyle!"

"Hurry up, Hamish!"

"Sorcha and milady are going with us to the river!"

Mary regarded the excited children, remembering the ones she'd seen playing beside the river the day Eaden had taken her to the cliff, showing her all of Craigievar. *The day I learned I would live here forever.*

She banished the memory and instead replaced it with the shrieks of laughter that had drifted to her ears that afternoon.

"All right," she agreed, touching the children's shoulders as they turned toward the castle gate. She glanced once at the sky, judging the clouds as they fled across the blue expanse, promising a beautiful summer morning.

"Let's go to the river!"

* * *

Hamish's aim went awry, and the ball, made of tightly bound rags, landed with an unexpected *plop* in the gently eddying water next to Mary. Intent on searching for pretty rocks for Ailie in the shallow pool, she jumped to her feet in surprise, whirling to face the perceived threat. And came face-to-face with five sets of frightened eyes.

The children stood in silence. Glistening specks of water dripped from Mary's nose and Ella laughed. Horrified, the girl immediately clapped her hands over her mouth, her eyes wide.

"Do you think I cannot retaliate?" Mary intoned, trying her best to keep the amusement from her voice. Slowly, she bent to retrieve the now-sodden ball and held it before her. All eyes turned on the bound rags as the river water sluiced from its mass.

With a sudden move, Mary drew her hand back and threw the ball unerringly at Geordie's chest. The dull thump as it struck the sturdy boy sounded unexpectedly loud in the silence and Mary could hold back her laughter no longer.

She whooped as Geordie reflexively clutched the ball to his chest, making a wet stain on his shirt that spread rapidly outwards. Relief lit their faces as the children realized Lady Scott enjoyed their play. They fell upon each other, snatching the ball away and squeezing its liquid contents on tousled heads. With screeches of girlish fright, Ella and Ailie darted away from the scrambling boys, taking refuge behind Mary's skirts.

"No fair!" Geordie panted, not brave enough to drag his sister from her hiding place.

Giggling wildly, the girls fled across the grass along the edge of the slow-moving river. Mary watched their antics, her entire body humming with contentment. She folded her arms, hugging herself to contain the moment of joy. As the children ran ahead, Mary followed, stopping to pick a handful of flowers from the plants growing beside the water. She held the blossoms to her nose, inhaling their sweet fragrance. Her eyes drifted upwards, thanking heaven for the beauty of the day.

A low purr of contentment thrummed in the back of her throat as she recognized the moss-strewn bower where Eaden had made love to her the night before. Following the children, she strolled further down river, until the men-at-arms on the wall of the castle were little more than shadowy marks against the clear sky.

A movement on the hill above the river caught her eye, the thud of pounding hooves growing loud as she spun to the left, peering intently in the direction of the sound. Two riders, urging their horses on, broke through the cover of the shrubs and Mary gasped in recognition.

"Ian!" Waving her hands in the air, she struggled to get his attention. He reined his horse to an abrupt stop. His searching gaze locked onto her, and to her horror, he wheeled his horse over the edge of the low cliff with a jerk of his hand, his shoulders nearly touching his horse's rump as he leaned back, helping his mount keep his balance on his downward plunge.

Mary clapped a hand over her mouth, her heart pumping wildly as Ian pulled his horse to a halt beside her.

"What are ye doin' out here, milady?" he shouted, trying to be heard above the excited cries of the children running toward them.

"We were playing, nothing more," Mary replied, startled by the force of his rebuke.

"Soldiers are coming. Mount up behind me!" Ian kicked a foot free of its stirrup and leaned forward, grabbing Mary's hand.

"No!"

"I must get ye to safety!" Ian's tone brooked no argument, but Mary snatched her hand away and stumbled away from his reach.

"I will bring the children. Go warn the castle."

Ian nudged his horse closer, but Mary took another pace back, battling her fear of the horse, warning Ian with a look that she would not come along quietly. By now the children clustered around her, their eyes on Ian and his prancing horse.

Ian scanned the trail to the castle, then glanced over his shoulder at the road he'd just left. Dust rose in the distance.

"Run!" Ian wrenched his horse toward the castle. Holding the steed to a pace even with the children, he followed, faithful as the deerhound guarding the children on their other side.

The children ran, Mary at their heels. Hooves pounded behind them, and Mary's heart leapt into her throat in fear. The gates to the castle were open wide, but the heavy hinges creaked as they began to close. Guards leaned over the edge of the parapet, urging them on. They held their bows up, arrows notched and ready, unable to fire upon the approaching intruders through the crowd of children.

Mary's breath came in hot panicky gasps as she realized the riders were almost upon them. The ground beneath her feet changed abruptly from grass to beaten dirt. Ahead of her, Ailie cried out, her hands flying out in front of her as she fell sprawling to the ground. Close on the little girl's heels, Mary tried to stop, but she tripped, rolling to one side to avoid landing on the child. The others ran ahead of them, but Ian wheeled his horse around. Mary scrambled to her feet, clutching at Ailie, dragging her upright.

Sobbing her terror, Ailie tripped again. Mary pulled the child against her, but they were now far behind the others. Ian reined to a stop beside them, his horse dancing against the pull of the bit. Looking over his shoulder, Ian maneuvered his horse back a step, putting himself between Mary and the soldiers on their heels.

"Here!" Mary thrust the child into Ian's lap. Startled, he tucked the girl before him in the saddle, snugging her tight beneath one arm. He leaned forward, reaching for Mary.

Mary shook her head wildly, unable to force herself to mount up behind Ian, regardless of the soldiers on their heels. "Go! I'll be right behind you." She caught her breath at the indecision on Ian's face, afraid he'd force her onto the horse. "Please," she begged him. "Save her."

Ian swore. His horse whirled in a tight circle, fighting his master's heavy hand. Mary jerked back, tucking her hands behind her, out of his reach. Ailie choked on a frightened sob, her dress torn, her tear-streaked cheeks red from her fall.

Ian glanced behind Mary, judging the advance of the intruders and Mary took his moment of inattention to dart further away. Certain Ian had the child safe in his arms, she faced the riders behind them. Their blue and yellow banner unfurled, and Mary stared, dumbfounded at the sight.

Her head high, Mary stepped to the middle of the road, flanked by the enormous dog at her side whose fangs gleamed white beneath snarling lips.

Chapter Twenty-One

Eaden paced the floor, his stride pounding out his anger. Wordless, Mary waited to one side of the room, staring at the rushes covering the cold stone. He could see her tiredness in her drooped shoulders, and she'd shuffled her feet more than once.

"What were ye doing outside the castle walls without an escort?" Eaden's voice sounded harsh, even to him, but at least he'd managed to keep from shouting.

Mary raised her head and sighed. "I was at the river with the children."

"Without an escort!" It was no use. He shouted at her. Shouting *was* better than grabbing her and shaking her, though his hands itched to do just that. "Ye gave me yer word ye would no' leave the castle without an escort." He bit back the rest of his words and spun his heel, coming to a stop as he shoved his hands through his hair, making clumps of it stand out on his head. "Ye could have been killed, Mairi."

"They did not know who I was."

"It dinnae matter. Ye stepped before four armed riders."

"They were from Bellecourt. I saw their colors." Her mouth tightened in a mutinous line. "No matter what you think of them, they are not evil. They would not hurt me."

"They dinnae know ye," Eaden mocked, throwing her words back at her. He sighed deeply and leaned his shoulders against the wall. "I should have told ye Ian was watching the Barde's men. They have been lingering on the border for two days."

"I would not have gone to the river had I known. But there was no indication from the guards we should not leave the castle."

"They were no' yet on alert." Eaden pushed away from the wall and stepped to Mary. "Ye dinnae understand, Mairi. I could see ye from the wall." He brushed an errant strand of hair from her face, tucking it behind one ear. "I watched the wee bairn fall, and ye behind her. It turned my bowels to water, watching ye offer yerself to those bastards who nearly ran ye down."

"I had to get Ailie away," Mary whispered. "Can you not understand?"

"I understand, lass. D' *ye* understand what I'm telling ye?"

Mary nodded slowly. "You're yelling at me because I frightened you."

He took her face in his hands. "Dinnae do that to me again."

"But I saved the children."

Eaden folded her in his arms. "Aye. Ye saved the children."

He held her against him for a long moment, savoring the warmth of her in his arms. He closed his eyes against the memory of the riders who had managed, with a rare feat of horsemanship, to rein their horses away from the tangle of woman, dog and children blocking their path. The ice in Eaden's veins began to thaw. For their skill alone, the men of Bellecourt would live this day.

"Ye won the favor of many who'd no' expected such a sacrifice from a Barde clanswoman," he informed her, his mouth against her hair.

"They are children of Craigievar. With our vows and my body, you have made them my children as well."

Eaden's heart burned with pride for his wife's words. "Well said, Mairi, love. Well said."

A knock on the door caught Eaden's attention and he glanced up. "Aye?"

"'Tis Ian, Laird."

Eaden released Mary and motioned her to the nearest chair. He strode to the door and opened it, beckoning the captain of the guard into the room. Ian ducked his head respectfully in Mary's direction and paused before Eaden.

"Ye have my most humble apology, Laird." He dropped his gaze. "An' my life as well, should ye require it."

Mary jerked her anxious gaze from Ian to Eaden. "What is he saying?"

"He dinnae protect ye," Eaden said over his shoulder, not taking his eyes from his captain. "An' his life is sworn to it."

"No! You cannot blame him. I commanded him to take the child."

Eaden crossed his arms over his chest. "He chose to follow yer orders above mine."

"He had no choice."

Eaden pinned her with a narrowed gaze. "Ye think Ian couldnae have dragged ye onto his horse and brought ye to the castle?"

Mary returned his look evenly. "No."

Eaden cocked his head at Ian. "Well?"

"Yer wife is verra convincing, Laird."

Eaden stared at Ian for a moment, then released an irritated huff. "Ye offer yer life for hers?"

Mary leapt from her seat. "No! If there is fault here, it is mine."

"It seems I have no choice, Ian Scott," Eaden pronounced. "Ye have a gift beyond all others."

Ian cast his wary gaze between laird and lady. "What is it, Laird?"

Eaden snorted. "Ye have the gift of making my wife admit her mistake. 'Tis something I've no' witnessed before."

"You will not punish Ian, will you?" Mary asked in a subdued voice.

"Beyond tasking him with standing guard over our guests for the duration of their stay, nay." Eaden sighed. "He may yet wish he'd taken ye up on his horse without trying to reason with ye." He nodded to his captain. "Go. I ken the lady well enough to know 'twas no fault of yours. Ensure our guests cause no mischief this night."

With a bow, Ian turned and hurried from the room.

Eaden turned back to his wife. "There is still the issue of leaving the castle without an escort."

"I understand, now. I will not leave the walls without an escort again."

"Ye put the children's lives in danger. There are those who would condemn ye had any harm befallen them."

"I said I was sorry, and I am."

"I will let it go this time. But understand ye are under the same laws as the rest of the people of Craigievar."

"What laws?"

"The laws of discipline. Of punishment, should ye willfully disobey." His voice was mild, but his words made Mary flush.

"I am not *willful*."

"Dinnae put others in harm's way again," Eaden lectured her sternly, ignoring her protest. "And remember, my men are sworn to protect ye. Dinnae put them at risk, either."

"Yes, m'laird." Her tone in direct opposition to the assent of her words, Mary bit her lip and Eaden wondered what she truly wished to say. Perhaps it best he didn't ask.

He carefully hid the admiration from his face, reluctant to see her spirit quenched with further admonitions. Instead, he reached into his shirt and retrieved a folded paper.

"This belongs to ye."

* * *

Confused at the change in subject, Mary stared at the parchment with The Barde's seal pressed in the wax. She cast a glance at Eaden. He smiled grimly at her and nodded, motioning with one hand for her to open the sealed letter.

"Read it then, lass."

Excitement jolted through her as she reached with suddenly trembling fingers to pick up the missive. She cracked the seal and unfolded the heavy paper, bending her head to read the words.

My darling Mary,

I was so dismayed to hear you were kidnapped by the barbarian Scott! Father did not tell me for many days after he found me married to Bennett du Melville, but after Bennett and I returned to Bellecourt, I soon discovered why you were not here for me.

Oh, my dear Mary. I know you are quite possibly in terror of your new husband, and I wish you'd found a proper husband as I have. I know Bennett is only Melville's fourth son, but I could never love another as I do him, and Father has been most generous to offer us residence at Bellecourt.

Should you need a haven of succor from the horrors of life and your barbaric husband, you will find your place here at Bellecourt waiting for you.

I miss you, my dearest friend.

Lady Miriam du Melville

Mary spread a hand over the short note as though she could blot the words from the page. Her cheeks blanched cold then flamed with heat. How different would things now be if Miriam's note had come to her weeks earlier? If she had been assured of her place at Bellecourt. It had hurt unbearably to believe she'd been abandoned by all she'd known, especially her closest friend, with no one to turn to, no place to go. Now she found herself irrevocably bound to the laird by not only her vows, but her body as well, and Miriam's belated promise of refuge fairly devastated her.

She glanced at Eaden. His eyebrow twitched upward with unspoken question. Battling the dismay welling in her, Mary gave a small shrug. The reasons leading to her decision to stay at Scott Castle hadn't been all bad.

"It is a note from Miriam," Mary said, her voice gentle but firm.

Eaden grasped her empty hand in his and turned with her to the door. "How does Lady Miriam fare?"

"She is married to du Melville's son and they now reside at Bellecourt Castle."

"And have ye also been offered residence at Bellecourt?" Eaden's hand clenched hers, but the pressure disappeared almost as quickly as it began and Mary couldn't say if it had been intentional or not.

She cut her gaze toward her husband but he stared straight ahead, his countenance giving away nothing of his thoughts. "Yes. She offered me a place at Bellecourt."

Would Eaden ask her to stay? Her heart raced, knowing his next words could alter their relationship in possibly irreparable ways. She had tried to show him her decision to stay by accepting her wifely duties, but she had yet to say the words. Having fought him for so long, the surrender came as bittersweet. Trying to judge his reaction proved difficult when his expression remained closed.

Eaden gave a slow nod, but still would not meet her gaze. "Will ye talk to me before ye make yer decision? I would like ye to remain."

Warmth swept through her and she squeezed Eaden's hand firmly. His soft words touched her heart, smoothing the dismay caused by Miriam's words. Giving her the letter from Miriam, likely guessing full well what it contained, he had to also know he'd given her the means she'd sought to be free of him.

He doesn't trust me not to leave him.

"If I see a need to return to Bellecourt, I will let you know." Mary sought to dispel the solemn mood.

The surprise—and perhaps relief—on Eaden's face caused Mary's cheeks to flood with heat. She hesitated only the briefest moment before she replied to his silent query.

"Is there still time to make a marriage of this?" Mary's voice grew hushed. This time Eaden's hand pressing against hers was unmistakable.

"Aye," he replied, his voice deep and approving. "There is the rest of our lives, an' should ye wish it."

Mary smiled. "I do."

Eaden's answering smile lit a smoldering fire low in Mary's belly.

Chapter Twenty-Two

"Where are we going?" Mary asked her husband.

After the morning's events, Eaden's invitation for her to join him caused a flutter of apprehension. Nonetheless, she walked at his side, glancing toward the Barde soldiers seated at the lower table in the great hall, well-guarded by Ian and his soldiers.

Eaden turned his head and she was amazed at the transformation on his face. He appeared to have shed years from his countenance and his habitual scowl had vanished. A teasing smile lit his face and his dark hair tumbled unheeded over his forehead.

"We're invited to visit the king, aye?" His eyes danced with mischief. For a moment, Mary felt certain it was Ranald beside her, not his dour brother.

"Yes," she replied hesitantly.

"And ye cannae ride a horse, aye?"

She shuddered, remembering he'd promised to teach her to ride. Eaden didn't seem to notice her less than enthusiastic response.

"This afternoon ye learn to ride, Mairi, love."

Mary bravely swallowed her fear at the sound of his endearment, and followed her husband to the stable.

A horse stood tethered outside to a post, head low, one rear foot cocked toe-down on the ground. He seemed harmless enough and Mary took heart. Ranald approached from the barn, saddle and bridle slung over one arm. With smooth efficiency, Eaden tacked up the horse, jerking firmly on the leather girth before tying it off. Mary hung back a couple of steps, eying the steed warily.

"There's no need to worry about this lad," Eaden said cheerfully. "He's much too placid to cause ye any trouble." He motioned for her to approach. She hesitantly touched the burnished red coat.

"Dinnae be so cautious, love. Horses can sense an' ye are afraid." Mary jerked back and Eaden hastily added, "Now, Starnie, here, is the exception. He's gentle enough for bairns to ride."

Giving the beast a cautious glance, Mary stroked the horse's shoulder, watching warily for the first sign of ill-temper. Starnie swished his tail lazily at a fly, but otherwise made no move.

After a moment, she offered Eaden a pleased smile. "He's nice. How do I begin?"

"Watch me. I want ye to learn to ride astride. Later ye can learn to ride sidesaddle if ye'd like. But I want ye sturdy in the saddle and confident, first."

"Astride? Like a man?" Mary's eyebrows flew upwards in shock.

"Aye. But a wee, beautiful one, forbye."

She searched his face, a flutter of warmth blooming inside at the unexpected humor lurking in his eyes. They twinkled and his lips twitched as he fought the smile.

She crossed her arms beneath her breasts and gave him a stern look. "Are you jesting me?"

"Nay, lass. I'd no' jest. But I'd rather have ye safe than fashionable. Now watch."

Eaden turned to Starnie and gripped the reins in his left hand, murmuring something soothing to the horse. Mary smiled. Starnie didn't appear to need any calming; any more at ease and the beast would surely fall asleep.

"Are ye watching, Mairi?" Eaden asked, glancing at her over his shoulder. Mary shifted her attention from the horse and glanced up and down Eaden's length, wondering if she had missed something in the past few seconds. The muscles in his shoulders bunched beneath the fabric of his shirt and she suddenly remembered the ropey feel of them beneath her hands. She quickly looked away, clenching her fists to tame the tingle in her palms.

"Yes," she replied, surprised to hear the breathless quality to her voice, wondering if Eaden had noticed. Lifting her eyes to his, she met his speculative look and ducked her head to mask the heat rising in her cheeks.

* * *

Eaden didn't bother to hide his grin at Mary's discomfiture. He damped down his reaction to the sound of her voice and turned back to the lesson at hand.

"Grasp the reins in yer left hand and place yer right on the back of the saddle." Eaden demonstrated. "Then place yer left foot in the stirrup and step up and into the saddle." With fluid grace Eaden suited action to his words, settling easily. He stared at her from his mounted height.

"'Tis no' difficult, ye know, lass. And Starnie hasnae even shifted his weight. He willnae even feel ye on his back. Are ye ready to try?"

Mary started to nod, but a fury of barking and motion snatched her attention away. From her right, a sturdy chicken half-flew, half-ran in her direction, apparently escaped from its pen. Wings held at angles from its body, its head tilted forward as it fled the dog mere inches behind it. The dog barked savagely at its prey. Feathers flew. Suddenly the chicken darted directly beneath Starnie who flung his head up with a piercing squeal.

In rapid sequence, the chicken sped beneath the horse, the dog skidded in the dirt to maintain his hunt, and Starnie lashed out a rear hoof with deadly accuracy. A resounding thud and resulting yelp of pain stopped the chase abruptly, and the chicken fled back to his pen, safe, at least for the moment.

Eaden, barely disturbed by the ruckus, rolled smoothly with the shift of Starnie's kick. In the instant it took the horse to settle, Eaden peered about, seeking the cause of the commotion. With a sigh, he noted the bare end of the fleeing chicken and turned to see the young dog slinking away, pausing once to shake its head. He glanced back to his wife, hoping the stramash hadn't frightened her.

Mary lay in a heap on the ground.

Eaden dove from the saddle and Starnie jostled easily to counter the move. At Mary's side, Eaden searched frantically for an injury, battling gut-wrenching fear. Had Starnie's hoof caught more than the thick skull of the dog? It wasn't possible Mary had been close enough to have been hurt in the melee.

"D'ye want me to fetch a burnt feather to rouse her?"

Eaden glanced at Ranald. His brother's face blanched pale with worry.

"Nay. I'll carry her inside the stable until she rouses. I dinnae think she's hurt."

Gathering her limp form in his arms, Eaden rose to his feet. Ranald hurried to open the double doors of the stable and Eaden claimed a bench halfway down the hall. Wide-eyed stares marked their entrance, but Ranald sent the stable lads scurrying outside with a jerk of his head.

Eaden sat carefully, Mary cradled in his arms. He smoothed tumbled curls from her face with trembling fingers.

"Wheesht, now, lass. Dinnae frighten me so." He slid the back of his hand down her cheek, silently urging color in the pale skin.

Suddenly Mary stirred and both Eaden and Ranald breathed a sigh of relief. The moment was short-lived, however, as her hand shot upward, grasping the front of Eaden's shirt in an unyielding grip.

"Don't kill him!" she sobbed, her eyes wide and unfocused.

Eaden drew back, aiming a puzzled look at his brother. "Dinnae fash, Mairi." Eaden pulled her against his chest as he ran a gentling hand up and down her back. "No one is being killed. I'll no' let any harm come to him."

"Who is she talking about?" Ranald asked, his voice a low undertone. Eaden shrugged in confusion and continued to croon words of comfort and assurance. Finally, she subsided into soft sobs.

"What could she be so upset about? Both the dog and the chicken got away. A bit fashed, but mayhap wiser. And Starnie is most likely catching a snooze outside right about now."

Eaden shook his head, careful not to dislodge Mary who had relaxed bonelessly against him. He gently eased her into a more upright position. "Mairi, lass. Talk to me." He jostled her gently.

Mary glanced around, her brow furrowed in bewilderment. "What happened?"

"Ye fainted. I brought ye in here away from the *stramash* outside."

Her cheeks flushed. "I'm sorry," she whispered.

"Lass, 'tis nay yer fault. But I would like to know what frightened ye so."

Mary looked away. "I don't remember."

Eaden rubbed a hand up and down her back again, trying to comfort her. "I think ye do. And I want ye to tell me what it was."

"I can't. I don't want to remember."

Eaden almost relented. But the memory of her lying senseless on the ground stabbed through him, and he pushed. "Tell me, Mairi. Ye're a brave lass, and I willnae let it hurt ye again."

Her muscles tensed beneath his hands and he tightened his grip, afraid she might bolt and run. She stared into the distance, but Eaden understood she did not see the wooden stalls or the horses' heads peeking over the open half-doors. Her eyes stared into some distance only she cold see, and she gripped his arm painfully, her knuckles white.

"He killed Miriam's pony." Her voice was a mere whisper of sound and Eaden leaned closer to hear the words. "His name was Prince, and he was the most beautiful pony in the world. We were barely old enough for a pony, but Miriam begged her da. We took turns grooming him and feeding him, and we loved him dearly."

Eaden cupped his hand at the nape of her neck, kneading the tense muscles, letting her tell the tale in her own time.

"Miriam was riding. She was so proud of what she'd learned, but Prince wasn't acting his best. She lost her temper and slapped his rump with her hand. He bucked and threw her to the ground." Mary's voice dropped again. "I thought she was dead."

She trembled and Eaden gathered her close, rocking her back and forth in his lap. "Wheesht, lass. I'm here."

Mary seemed to regain her composure and struggled to sit up. "Prince raced around the paddock. A groom grabbed his reins, but before he could lead him away, Laird Barde stormed over. His face was black with rage. He snatched a dagger from his belt and I thought he meant to cut the reins free . . ."

Mary's voice choked on a sob and Eaden saw tears stream down her face. "He slashed Prince's throat. Blood spurted everywhere and I choked on the smell of it. Prince screamed and I couldn't shut out the horrible sounds as he died."

Eaden could do little else but hold her as she cried. His gaze met Ranald's bleak look and he wanted nothing more than to meet for a moment with the loathsome man who'd committed such an atrocious act before a young child.

Mary's sobs eased and she pushed herself into a sitting position, brushing at the tears with her hands. "I'm sorry. I hadn't remembered it in a very long time."

"Probably no' since it happened, though ye've most likely had nightmares ye couldnae recall. Starnie squealed and kicked the *glaikit* dog. The sounds must have been enough to jerk ye back to that day." Eaden cupped Mary's face in his hands. "Small wonder ye were afraid of horses." He kissed the tip of her nose. "'Twill never happen again."

* * *

"I want to learn to ride," Mary insisted as they left the stable. "I don't want to go back inside."

Eaden rubbed the back of his neck in frustration. "But ye fainted, lass."

"I was frightened, not hurt."

"Ye're a stubborn lass, I'll give ye that." He turned to Ranald. "Bring Starnie back outside. Lady Scott wants to learn to ride."

Sketching a jaunty salute to his good-sister, Ranald turned the horse back through the stable doors. Mary walked up to the animal who eyed her benignly as she stroked his neck. "You're a good one," she crooned. "You and I will get along fine."

"Take the reins like I showed ye and get yer balance." Eaden placed his right hand on hers and set it on the back of the saddle. "Now, yer left foot, good. Step up and there ye go!"

She could barely reach the stirrup, and bounced once on her right foot before she got enough momentum to scramble up the horse's side. She landed on her belly, not quite high enough to reach the saddle's seat. Eaden planted a hand on her bottom and boosted her the rest of the way. He chuckled at Mary's gasp of surprise as she landed in the saddle and turned to look at him.

"How does it feel?" he asked, a wicked quirk at the corner of his mouth. Her eyes widened and she shifted in the saddle. "To be riding. Not to have my hand on yer arse. Though ye could tell me if ye please," he drawled, liking the way her skin pinked in embarrassment.

"I'm not riding, I'm sitting," she responded loftily.

"Then pick up yer reins, lass, and ride."

Eaden grasped Starnie's reins beneath the shank of the bit and led the docile horse to the paddock beside the stable. He was pleased to find Mary a quick learner. Now that she'd apparently shed her fear, her natural affinity for animals helped her to respond to Eaden's instructions, and soon she rode confidently around the worn path on the inside of the paddock rails.

"Ranald! Bring Duff out." A few minutes later Ranald led Eaden's horse from the stable, tacked and ready to ride.

He gave the girth on Duff's saddle a quick tug, pulling the slack out of the soft leather. Gathering his reins, he stepped effortlessly into the saddle and turned to his wife. "Come along, Mairi. 'Tis time to further yer education."

He grinned at the bemusement on her face. Whistling airily, he kicked Duff forward.

Chapter Twenty-Three

Every muscle in Mary's legs and buttocks screamed, tight with unaccustomed exercise, as she bravely fought the urge to lie down and cry. She'd barely had enough time after her riding lesson to wash her face and change her gown before supper. She sat stiffly beside Eaden during the interminable meal, waiting for her limbs to crack and fall off, rather hoping they would. Surely being legless would be better than the pain she currently endured.

"Well, are ye finished?"

She looked at her husband and nodded briefly, the short jerk of her head all her neck muscles would allow. He rose and grasped her chair, pulling it back from the table to help her rise. Mary unbent her body from its seated position, a cry of pain escaping her lips before she could stop it. She stumbled forward, her muscles not answering her command to stand.

"Wheesht, and I'm a fool!" Eaden hissed beneath his breath. "Can ye stand if I help ye?"

"Yes." She rose to her feet, biting her lip to keep the tears at bay.

"I'm sorry, lass." Eaden took her arm in a strong grip, turning her gently from the table and keeping pace with her halting stride. By the time she reached the stairs, her muscles had loosened somewhat.

She offered Eaden a forced smile. "I'll be fine, now. I think I just sat too long."

"Ye were too good a horsewoman today and I forgot ye'd no' be accustomed to using those muscles." He eyed Mary's derriere, a speculative look on his face.

He accompanied her up the stairs, stopping a moment to murmur a few words to Ina. Mary was grateful for the support of his hand on her arm as her knees threatened to buckle beneath her. Despite the protest of her body, pained as though she'd received a thorough beating, she wouldn't let him know how much she hurt.

"I enjoyed the ride. Perhaps we could go again tomorrow?" She sought to keep her voice light and hopeful.

Eaden gave a low chuckle. "Ye'll be in no shape to get out of bed tomorrow, much less swing a leg over Starnie's back."

He ushered her inside their bedroom. She eyed the bed and felt the slide of his hand down her back. Her muscles screamed in silent agony and she choked back a moan. Eaden closed the door behind them and began unfastening his clothes as he crossed the room. He stepped out of his breeches, leaving his shirt hanging nearly to his knees.

He turned back to Mary. "Here, and I'll unlace ye," he said as he placed a hand on her shoulder. She flinched and bent her head.

"Could we . . ." Her voice trailed off in uncertainty.

Eaden brushed her hair from her cheek and tucked it behind an ear. "Could we *what*, Mairi?"

She sent Eaden a pleading look. "Could you not . . . not touch me . . . just tonight?"

Throwing his head back, Eaden gave a great shout of laughter. Mary shrugged beneath his hand, unsure if he scorned her or agreed with her. Giving both of her shoulders a quick squeeze, he lifted her hair out of his way and loosened her laces. She steeled herself against the caress of his fingers.

"Mairi, ye do intrigue me. I've never been asked so nicely to keep my attentions to myself before." He pulled the edges of her gown apart and drew it over her shoulders. Without further comment, she stepped woodenly from her gown as it pooled at her feet, letting Eaden hold her arm to keep her balance. To her surprise, he handed her the pale green velvet robe draped across the foot of the bed.

"Slip into this. Ye willnae want to shock the lads."

Mary's eyes widened at his comment, then wider still at the knock on the door. With a motion for her to belt the robe securely, Eaden opened the door to admit three strong lads carrying buckets of steaming water. They set the buckets on the hearth and, without so much as a sideways glance, hurried from the room. Eaden disappeared into the bathing chamber and dragged the tub across the floor, positioning it before the fire.

Rustling sounds in the basket on the hearth caught Mary's attention. She walked to the hearth and reached inside for the puppy. He rooted against her hands, searching for sustenance. She picked up a folded scrap of rag from the stack beside the basket and dipped it in the little pot of milk Kirsty had left warming near the fire. Settling the puppy on her lap, Mary touched his nose with the false teat, encouraging him to suckle.

The tiny mouth opened and latched on the saturated fabric, but he did nothing more than mouth it aimlessly. He swallowed a couple of times then let the teat fall from his mouth as he lay passively in Mary's hands. The sounds of her bath being prepared faded into the background as she held the puppy to her face, whispering into the tightly closed ears.

"You will grow strong and happy. You will make my life bearable here and become a companion for the baby I know will someday be mine."

Mary mulled over this thought. From the moment she'd made her decision to stay at Scott Castle, she'd known what the results would most likely be. A baby would bind her to Eaden further, and such knowledge had ceased to be an unthinkable thing. She flushed happily with the knowledge.

She smiled against the puppy's soft coat, feeling his tiny, warm breath against her cheek. Were it not for the troublesome way men had of enjoying themselves with their proper, sedate wives, as Isobel had confided to her, she would welcome the laird's attentions. Her smile faded. He must never suspect the lack in her, the increasing difficulty she had keeping her mind focused on producing an heir. Never would she allow him to think her less than a proper wife nor let him see this wanton side of her that longed for his touch.

The lads returned with more buckets, Isobel on their heels. Eaden quirked an eyebrow at the woman as she lingered inside the door, wringing her hands in indecision.

"Could I help milady with her bath?"

Eaden gave Isobel a steady look. "Nay."

"But Kirsty . . ."

"Kirsty isnae needed, either." He motioned her out the door.

Mary puzzled the interaction between Isobel and Eaden, remembering Ina's warning against Isobel. She smiled faintly. Isobel tried so hard to help. Ina had to be wrong about her. Besides, Eaden did not seem discomfited by her presence or friendship.

"Thank you, Isobel," Mary called as she replaced the sleeping puppy in his basket. "I can look after myself."

Isobel stared at Mary, her brows pulled together in concern. Mary gave a discreet shake of her head. *I remember your warning*, she meant to convey. With an answering nod, Isobel turned and left the room.

Eaden thanked the lads as they finished their chore, this time latching the door behind them as they left.

"Ye can remove your robe, now," he informed her as he added the steaming water to the tub, testing the temperature with his hand. Mary stared at him, completely at a loss for words. Did he expect her to take a bath now? In front of him?

Eaden glanced up, wiping his wet hands on his shirt as he rose to his feet. She eyed him warily as he approached her. He gently tugged the belt from her hands, loosening it to let it fall to the floor.

"There are many different ways to love," he whispered. "Ye *do* trust me, don't ye?" He frowned at Mary's slow nod and sighed. "Och, well. The heat from the water'll loosen yer muscles and the fire will help keep ye warm."

He bowed in a grand gesture, inviting her to climb into the tub. She looked down, trying to ignore the way her heart pounded in her chest as she climbed over the rim. The water simmered hot against her skin, but Eaden quirked one eyebrow, challenging her to complain. She sank beneath the surface of the water, groaning as the heat bit into her sore muscles.

"Lean forward."

Feeling too utterly weary to question him, she rested her arms on her bent knees, cradling her cheek against her forearms. The scent of roses drifted on the steam and she cracked one eye as Eaden slowly rubbed her back with the soapy cloth. Her breath left her in a purr of pure bliss as he moved his hands slickly up the column of her neck. She rolled her head to give him greater access.

As she surrendered herself to the slow, soothing motion of his hands, one by one, her muscles relaxed.

* * *

"Are ye better?" Eaden murmured against her hair. He idly continued to soap Mary's body, allowing himself the growing warmth in his belly.

Remembering how sleep softened her defenses against him, he wondered if she had relaxed enough to respond to gentle lovemaking this night. He breathed deeply, the scent of flowers rising from the water and Mary's moist skin. Quickly he rinsed the soap from her, brushing his hands down her arms as he worked. The water lapped softly over her skin, and Eaden decided he couldn't wait.

"Mairi?"

A faint sigh escaped Mary's lips and Eaden stared at her in wry disbelief as his stirring passion faded dejectedly beneath his wife's delicate snores.

Light from the fire licked across her wet skin and Eaden gently wiped a bit of soap away. His fingers smoothed across dainty muscles, slick with bathwater, and he sighed as his ministrations elicited no response from his wife.

"Ye are a vexation to me, lass." He grabbed a linen from the stack on the hearth and shook out the folds. He tossed it over one shoulder and bent to lift Mary from the tub. Cradling her against him, he wrapped the warm cloth about her, ignoring the water soaking his shirt. He carried her to the bed and, pushing back the coverlet, laid her on the cool sheet. With a lingering hand, he finished drying her.

"Ye would enjoy this more were ye awake," he mourned. He lifted her arm and admired the smooth skin. "I know *I* would enjoy it more if ye were awake."

He eyed his wife, but there was no response. He sighed. "I promise ye a good marriage—a good life for ye and our bairns should we be so blessed." Giving her a kiss, he tucked the covers around her.

He rose from the bed and stripped away his shirt. Taking a square of thicker linen, he wet it and quickly washed himself, then dried off and crawled beneath the coverlet. Wrapping his arms about Mary, he pulled her against him. She nestled her back against him, and for a moment he thought she would wake. But with a faint hitch of breath, she settled in his arms.

"Ye will come to me willingly, Mairi. One day soon, ye will forget what holds ye back and accept me. This I promise ye." Eaden hugged her tightly, breathing in her scent of flowers, and tried to convince himself they would someday have a true marriage between them.

Chapter Twenty-Four

Heavy pounding rattled the wooden door in its frame. Ignoring the faint protest from her muscles, Mary rolled over, wide awake in the next instant. Already out of bed, Eaden crossed the room, sword in hand. A reddish glow lit his skin, the pale moonlight from the window tinted a curious golden shade, mingling with the smolder from the hearth. Her heart pumped in alarm as Eaden yanked the door open.

Ian hovered in the portal, his face a pale oval in the shadows. "The stable's on fire!" he barked.

Cursing, Eaden set his sword against the wall and collected his clothes as Mary scrambled to a sitting position, clutching the blanket to her chest. Eaden shoved one arm into a shirt sleeve and leaned across the bed. He gave her a hard, brief kiss then looked her straight in the eye.

"Stay here."

Mary bristled at his presumptive tone, but swallowed both her hasty retort and her fear, nodding in assent. A surprised look came over his face at her easy compliance, but whatever else he might have said was interrupted as screams broke out below. Eaden lunged away from the bed and bolted out the door, shoving his sword into its scabbard at his side.

Willing her legs to stop quaking, Mary threw back the blanket, reaching for her shift and robe at the foot of the bed. Her hands cold with apprehension, she belted the robe snugly about her waist, feeling somewhat better to have even this much protection around her.

Hurrying to the open window, she could see nothing but the twisting red and orange shadows writhing across the pale grey stone of the castle walls like an enormous beast caught in its death throes. Frustrated, she stared at the fire's reflection against the stone. A stable lad burst into her line of sight, leading a frightened horse. Hooves flailed the air as the horse plunged and reared, trying to break free from the boy's determined grip. Other shadowed figures emerged to join them, the horses' coats ablaze with reflected light, the stable lads thrust into darkest silhouette. Watching helplessly as they struggled to save their charges, Mary pressed against the stone, trying to see as far beyond the wall as she could, certain Eaden stood in the middle of the madness. Her blood ran cold as her imagination fed her fear.

With all her concentration centered on Eaden's safety, she was unaware she was no longer alone until she heard the small creak of the door. Frightened, Mary whirled to face the intruder. Her knees buckled in relief as she recognized Isobel standing in the doorway, the candlelight from the hallway framing her black cloak in a swirl of yellow and gold.

Isobel beckoned frantically to her. "Hurry, milady!" she hissed. "Come with me."

Mary hesitated, remembering Eaden's words. "Laird Scott told me to stay here."

Isobel moved away from the door, giving Mary room to pass her. "Ye must come now! Ye can see from the parapet."

It wouldn't be exactly disobedience for her to go to the parapet, Mary reasoned quickly. Surely, he simply didn't want her near the fire. If she could only see what was happening, she wouldn't be so frantic with worry. She grabbed the front of her night shift and robe with one hand, lifting the hem from the floor, and hurried out the door. Isobel took a candle from the sconce at the doorway and held it high, lighting Mary's way.

Together they slipped down the stairs and skirted the edges of the great hall. Bustling servants ignored them, careening about the room, carrying buckets of water and other items Mary did not stop to wonder about. A large well in the bailey lay near the stables and Mary shuddered to think of the dangerous flames requiring so much water taken from the cistern near the kitchen.

She scarcely spared a thought to the activity in the hall, intent on making her way to the parapet so she could find Eaden in the crush of frantic activity outside. For a moment, she was separated from Isobel as a servant stumbled, spilling a flagon of water on the floor between them. Mary halted uncertainly at the bottom of the narrow stairway, the way blocked by darkness unlit by either candle or torch.

Mary waited for Isobel, but the woman swept her cloak away from the puddle of water and gestured impatiently. "Go!" she cried, lifting her candle high. Mary peered at the stairwell where the dancing flames of the room's candles did nothing more than intensify the shadows beyond their reach, giving life to the ghostly stories that haunted the castle. Chiding herself for her superstitious fear of the ghost of Lady Fenella, she gulped a deep breath and fled up the stairs, fright for the unknown mingling with the fear for those who battled the fire raging below.

Mary reached the top of the stairs and rushed into the smoke-filled night. The stars and moon were vague points of light veiled behind thick wreaths of smoke, tinted red and gold by the flames shooting into the midnight sky. Far ahead, a soldier stood guard on the parapet, his attention torn between his duty and the activity in the bailey.

Mary fled across the stone floor and leaned over the high wall, searching the swarming mass of bodies far below. They formed lines with buckets passing from one man to the next. In their haste, they splashed water onto the ground and it shimmered in the firelight with the dark viscosity of blood.

The stable lads were young and slight of build. She quickly dismissed them, looking for the tall, muscular form of her husband.

"Keep the water coming!"

Suddenly, she spotted him next to the stable, his arms waving, directing the action. Stripped to the waist, dark smudges streaked his torso. Mary prayed the marks were soot and not blood, but she had no way of knowing for certain.

An ominous rumble filled the night and Eaden threw an arm over his head defensively. The eaves of the stable split with a rending shriek and fell in a shower of sparks and flames. Mary screamed in terror and flung a hand toward Eaden, denying the nightmare unfolding before her.

"No!" The single word, so loud in her ears, was swallowed up by the voracious crackle of the fire and the shouts of the men in the bailey. Frantic, Mary glanced around, but, save the guard who could not leave his post, she stood alone on the parapet.

Something pale fluttered in the wind, catching her attention. She swung toward the stairwell opening where a form, clad in white, billowed and swayed. An unearthly keening filled the air and Mary clapped her hands over her ears, backing away in fright from the apparition.

The figure lifted a draperied arm, pointing toward the fire in the bailey. Unable to help herself, Mary turned her attention back to the scene below. Eaden sprawled in a heap on the ground, smoldering timbers rolled to one side.

Mary trembled, fighting the panic rising in her throat. Beside her, the ghost approached the parapet wall and Mary shrank away, a hand to her throat in terror. The spirit turned to the scene below, but Mary was unable to look away from the figure, the cowl of her gown pulled around her head, setting her face in impenetrable shadow. The apparition leaned far over the edge of the wall and her draperies floated on the updraft, making her seem as though she were about to take flight.

Lady Fenella's story slid through Mary's mind and she gasped as the ghost bent even further over the wall, moaning and wailing the loss of her love. Mary tore her gaze away, searching for Eaden's fallen shape. He was not there.

Abruptly the keening sound ceased and Mary caught sight of the white form as it pitched over the edge of the parapet, the gown floating for a moment on the rising, heated air of the blazing fire below.

With a horrified cry, Mary lunged forward, reaching for the fabric as it floated toward the ground. Her momentum caused her feet to leave the floor and she grabbed in panic at the smooth stone wall. She teetered over the edge a moment before losing her balance altogether. Her fingernails frantically scrambled for a hold on the stone and she cried out in fear.

"Mary!"

Hands grabbed at her, pulling her back inside the parapet, and she clutched her rescuer's arm.

"Milady!" Isobel's voice hissed in her ear. Tears of relief sprang to Mary's eyes, blurring her vision.

"Mary!" Ranald shouted again, his voice sharp with fear. Mary wiped her eyes and turned to face him as he hurried toward her.

"Where is Eaden?" Mary gasped.

"He's gone to question the men from Bellecourt about the fire." Ranald grabbed her upper arms and shook her. "What are ye doing here?"

"I had to see. I had to know he was all right."

"Ye nearly fell over the wall," he raged, and Mary looked closely to be sure it was Ranald and not Eaden who railed at her.

"I saw Eaden." She gestured helplessly. "I saw the ghost . . . she fell over the edge . . ."

"Dinnae be daft," Ranald retorted. "'Tis no ghost up here. She's no' but a story to keep the bairns off the stairs at night."

"But I saw her—and Kirsty said . . ." Mary paused, seeing the dark frown on Ranald's face. He was more than cross with her, and in no mood to discuss the merits of a ghost story. She turned to Isobel. "Did you not see her?"

"Nay, milady. I saw ye leaning too far over the wall, but ye were alone."

"But, she fell." Mary snatched her arm away from Ranald's grip and ran to the wall, peering over the edge, ignoring the gasp and hot words of warning from both Ranald and Isobel.

Ranald bolted to her side, jerking her away from the edge. "Ye muckle-headed . . . What are ye doing?"

Mary motioned to the ground below. "I saw her fall. I know I did. She should be on the ground right there."

Ranald leaned over the wall. He shook his head. "Lass, there is nothing there. If a ghost did jump, there's no reason to believe ye'd see her lying on the ground." He loosened his grip on her arm. "Come away, now. Eaden will want to know ye're safe."

With a final glance below, Mary reluctantly turned away, rubbing her arm where Ranald's fingers had gripped. "I know what I saw," she insisted stubbornly.

Ranald sighed. "Lass, it doesnae matter what ye did or dinnae see. What matters is ye could have fallen to yer death."

"Why did you come up here?"

"I was returning to the hall. I looked up and saw . . ." His voice trailed away as he stared at her.

"What did you see?" Mary whispered as the bottom fell out of her stomach at his expression.

Ranald scrubbed his head. "I saw something white fluttering on the edge of the wall." He stared at Mary. "It could have been ye, no' a ghost."

Mary glanced at her robe. Its pale green velvet fabric was heavy and unlikely to flutter in the wind. She turned to speak to Isobel, but the woman had vanished.

"Isobel wore a black cloak. Mine is too heavy to flutter. Do you not believe me?"

Ranald's face set in grim lines, and even in the dark Mary could tell he would not comment further.

Mulish ass, she thought with a sigh of discontent. A frisson of warning slid down her spine and she turned once more to look into the bailey yard below. She saw neither fabric nor body lying on the ground below. Where could it have gone?

And, if not the ghost of Lady Fenella, who, or what, was it?

Chapter Twenty-Five

Eaden closed the bedroom door, weary and troubled by more than the burning of the stable. He rubbed the back of his neck, trying to ease the tension across his shoulders. A hot bath and a warm woman would be high on his list of priorities right now, but a moment of peace would have to do while he sorted out the rest.

Out of the corner of his eye he watched Mary cross the room to the puppy's basket. He took refuge in the cushioned chair near the window, angling himself so he could see his wife and still prop his feet on the edge of the bed.

She rested a finger on the lip of the basket, tilting it slightly toward her as she peered inside. Her shoulders tensed and she let out a cry of distress. Bounding from his chair, Eaden strode quickly to her side. Looking over her shoulder into the basket, he saw the unnaturally stiff body of the puppy and needed no explanation.

He laid a hand on Mary's shoulder in mute sympathy. She turned to him, hiding her face against his chest as she sobbed out her broken heart.

"There, there, lass." Helplessly, he patted her shoulder. The puppy had apparently meant more to her than he'd realized, more than it should have, considering its tenuous hold on life. He smoothed her hair, trying to ignore the stirrings of passion deep inside him at the feel of her body against his. He meant only to comfort her; instead he wished he could take her to bed and make her forget the pup ever existed.

He didn't want to be impatient, either, but he despaired of crying women, especially when they sounded as completely heartbroken as his wife did. He'd much rather have her railing at him.

Soothing her wasn't helping. Perhaps a little challenge would dry her tears. "Wheesht, now, lass," he chided her gently. "What's happened to my Mairi? Where's the brave Mairi I know? She is a strong lass and wouldnae *haver* so."

With a snarl Mary pushed away from him, wiping her eyes with the back of one hand. "Your *Mairi*," she flung the name at him, "wants to go home!" She took two steps backward as he raised a hand in protest. "Your *Mairi* is tired of not belonging here. Your *Mairi* is finished pretending everything is fine."

She stared at the still form in the basket on the hearth, tears streaming down her face. Shoving a fist into her mouth, she choked back a sob.

He gaped at her. He'd certainly stopped her tears *and* provoked her to anger, though he hadn't expected her to change so quickly. Realizing he was holding his breath against her unexpected tirade, he let it out in a *whoosh*, startling her into looking at him. He wanted her to be happy. But he was not willing to let her go.

"This is yer home, Mairi," he reminded her in a firm, quiet voice. "I willnae let ye go back to Bellecourt." He moved toward her as her face crumpled, threatening tears again.

She scuttled away from him. "I cannot do this any longer, Eaden."

"'Tis more than the puppy, aye?"

She hugged herself, as though to ward off his touch, and irritation surged through his veins. Reaching for her, he held out his arms. "Ye told me ye wanted to make a marriage with me. We cannae, an' ye no' tell me what is troubling ye." He motioned for her to come to him with a slight wave of a hand.

The way she eyed him, so warily, turned his frustration to bitterness. "Why do ye still turn from me? I've felt ye tremble in my arms, yet ye take no pleasure in being my wife. Why?"

She looked away, wiping her tears with the backs of her hands. "I will do whatever you ask." Weary resignation muted her voice. "I am tired and the puppy upset me, is all." She turned to him, head tilted up. "What do you want of me?"

Eaden shot a hand through his hair, provoked beyond reason. He opened his mouth to speak, then shut it and spread his hands in supplication, searching for better words to bring him the answers he sought.

"I dinnae want to *ask* ye to let me hold ye. I want ye to walk into my arms, to smile when I touch ye." He gave her a pleading look. "Why can ye no' do that? Am I that repulsive to ye?"

Her eyes wide, Mary protested, "Nay, m'laird. You are not repulsive to me. It's . . ." She frowned and turned away.

"Then tell me, Mairi," he begged her. "Tell me what is lacking between us."

"I cannot."

"Be damned, but ye can!" He roared. His face flamed with the sudden heat of anger but he could do nothing to stop it. Mary stiffened at his outburst, but continued to stare stoically ahead.

Weary of dancing around her feelings, of wishing he'd acted differently on their wedding night, he realized he'd rather take a hard beating than continue living like this. He closed the distance between them and grasped her shoulders as he turned her about. Her face was a mask of defiance and resolution, trying vainly to cover the wariness and pleading in her eyes.

Trying not to curse aloud, he urged, "Ye like my kisses well enough, aye?"

Mary nodded slowly.

"Then ye will tell me why ye hold yerself from me."

Mary stiffened in his hands, and they stood at an impasse for a moment before her shoulders slumped in defeat. He brought her gently to him, folding her into his arms, taking heart when she didn't pull away. "Come, lass, and talk to me." He led her to the big chair by the window, turning it away from the sight of the basket.

Sinking into its thick cushions, he settled her on his lap and cradled her head against his shoulder. "Whatever needs be said, it may be easier if ye dinnae have to look at me."

Mary nodded, shifting slightly in his lap. Eaden gritted his teeth at the gentle movement of her bottom against his groin and wished he'd chosen a different way to be sure she didn't run from him this time.

He marshaled his thoughts. "Tell me."

At first, she said nothing. He heard her breath catch as she tried several times to speak, and he did not scold her further. With firm resolution, he waited.

"It's not that I don't *want* you to touch me anymore," she finally said, hesitation hitching her voice. Eaden held his tongue, vowing to hear her through.

"I'm afraid."

He battled down the first words that leapt to his mouth and instead chose a more diplomatic way. "I've told ye I willnae hurt ye again."

"I know." She lifted her head from his shoulder and looked him in the eye. "I know. And you've kept your promise." She touched the spikes of his hair and smoothed a few against his head.

Eaden struggled to keep his mind off the soft motion of her hand against his scalp sending streaks of fire racing beneath his skin, and on the question at hand. "Then, what are ye afraid of, lass?"

Mary frowned suddenly. "I'd rather have married a peasant!"

Eaden drew his head back in surprise. "What?"

"There wouldn't be this, this wall between us if I didn't . . . if you didn't . . ."

"For the love of Saint Andrew!" he exploded. "What are ye talkin' aboot?"

Mary jumped from his lap, clasping her hands over and over in agitation as she paced. Eaden scraped a hand through his abused hair, undoing what repair her soft fingers had accomplished.

"I know you want an heir," she finally said, stopping before him. "And I promise you will never have cause to doubt the child is yours."

Eaden's eyes popped open wide. "Are ye thinkin' of takin' a lover?" The edge to his voice caused Mary's mouth to round in surprise.

"No!" she stammered. "But I know if you think I enjoy .
. ." she spread her hands helplessly toward the rumpled bed,
her cheeks flaming as she sought the words, ". . . then you will
worry I will seek others."

He rose menacingly to his feet. She hastened to
reassure, "I would never do that!"

"'Twould be best if ye remember it so." He stood before
her, his stance predatory and possessive.

Mary stomped her foot. "See why it's so hard to be
married to an earl?"

"Can ye explain this to me? For I cannae see a peasant
would be any happier to have his wife sharing her bed with
others."

"No. But 'tis only the nobility who worry about such
things. A lady must not let herself be thought of as . . . as a
whore." Her voice choked and dropped, but Eaden heard her.

"A whore!" he shouted. "Who has told ye such drivel?"

Mary flushed. "Well, you see, I did not know how to
respond to you, and you are so large . . ."

It was Eaden's turn to flame with sudden heat. He
glanced down at the front of his breeches.

Mary gasped out a laugh. "No! Though that, too. I only
meant I felt trapped and breathless whenever you were near
me. There was little hope I could return to Bellecourt, and I
finally resolved to make myself such a life as I could here,
with you."

Eaden eyed her narrowly. "Ye still havnae told me
where ye got such an outlandish idea."

"Is it? You seem to be willing to shout at me for telling
you what I believe to be true."

"I shouted because ye are driving me to madness." Eaden drew in a breath against impending insanity. "Tell me, now."

"Does it matter who told me you would not like me too eager in your bed?"

"Aye! It does!"

Mary stared past him, her breath quickening. With a raised eyebrow, Eaden watched her agitation increase. Her eyes flashed and her lips thinned. His tension mounted, and he was unprepared for Mary's next words as her eyes suddenly snapped to his.

"Your mistress!"

It took Eaden a moment to recover his wits. "My mistress?" he roared. "What game are ye playing, now?"

"No game, m'laird. But there is a woman who seems to like you overmuch who has gone to great lengths to keep us at odds."

"Who are ye talking about?"

"Who? Are there so many, then?" she flung at him, her temper and color high. "Do you have time to pick and choose between them?"

"Be damned, woman! I have no time to spend hopping from bed to bed! I spend too much time trying to get into yers!"

Mary threw her hands up in response and whirled around, her skirts billowing.

"By St. Andrew's teeth, Mairi. I have no desire to lay claim to any woman but ye. And ye are the most difficult woman I've ever tried to bed."

"Do you swear you've not encouraged her?" Mary's hands clenched, her shoulders drawn in a taut line.

With a silent prayer for patience sent heavenward, he forced the anger from his voice. "I have neither encouraged nor brought a woman to my bed except you since our marriage. Tell me her name, Mairi. Dinnae let there be any more uncertainty between us."

It took every ounce of willpower Eaden possessed to keep still and not grab his trembling wife. He would not play guessing games with her. She must tell him of her own accord, but he could sense the admission cost her dearly.

Finally, she took a ragged breath and bowed her head. "Isobel."

Eaden settled his hands on her shoulders, squeezing gently. "I thought perhaps 'twas her. I couldnae think of another I'd known in the past who cared enough to hurt ye. It bothered me when I returned from Edinburgh and found her here in the castle. But ye seemed happy and she acted differently. She even helped make ye a dress I could see pleased ye."

He moved even closer, feeling the warmth of her against him. Resting his cheek against the top of her head, he breathed deeply of her fragrance. "I wanted to challenge her. I should have at least warned her should she hurt ye in any way. But I wanted ye to be happy. And if it meant seeing Isobel in the castle as yer friend, then so be it."

"She was so nice to me," Mary whispered.

"She used ye to get to me. I see it now." Eaden sighed. He ran his hands slowly down her arms. "Did she really tell ye I'd think ye a whore if ye liked me loving ye?"

Mary nodded wordlessly.

He kissed her cheek, his lips against the soft skin, drinking in the scent of her. His thumbs traced gently against the warmth of her neck beneath her heavy hair.

"I'd be more than happy to prove her wrong."

Chapter Twenty-Six

Shivering beneath Eaden's touch, Mary turned to him. His face and chest still bore the stains of the fire and his hair stood out from his head in a most ridiculous manner. He looked like a man sorely beset by his trials and she hid a slight smile as she drew a forefinger through a patch of soot on his chest, lifting the finger to inspect the blackened tip.

Leaning up on her toes, Mary placed her lips against his, tasting the smoke heavy on his skin. "There are many ways to show love, m'laird," she whispered, the words an echo of his own promise to her hours, or perhaps a lifetime before. Glancing at the tub still beside the hearth, she canted her head in invitation.

Silently, Eaden loosened his breeches and let them fall to the floor as she picked up a pail of steaming water and added it to the tub. Eaden eased over the edge of the tub and this time Mary did not avert her eyes from the golden ember-glow playing gently across the muscled planes of his body. Her breath caught and her skin warmed as she noted what she'd instigated.

"The water is not yet warm, m'laird," she warned him.

Eaden met her gaze evenly, the slight upturn of his lips attesting to his humor. "'Tis warm enough, Mairi," he avowed as he sank into the tub. "Warm enough."

She picked up the bar of fragrant soap and a square of coarse linen, approaching the tub and halting behind Eaden's shoulder. Dipping the cloth in the water, she worked the soap into a thick lather, then squeezed the linen, dribbling soapy water across his broad shoulders. His muscles bunched and smoothed as the tepid water made contact with his skin. Mary smiled.

She boldly splayed her hands over his skin, warm and tight beneath her palms. She massaged the thick muscles, remembering, with a delicious shiver, the heat of his hands on her own aching limbs.

Eaden groaned in contentment and slumped forward as Mary rubbed the soap into the soot and grime on his body, sliding her hands up and down his back. Each time she plunged a little deeper in the tub, scooping handfuls of water to pour over his skin. Her hands slipped around his sides, bumping over the hard line of his ribs to meet on the taut muscles of his stomach. She gasped as Eaden's hands caught her wrists, keeping them from dipping lower.

"No' yet, Mairi." His voice was rough with checked passion. She cut her gaze into the water below their hands and her cheeks flamed hotly as she realized what she had almost done. She pulled gently from his grip, careful to slide her hands up his chest, rubbing in a circular motion as she loosened the soot and grime from his skin.

Rinsing the piece of linen in the water, she leaned over his shoulder and wiped his face clean. She ran her fingers through his hair, pulling lather through the night-dark strands. A moan of pleasure escaped his lips and Mary felt a peculiar tug deep inside. Warmth spread through her belly and legs, tingling in her breasts grown suddenly tight against the fabric of her robe.

"Tilt your head back," she whispered. Eaden obliged and Mary used the bucket to dip into the tub, rinsing the suds from his hair. She leaned forward, running her fingers through the wet strands, feeling for lingering evidence of soap.

Eaden caught her hands, pulling her to the side of the tub. Her breathing grew rapid and deep as he tugged at the cuff of her soft, green velvet sleeve. "Lose your robe, Mairi."

Mary untied the belt and let it fall to the floor. She shrugged and the robe joined the belt at her feet, leaving her clad only in her thin night shift. A grin slashed across Eaden's face as he grabbed her arm and turned her around, her back to the tub. With a quick jerk, he pulled her into the tub with him, sending water sloshing noisily onto the wooden floor.

Mary shrieked in surprise as she tumbled into the water, the tub barely large enough for her bottom to fit between his feet. A glance at him confirmed the merriment in his eyes.

It suddenly occurred to her this time things were very different between them. Theirs was no longer a relationship of duty and distrust. A new, intriguing element had arisen. It was not Eaden's fault she'd sought information on how to please him from a completely unreliable source, though the thought of Isobel's audacity and deception still galled her sorely.

There was a way, however, to beat Isobel's treachery. Mary's body flushed with anticipation, suddenly longing to discover what Isobel sought to hide from her.

Without warning, Mary heaved a handful of water into Eaden's grinning face.

"Ye imp!" he sputtered as he grabbed Mary's bottom, jerking her toward him. Off balance, she slid through the water, hands flailing wildly for the edge of the tub. Eaden roared with laughter, and to her surprise, she didn't want to throttle him for nearly drowning her. Instead, she grinned back at him, pushing away so she could stand.

His smile faded as she rose over him, water dripping from every part of her. For a moment she paused, nonplussed. This new game they played had much to teach her. She studied the way his eyes darkened as his gaze met hers and she looked down, trying not to be self-conscious of how the wet, filmy fabric molded itself to her, as intimate as a caress.

She grasped her shift, pulling it slowly over her head to let it fall carelessly to the floor beside the tub. Eaden's breath rasped and her heart, already racing with her daring, sped up a notch.

"Come to me, Mairi." Eaden pulled her back into the water. He stretched his legs as far as he could, making room for her knees on either side of his hips. She straddled him, the heat of him, full and tight, against her skin. He slid one hand between them, his fingers finding the swollen, hot core of her. Mary closed her eyes, savoring the strange, new sensation streaking through her.

He shifted beneath her and sat straighter, leaning forward to kiss one breast, his lips nibbling her sensitive skin, his tongue drawing her nipple into his mouth. She grabbed his shoulders to steady herself, her muscles relaxing beneath the onslaught of his caresses.

He moved his attention to her other breast and Mary gasped as her entire body clenched and eased with the tempo of his suckling. Tightness built within her and she panted in a struggle to meet her body's demand for air.

Eaden slid his hand from her and she uttered a small cry of regret. He lifted her hips and her eyes flew open as the swollen head of his cock probed her opening.

"I want to pleasure ye."

Mary shuddered at his husky voice promising her something new and exciting. And previously forbidden. She gasped at the slightly burning, stretching sensation as he slowly lowered her onto his shaft. He rocked her against him and she caught the rhythm instantly, needing no further encouragement. With the tips of his fingers, he stroked her again. A cry of surprise escaped her as she shook against him. Eaden gave a shout and stiffened suddenly beneath her, his head thrown back against the edge of the tub as his own release claimed him.

Time stood still. Mary didn't know if she'd been lying against Eaden's chest for minutes or hours, his arms wrapped tight around her, but her heartbeat had slowed and the water cooled around her. She sat up slowly, placing a hand on his chest, and he shifted so she could rise. The muscles in her legs quivered.

"Wait, lass." Eaden rose to his feet and heaved himself out of the tub, then held her arm as she joined him. He pulled a thick linen from a stack on the hearth and Mary leaned gratefully into the warm folds. He dried her gently, making sure he missed no spot, and Mary's skin heated from more than the cloth by the time he finished.

Eaden grinned at her and quickly wiped himself down, giving no more than cursory attention to his own damp limbs. Ignoring the water puddled on the floor, he scooped Mary into his arms and carried her to the bed. He yanked the covers back and laid her on the cool sheets.

Mary sucked in a breath against the chill, but he covered her with his body, reaching behind him to drag the coverlet over them. She felt him warm and hard against her thigh, and knew he wanted her again. To her surprise, she wanted him, too. She curled her arms around his neck, arching her body into the curve of his. Eaden nibbled her ear.

"Are ye sure, Mairi?" he murmured. "I can wait if ye wish." He drew his head away, letting her see the grimace on his face as he laughed at himself for such a blatant lie.

She tightened her hold on him and kissed the rough line of his jaw. "Nay, Eaden. I believe you've proven Isobel wrong. But you could try again just to be certain."

Chapter Twenty-Seven

Mary remained snuggled against him the next morning. Pleased to see his wife had not run from him this time, Eaden grinned broadly as he held her gently in his arms. No surprise she was not yet awake. They'd slept little in the hours before dawn, too wrapped up in each other to notice the passage of time.

He lifted his head from his pillow and sniffed the air. The lingering odor of smoke was damped down by the rain plinking against the partially-open glass window. The entire castle could have burned to the ground last night and he doubted he or Mary would have taken notice. He spared a glance at the drops of water on the floor beneath the open window and, deciding they were of no major concern, settled his head back on his pillow.

He sighed. He had no qualms about putting Ranald and Ian in charge this morning, leaving himself free to make love to his wife in the light of day. But after the events of the night before, he would need to be up soon to see about the damages to the stable and other buildings, as well as the men and lads who'd come to his aid. He did not know who or what had started the blaze and needed to question the stable lads while their memories were still fresh.

Mary stirred, sighing softly as she cuddled closer. He thought to rouse her, his own body jerking pleasurably to wakefulness as she moved against him. Caught between regret and compassion, he softly brushed his lips over her forehead, remembering the barest edge of pain to her cry of pleasure as they'd made love again a short time ago.

Slipping from the bed, he tucked the blanket snugly around her, assuring she was warm and comfortable. He managed to get his breeches settled on his hips, hoping the fit would ease once he set about his morning business. Pulling on his shirt, he turned back to the bed and kissed his wife once more. This time her eyes fluttered open, her sleepy smile becoming a puzzled frown as she realized he had dressed.

He touched the tip of a finger to her lips, forestalling her words. "I hate to leave ye, Mairi, but I need to see to the stables, and ye need some sleep." He chuckled as her cheeks pinked with sudden color. She slipped a hand free and caressed his face. Heat rushed through him at her silent promise and turning his head, he pressed his mouth to the palm of her hand.

"Sleep, Mairi, love. No one will disturb ye before ye wake again." He couldn't resist a final parting shot. "Ye will need yer rest, my love."

* * *

The answers he received were less than satisfactory. The men from Bellecourt, thanks to Ian's sharp eye, had alibis for the night. Reluctantly, Eaden had to admit the culprit, however unintentional they may have been, could be someone from Craigievar. But who? The stable lads knew the safety rules for their domain. Not even the greenest among them would dare light a lamp in or near the barn without keeping a close eye on it. It was an unforgivable offense to leave a lantern unattended near the dry hay and wooden timbers.

He studied the lads arranged before him. Haggard and bleary-eyed after being roused from their exhausted sleep, most had yet to accomplish all but the most perfunctory ablutions. Soot clung to clothes and elbows, the scent of smoke wafted from their bodies. One lad shuffled his feet tiredly, another coughed into his closed fist, but none exhibited the tenseness or furtiveness of someone trying to hide guilt or information he'd rather not share.

"Check on yer horses, lads," Eaden said, realizing he would get no more information from the weary young men. "Feed them and turn them loose in the paddock furthest out to work off their energy. Grab some food as ye go, then get a couple hours' sleep. Master Camran will be wanting ye to look sharp soon." He dismissed the lads with a nod of his head and they shuffled away, their normal, jaunty steps dulled by the previous night's exhausting work.

Eaden turned to his brother, catching him mid-stretch, joints popping. Ranald lowered his arms with a shrug, bringing his shoulders forward to pull the tension from them.

"Those most likely to have started the fire are all accounted for, aye?" Eaden reiterated, more to gather his thoughts than as a question he already knew the answer to.

He sank into a nearby chair, propped his feet on the bench next to him, and sighed. "Is there anyone ye've heard grumbling lately? Anyone who wouldnae have a care the horses could be injured?"

Ranald scrubbed his face tiredly with the heels of his hands. "Nay. I'd have pegged Barde's men an' had I not known Ian was sitting on them. There's been no grumbling above the normal at the castle for some time." He glanced at Eaden. "Most of which are opposed to yer marriage to the Barde lass."

Eaden's jaw clenched. "Anyone in particular?"

"Nay. The lass has charmed nearly everyone here."

Eaden stared into the distance and the silence lengthened.

"Thinking of someone?" Ranald queried.

"It couldnae be," Eaden murmured. "She wouldn't dare . . ."

Ranald sat up in his chair. "She?"

Eaden turned to his brother. "Isobel has befriended my wife."

"Aye. And I dinnae trust the woman."

"Nor do I."

"She's ambitious, Eaden. Though I'm no' sure I'd believe her capable of firing the stables." Suddenly, Ranald jerked his head up, as if caught by an unexpected thought.

Eaden eyed his brother narrowly. "What?"

Ranald rubbed his chin. "She was on the parapet with Mary last night."

"They were on the parapet?" Eaden's voice snapped, sharp with anger. He wasn't tired enough or sated enough to forget he'd specifically told Mary to stay in their room.

"Aye. Mary said she'd needed to see ye safe." He waved a hand as Eaden opened his mouth, stalling his next words. "Something caught my eye as I headed back into the castle and I looked up and saw her. Someone stood next to her, something fluttering pale in the torchlight."

"There's no ghost at Craigievar, Ranald," Eaden replied chillingly.

"Nay. There were two women on the parapet. Yer wife and Isobel. And neither was dressed in something pale and fluttery."

"Ye're not suggesting a ghost set the fire, are ye?" Eaden scoffed.

Ranald shook his head. "Someone flesh and blood set the fire. But something nearly sent Mary tumbling over the wall."

Eaden jerked at Ranald's words. "What?" Rage slammed through him. He rounded on his brother. "Why have ye no' said anything?"

"Well, mostly because we've been focusing on the fire, no' Lady Fenella's ghost," Ranald retorted, scowling his irritation.

"Tell me," Eaden demanded.

"I saw Mary clearly on the parapet. Next to her stood a dark form . . ." His voice trailed off and he glanced away. After a moment, he turned back to Eaden, his face bleak. "The pale, fluttery movement caught my eye. And so did Mary. I dinnae remember the dark form until now. I ran up the stairs, not sure what I'd seen. Mary leaned far over the wall, her arm outstretched, her feet no' touching the floor."

Ranald ducked his head, staring at the worn stone at his feet. His fists clenched and relaxed. Whatever he had witnessed had apparently disturbed him greatly. He continued his tale, his words slow and thoughtful.

"The ghost, or whatever, wasnae there. The one in the black cloak reached a hand toward Mary. I shouted and saw her grab Mary's arm, pulling her back."

"Who was it?"

Ranald looked at his brother, his face stricken. "It was Isobel. And she wasnae pulling Mary back. She was braced to push her over the edge."

Chapter Twenty-Eight

Mary stretched languidly beneath the soft coverlet. Soreness pulled at the muscles on the insides of her legs, causing her face to heat with the memory of what she and Eaden had shared. A smile bloomed on her lips as she remembered the warmth of his body on hers, the heat of his hands, and the fullness of him inside her.

The glow of sunlight danced across her closed eyes, and she cracked one lid experimentally. The angle of the sun canted high through the window, and she realized with a jolt the hour was close to noon. She sat up, pushing the covers away to swing her legs over the side of the bed. Cool air touched her bare skin and she shivered as she scampered across the stone floor to the bathing chamber.

"St. Andrew's teeth, but 'tis cold this day!" Her teeth chattered and goose bumps rose high on her skin as she finished her ablutions. She turned to the doorway, stopping as she spied Kirsty milling about the bedchamber, moving toward the rumpled bed as she picked up the clothes lying scattered across the floor.

Self-conscious, Mary didn't move. She hadn't anticipated how her nakedness would remind her of the passion of the night before, embarrassing her before her maid. Warmth crept beneath her skin as she remembered the fevered way Eaden's hands had roamed her body.

As Kirsty reached for the embroidered coverlet partly pooled on the floor beside the bed, she looked up with widened eyes to see Mary's lack of clothing. Flushing hotly, Kirsty whirled about, grabbed Mary's robe, and rushed to envelop her in its soft, concealing folds.

The click of the door latch surprised both young women and their heads swung in unison to the opening door.

* * *

Isobel entered the room, her step arrested as she saw Kirsty and Mary. Her eyes slid from Mary's naked body to the laird's rumpled bed, whose state bespoke far more than simple sleep. She carefully schooled her expression to a calmness she didn't feel and forced her lips into a slight smile.

"Sleeping late, milady?" she asked, unable to keep the challenge from her voice.

Mary stiffened as she slipped her arms into her robe. Belting it snugly about her waist, she crossed the room to Isobel, closing the distance between them in quick, purposeful strides. The resentment on the younger woman's face sent warning tingles racing along Isobel's spine.

Mary halted mere inches from Isobel, her face registering more than mere hostility, and Isobel eyed her warily.

Mary drew back a hand, fisting it in mid-air as she swung an arc toward Isobel's face. The force of the unexpected blow felled Isobel and she crumpled in a heap onto the floor. Pain exploded in her head and she reeled, dizzy with shock.

How dare the little bitch hit her? She cringed against the throb blossoming in her head and rose slowly to her feet. Mary stood before her, balanced on the balls of her feet, leaning slightly forward, her hands clenched at her waist.

Prepared to strike her again.

Isobel rubbed her jaw gingerly. Her gaze slid to the bed, taking in the jumble of bedding clinging precariously there. Well did she remember the intimate joke between herself and Eaden in months past that it had been pointless to keep covers on their bed. The heat between them had been fierce, and it was far too easy for Isobel to recognize the jumble on the laird's bed for what it was this morning.

Isobel seethed with anger and outrage. Damn Eaden! It had to be his fault. She had taken great pains to assure Mary would never turn to him of her own accord.

She struggled to maintain an expression of innocent shock, needing time to repair this setback to her plans. "I am truly sorry, milady, if I . . ."

"Don't speak! Don't move and don't try to explain. Listen. Carefully." Mary's voice sounded strong, biting, furious . . . but her weight eased down to the soles of her feet and Isobel breathed a discreet sigh of relief.

"I am Lady Scott. I demand you leave Scott Castle. Immediately. Should you ever show yourself again here or to me or Laird Scott, I will have you beaten. You will receive no further clemency for the damage you have attempted between me and my husband. I have no control over what happened before I married him, but I will not allow you near him ever again. Do I make myself clear?"

Isobel meant to smile reassuringly, but only one side of her mouth curved upwards, forming a sneer, betraying her contempt. She straightened her shoulders, tossing her head so her heavy mass of shining black hair slid voluptuously across her back. Despite Mary's words, Isobel would not believe Eaden to be out of her reach. There would be another time, another chance. He loved *her*, not this child-bride.

"As milady wishes," she murmured, her eyes narrowed with spite. "But know this. Eaden will be mine again. Ye dinnae know what attracts him to me, but 'tis something ye dinnae have." She flicked a scornful glance over Mary's slender body, her hands smoothing her body's own ample curves in emphasis. "And never will."

Isobel lifted her chin, her voice full of malice and lies. "He has come to me often since your marriage. Why would he, if ye pleased him?" She nodded toward the rumpled bed. "Ye will bore him soon enough. He will come to me again. 'Tis only a matter of time."

"Get out!" Mary hissed, surging forward as she pointed to the door with an out flung hand. "Do not let me hear you lingered to leave the castle."

Holding her tongue against a further retort, Isobel spun on her heel and left the room. She stormed down the hallway, a bitter scowl plastered to her face.

So the bitch has decided she likes Eaden's hands on her. Why had Eaden kept trying? He had no real claim on her beyond vows spoken with the wrong bride. It was no secret she was only Lady Miriam's companion, of no breeding or status—of no consequence at all. And while Eaden was not one to let such things stand in his way for something he wanted, the question remained. Why did he want *her*?

Isobel opened the door to a small bedchamber she'd secretly claimed for herself at the end of the hall. It was far enough from the laird's bedroom so he wouldn't take note of her if she remained in the castle overnight, yet close enough she could still savor his nearness. She'd told Paedrus she was occasionally needed by the laird's lady, and he was sufficiently impressed that he'd raised no objection when she'd spent the occasional night away from home.

She'd have liked nothing better than to slam the door shut behind her, but thought better of it. The noise might attract unwelcome attention, and she needed time to think.

Pulling a bag from a wooden peg on the wall, Isobel opened the drawstring neck, shoving her night shift and a few other items she'd brought with her inside. She flung the bag on the bed and collapsed beside it, bouncing on the soft mattress. What could she do? The lass was pretty enough, and Eaden apparently besotted enough—a dangerous combination, in her opinion. She would have to work fast.

Lady Scott was angry, but how secure was she in her belief her husband would remain true to her?

Chapter Twenty-Nine

"Hurry." Mary fidgeted as Kirsty laced her gown. She needed fresh air or she knew she would scream. Reliving her husband's amorous attentions the night before had put her in no mood to confront his mistress this morning. *Former* mistress, she firmly reminded herself. There was no longer any room for *that* woman in his life. Or in hers. She'd done quite well for herself at Bellecourt Castle and if Kirsty was not available as her maid, she'd simply do without.

Had Eaden lied to her? Had he made love to Isobel since their marriage? It was obvious he enjoyed the pleasures of the flesh. While the two of them were estranged, would he have gone without, or would he have sought comfort elsewhere?

Isobel has no loyalty to me. She would have no problem betraying me by taking Eaden to her bed.

Mary fisted her skirts and ran from the room, stifling the scream rising in her throat. She fled down the stairs and through the great hall, not stopping to speak to the people lingering there. Entering the bailey, she coughed at the bite of the smoke-tinged air. Remembering the devastating fire at the stables last night depressed her further.

She noted a group of men standing to one side of the yard. Their backs were to her, but she could not fail to recognize her husband's stance and form. Not quite ready to face him, she turned in the opposite direction and made her way toward the far pasture where the lads had turned the horses out for the day.

Burnished coats gleamed in the late morning sun, shades of copper, gold, and one of darkest night. Two foals frisked about on stiff new legs around their dams and Mary smiled, her headache draining away in the clear, spring air. Starnie raised his head, nickering softly in greeting. He flicked his ears forward and ambled to the fence, lifting his head over the railing, snorting once.

"Greedy lad." Mary laughed and ran her hand obligingly over the long straight bone of his face. Her fingers came away covered in loosened winter coat and she dusted her hands together to dislodge it.

She moved toward the stable and frowned at the charred skeleton-like spars of posts and ruined rafters at the near end of the building. For an instant Mary again saw the flaming timbers, smelled the harsh smoke, and heard her own voice shout against the torched wood as it burst apart in a rain of sparks and embers, threatening to fall on Eaden's head.

A hand rested on her shoulder and Mary nearly fainted with fright. She jumped beneath the gentle stricture and heard the soft murmur of Eaden's voice.

"'Tis a right mess, aye?"

"I didn't know you were here. I was just remembering . . ." She shuddered beneath his hand.

"Aye. It takes ye like that, the realization." He rubbed his hand along her cheek as she turned to him. "I need to clear my head. Will ye ride with me?"

Mary nodded eagerly and he twined his fingers intimately with hers as he led her to the armorer's building. Warmth instantly suffused her at his touch and she stifled her protest as he broke the connection.

"We moved the tack and equipment here so we could start tearing the stable down tomorrow." He ducked beneath the low lintel, motioning Mary to wait outside. Returning with his arms laden, he dumped the saddles and blankets to the ground, unwinding a slim piece of rope as he climbed through the fence rails. Walking calmly among the horses, he touched one on the neck, another on its rump, as he moved to Starnie's side. He slipped the slim piece of rope around the horse's neck and led him unresistingly to the gate. "Hand me his bridle, lass."

Mary separated the tangled pieces of leather and held one up for his use. His hand closed over her wrist and pulled her to him as he stole a quick kiss before he took the bridle from her. With a wink, Eaden set Starnie's bit, and Mary's heart raced as he gave the horse's neck a fond slap and handed her the reins.

Eaden let out a sharp whistle. The horses stirred in the paddock and Duff barreled his way through them to the gate. The stallion nudged him and Eaden offered a small, wizened apple from his pocket, unembarrassed to be seen spoiling the beast. Warmth tugged at Mary's heart to see this side of her stern husband.

He quickly saddled both horses, his forearm muscles rippling, shirt sleeves rolled above his elbows. Mary was content to watch appreciatively, remembering the gentled strength he'd shown her the night past. How could she have believed Isobel's lies?

Eaden's task complete, he helped her mount, the action accomplished with more ease than she'd shown the day before, though Eaden still had to give her a boost, his hand planted familiarly on her bottom. She settled into the saddle and he moved his hand caressingly down her leg, giving her ankle an affectionate squeeze.

"Ye did well," he told her, his face creased in a smile. Picking up Duff's reins, he led him forward, springing into the saddle without bothering with the stirrups. Mary heeled Starnie gently and he followed Duff beyond the castle gates.

* * *

The horses' hooves pounded in the water along the edge of the river, sending spray like diamonds over their riders' legs. They pulled at their bits, straining against the moderate pace Eaden set. Long before the horses were winded, he reined them to a halt.

"Do we have to stop?"

Mary's face flushed with the excitement of the ride, her hair spilling from the confines of her thick, shining braid. Eaden threw his right leg over Duff's withers and slid lightly to the ground. Moving to Mary's side, he slipped a hand up her leg, grinning as she twitched at his touch.

"Nay. We dinnae have to stop."

Mary laughed and held her arms out, accepting his help to dismount. He grasped her waist and pulled her forward, letting her land against his chest as her legs slipped from the saddle. She slid the length of him, her soft breasts pressed against him, and he savored the heat of their contact. Her arms twined about his neck as she tilted her face to his invitingly, and he nibbled her lips until she giggled.

There was nothing funny about the way he now hungered for her, and he crushed her close as his mood changed from playful to demanding in the power of his kiss.

When he released her, Mary took a balancing step backward, a hand lingering on his chest for support.

"Turn around, Mairi," he whispered hoarsely. "Let me untie ye."

She jerked shocked eyes to his, cutting her gaze around them. "Here?"

He raised an eyebrow.

"It's daylight! What if someone sees us?"

Eaden's lips tilted up. "No one will follow us, lass."

"How do you know?"

He kissed the top of her head. "Ian will make sure of it."

Mary drew back, astonishment plain on her face. "Ian knows what you're about?"

"What *we're* about," Eaden chuckled. "'Tis no fun without ye."

He slid one hand to cup her breast, his thumb caressing the nipple straining against the fabric of her dress. Lowering his head, he kissed her again, nipping his way from her lips to the slim, warm column of her neck. Mary shivered and tilted her head back, her breath quickening as his kisses rained above the low neckline of her dress.

Her breasts threatened to spill from the top of her gown, and she gasped as his tongue swirled across the swelling skin, her fingers gripping the front of his shirt. He caught her close, reaching behind her to tug at the lacings of her dress.

"Don't," she whispered, her voice a low moan of mingled desire and regret.

"No one will see, Mairi."

"I can't undress out here in broad daylight!" She pushed away from his grasp, her eyes suddenly wide and clear with certainty.

At the pleading in her eyes, Eaden let her slip from his hands. He briefly pitted her request against his desire to see the sunlight on her skin, then eased her into his embrace, settling his hands familiarly on her bottom. He gathered her skirt in both hands and with a quick tug, jerked it up her legs.

With a gasp of surprise, Mary batted at his hands. "What are you doing?"

"Ye dinnae have to undress, ye know. 'Twill *ruckle* yer dress a bit, but no one will see yer pretty bum."

"Stop!" Her gasp was half laughter, half outrage.

"I swear, I dinnae know which shocks ye more. Making love with yer clothes on or baring yer bum to the sun."

Eaden dropped her skirt, shoved his hands behind his back and circled her, finally halting against her shoulder, his breath lifting the tiny curls at the side of her face.

Eying the rise and fall of her breasts, he whispered in her ear. "Before ye leave this place, Mairi, love, ye will take yer own clothes off."

* * *

Mary released her breath in a *whoosh* of surprise at his words. A wolfish grin spread across his face as their eyes met. She glanced down, his impatience evident beneath his tented breeches, and wondered how long his temper would last.

Before she could speak, his hands claimed her, warm, open palms sliding up her arms, slowly, softly, raising the fine hairs and goose bumps along his path. She jumped at the sensation and twisted beyond his grasp.

He chuckled, a seductive glint lighting his eyes. "No fair! Ye cannae run away."

Mary tossed a smug smile over her shoulder as she darted toward the river bank. "Yes, I can!"

Her heart stuttered at his seductive laugh as he accepted her challenge. She dodged behind a nearby tree, swinging around its trunk, needing to see how close Eaden followed her. Sliding to a stop, she found herself face to face with his grin. He'd anticipated her move and there was now only the thickness of the tree trunk between them. She feinted to the right, barely eluding his grasp.

Skidding down a low embankment, she stumbled against a rock. She felt his steadying hand on her arm, grateful for his support, though it forced her to give up the chase.

Her heart raced and she sucked in a gulp of air. Eaden brushed strands of hair from her face and she settled the mass over her shoulders with a toss of her head.

"Now I have ye, love, what would ye like me to do with ye?"

Mary bit the inside of her lip, his husky voice sending tremors of anticipation through her. The sun rippled through the trees in the glen and glinted off the gentle current on the river. Daylight shone brightly around her but she teetered perilously close to abandoning her ingrained inhibitions on the edge of the glen where anyone could see. Desperate inspiration struck and she lifted her face to his, kissing the rough line of his jaw. If she could kiss this insanity away, perhaps he'd take her back to the castle where she could love him as she longed to do.

"Aye, it's kissin' ye want, then?"

She heard the low rumble of his voice, but scarcely heeded the warning.

"Then it's kissin' ye'll get." Eaden lowered his head and sealed his lips to hers, all the teasing gone in the instant it took Mary to realize her mistake. He drank deeply from her lips, stealing the very breath from her. She arched up on her toes, molding herself closer, fitting her body against the hard lines of his muscles. Her fingers twisted in his hair, drawing little growls of pleasure from deep within his throat.

* *

Panting, Eaden broke the kiss. His hands cupped her breasts, this time spilling them from the silken confines of her bodice. He fastened his mouth hungrily on a nipple, his thumb teasing the other to stiff attention. He pulled at the swollen flesh as she swayed in his arms. Wrapping one arm around her waist, he held her upright. He closed his teeth gently on her nipple and she whimpered, her fingers digging into his shoulders. Moving to the other breast, he paid it similar homage as her nails bit against his flesh through the fabric of his shirt.

Eaden lifted his head and with singular purpose backed her against the trunk of a nearby tree. He pressed his throbbing manhood against her leg, unable to ease the pressure building intolerably against his breeches. Pulling at her gown, he raised the hem until he reached the silken smoothness of her thigh, sliding one hand along the curve of her leg to the juncture of her heat.

"Let me love ye, Mairi. D'ye no' ken what ye do to me?" he breathed against her hair.

Mary pushed her body against him and he clasped her buttock, massaging the muscle with firm strokes. She moaned, her hands gripping the tree at her back.

Suddenly she broke away. Her hands flew to the laces at her back, clawing at them in her haste to be free. With a wrenching tug, she released the ties and her dress sagged forward as she brushed the sleeves down her arms, shoving the crumpled fabric over her hips. With a wriggle that caused her breasts to sway and Eaden to fight for control, she fought free of the gown. It took less than a second for her nearly transparent shift to follow the dress, and she threw herself back into his arms.

Kicking the gown away from the knobby roots of the tree to the thick grass a few feet away, Eaden lowered her to the soft, silken folds. Sunlight warmed his shoulders as he yanked his shirt over his head. His breeches were harder to dislodge and he offered a wry grimace as he worked them over his hips. The sultry smile she gave in answer made his breath clog in his throat, and then he came over her, nudging her knees apart.

She opened to him, clasping him to her eagerly, and he buried himself in her welcoming warmth. With a shudder, he tried to slow down, wanting to be sure she kept up with him, but she writhed beneath him, keening her rising passion.

Light burst through his skull and pleasure streaked from the base of his spine. Mary's fingernails bit into his back, but he paid them no heed. Her voice sounded in his ears, though he barely heard her. She clenched around him, so tight and hot, rippling over him, drawing his response again and again. He collapsed into sweet oblivion.

* * *

Something lit lightly on his nose. Eaden wrinkled his face, trying to dislodge the bothersome pest, but it returned with aggravating speed. Eaden thought to wave it away with his hand, but one appendage lay trapped beneath something warm and soft, and the other seemed too heavy to lift. He cracked an eyelid open.

Merry green eyes met his and he blinked, focusing on the long blade of grass dangling from slender fingers above him. The edge of the blade touched his nose again, and he growled in mock displeasure.

He tried to swat the stalk of grass away, but Mary lay across one of his arms, pinning it beneath her. He flexed his free hand, reveling in the sated laxity of his muscles. Closing his eyes, he gave himself over to the contentment rippling through his body.

"You're lying on my dress," Mary whispered in his ear.

Eaden could hear the laughter in her voice and his lips twitched in a smile. "Aye. Are ye cold, love?"

"No. But how long will Ian keep people away?"

"I dinnae think I can rise just yet." He clenched the hand beneath her against the smooth line of her bottom, remembering well the baring of it. He wanted to tell her *I told ye so*, but even drowsy and sated he was not such a fool.

His smile deepened when his cock twitched agreeably. He opened his eyes and found Mary staring at him, watching as his manhood swelled larger. Speculation twisted her lips and she touched him with the dangling end of the blade of grass. A startled shout escaped him at the delicate challenge, and he jerked mightily in response.

"Your turn, Mairi," he said with a wicked grin.

"What?" A look of bewilderment crossed her face.

He grasped her arms and dragged her over him, groaning as she settled herself on his rigid shaft. She bent to him, her hair falling forward as she rocked back and forth, picking up the rhythm at his encouragement.

He watched her through the partial veil of her gold-threaded hair as she reached for her release. His hands cupped her breasts, swaying above him, and her breath caught in a cry. Waves of passion washed over him and he grabbed her waist, yanking her firmly down onto him as he gave one final thrust before he lost all control.

Chapter Thirty

Early morning mists surrounded the castle walls, creating a shimmering faerie land of grey and white, the sun a faint pink and yellow stain on the shrouded horizon. Mary leaned against the parapet wall, her thoughts as ethereal as the swirling haze of morning.

The soft clop of the sentry's boots echoed nearby, but he'd seen her and acknowledged her presence with a short nod before returning to his rounds. Impossible to see him except as a faint shadow behind the ghostly curtain of mist, Mary pretended she was alone with her thoughts.

The dewy wetness clinging to the stone seeped slowly through her heavy velvet robe. She inhaled deeply, feeling the cool, moist bite in her chest. An early breeze caught the morning vapor, swirling it between the crenellated stones, twisting it into garish shapes swaying just beyond her reach.

The soft sound of footsteps behind her broke into her fanciful thoughts and she turned at the approach. A form materialized out of the mist and Mary's lips curved in a slight smile as she recognized Eaden's brother.

Ranald halted abruptly, obviously surprised to see her. "Wheesht, lass! Dinnae scare me so!" He came closer to peer over the parapet wall.

Mary laughed softly. "Don't worry. I'm not about to jump."

Ranald nodded. "'Twould be a fair mess on yon cobblestones, to be sure, seeing as ye are no ghost. What brings ye up here this fine morning? That pirate bothering yer dreams?" Ranald cocked his head toward the stairwell and presumably at Eaden beyond.

"Pirate?" Mary exclaimed, amused at Ranald's description. "Whatever makes you call him that?"

"Och, our mother hailed from the Kintyre peninsula. Her people were seafarers." Ranald shrugged. "Pirates."

"And has he shown any inclination to follow in his ancestors' footsteps?"

"Nay, but her clan 'tis no' so far from King Robert's castle at Troon. Eaden was but a lad fostering with an uncle there when he first met the king."

"He became a herald at a young age, then?"

"Aye. He's always had a gift for remembering things. He'd watched his uncle divest a less wary man of his coin in a game, and was able to recall the wager, drunken though it was, in great detail." Ranald grinned. "He won his first horse and the attention of the king that day."

He turned back to Mary. "So, all yer dreams are good now?"

Mary's cheeks flushed, thankful for the mist shrouding her, veiling her from Ranald's astute gaze. "Aye. My dreams are fine."

"Good. I hoped ye were the reason for his improved mood these past two days. He's come close to losing his temper several times lately."

"What do you mean?"

"He's been sore wanting ye and making no apology for it. And he can be a right bear when he cannae have something he wants." Ranald rested his elbow against the stone. "Ye've softened him, and I'll be the first to thank ye for it."

Mary laughed. "Well, perhaps we can all get on with our lives now."

"Ye'll be stayin' at Scott Castle, then?"

Ducking her head to hide the heat rushing to her cheeks anew, Mary nodded. "Yes. I'll stay."

The companionable silence between them lingered. Mary watched the mists ebb and flow, only to shred apart as the heat of the sun at last defeated them.

"What *does* bring ye out here this morning?"

Mary sighed. "It's difficult to explain. I'm quite contented now as Eaden's wife, and I suppose I should still be asleep . . ." She heard Ranald's startled cough and chuckled. "I only meant I am not usually such an early riser. But I wanted to be by myself for a while and think, and it is difficult to think with Eaden and Sorcha snoring."

"D'ye wish me to leave ye?"

Mary made a dismissive gesture with one hand. "Oh, no. I'm all thought out. I was simply admiring the mists when you arrived."

Ranald turned back to the view from the parapet, the smoke rising from the cooking fires, twining darkly with the white feathers of the lingering morning mist.

"I do need to thank you, though," Mary added.

"Aye? For what?"

"For reminding me I should accept what I cannot change and make good use of what I have."

Ranald nodded. "I couldnae bear to see ye so sad. I knew Eaden could make ye happy if the two of ye would put aside what brought ye here and focus on each other. 'Twas clear to see ye suited each other."

"Suited each other? Are you mad?"

"Nay. I've been called an *amadan* on occasion, but never blind."

Mary laughed. "An *amadan*?"

"Aye, a fool."

"Who would call you such?" Mary bristled in sisterly outrage.

"Mostly my kind brother—when he couldnae think of anything else to say. An' he's a fair hand with words. I've been cursed by him in as many as four different languages."

Mary shook her head. "'Tis amazing the two of you get along sometimes."

"Och, ye just need to realize he's not the perfect man our father raised him to be. Eaden knows this, but tries to hide it. Our da wouldnae let him be anything but the best at whatever he did. Eaden had to be the best swordsman, the best scholar, the best sailor . . ."

"Sailor? Why a sailor?"

Ranald shrugged. "He had an opportunity to train with our uncle, so Da sent him to learn to sail. Sometimes I think Eaden became the king's herald to stay out of Da's reach. It was mayhap a way for Da to be proud of him without being under his thumb all the time. Smart man, my brother."

"And how was life growing up for you?"

"Fine. Living in my perfect older brother's shadow gave me plenty of freedom. Sometimes I wonder if he resented me for it." Ranald stared off into the distance. After a moment, he shook himself as though clearing a particularly unpleasant memory.

He faced Mary again. "Enough about me. Are the two of ye still leaving to visit King Robert today?"

"Yes. Kirsty packed most of my things yesterday. We only wait for yon pirate to wake and break his fast."

Ranald motioned Mary from the wall. "Away then. I'll walk ye to yer room and help ye roust the blackguard. Daylight is here."

"You're right. I suppose it is time."

"Not nervous at meeting the king, are ye, lass?"

"Oh, no. Just a bit overwhelmed, 'tis all."

Ranald made a satisfied sound in his throat as he paused to let Mary precede him down the stairs. "I suspected ye had a bit o' steel in ye."

"You did?" Mary glanced over her shoulder at the bottom of the steps. "And why is that?"

"'Tis no but a rumor, but I hope 'tis true."

Mary narrowed her eyes. "A rumor?"

"Aye. 'Tis said ye've sent the sloe-eyed witch, Isobel, away from the castle." Ranald gave a nod of approval. "And about time, too, I say."

Silently Mary crossed the great hall, Ranald beside her. When they were at last in the privacy of the upper hall, she ventured, "What do you know of Isobel?"

"Enough to ken she was up to no good. I told Eaden yesterday she could easily have pushed ye from the parapet the other night."

Mary gasped. "What are you saying?"

"Dinnae fash. If ye hadnae sent her away, Eaden would." Ranald scowled before he added, "Neither of us realized how far she would go to be rid of ye. She wants Eaden badly, ye ken."

"She told me she and Eaden were still . . ." Mary dropped her gaze to her hands, twisting them together in agitation as she remembered Isobel's spiteful words.

"I hate we dinnae do something about her sooner. She seemed to be trying to make amends by befriending ye, and I was wont to let it lie."

"'Tis what Eaden told me, as well." Mary sighed. She stopped outside the laird's chamber, her hand on the door latch. "Perhaps Isobel only tried to hurt me with her lies."

"Whatever ye've been told, Eaden has no' lied to ye."

"But . . . No, never mind." Mary's lips thinned. She would not repeat the words that had cut her so deeply. Just thinking of Isobel in Eaden's arms made her stomach clench painfully.

She squared her shoulders, shoving the image from her mind. "She is gone and cannot hurt me any longer. Whatever happened between them is past, and I know Eaden would never betray me."

Her eyes softened and she smiled a secret smile, thinking of the night just past and the words of endearment that fell so easily from Eaden's clever lips. "I think he is in love with me."

Turning the latch, Mary opened the door, and her world came crashing down.

Chapter Thirty-One

Eaden woke as heat spread through his groin. Warm fingers fondled him, stirring his flesh. Eyes still closed, he let his legs sprawl open, giving the fine-boned, nimble fingers room to work their magic. This was an excellent way to start the morning, he decided, lazy and amorous at the same time. Married life was definitely improving.

He felt himself fill within the spread of her hands. A few minutes ago, he'd have sworn he was too sated to consider making love to his wife again, but thankfully she hadn't stopped to ask. Eaden cracked one eye open and dimly saw the top of her dark head and the pale gleam of her naked shoulders, partly hidden by the early morning shadows and the bed sheet flowing from her waist to the floor. He moaned, closing his eyes as her warm hands closed over him. Gripping the mattress, he gave himself up to his wife's unexpected innovation. Who'd have thought she'd be so bold?

"Och, Mairi," he groaned, ignoring the feeble warning in his head. He didn't want to question the fire of his response streaking through him. Thinking was not on his list of priorities at the moment. He arched his back, closing his eyes tight against the heavy pulse beating strongly at the base of his spine, straining to make the sensation last. His blood pounded in his ears and fire flashed through him with quicksilver heat.

Dimly he heard the snick of the door latch, and a noise somewhere between a shriek and a gasp intruded on his concentration. He grunted in protest. Who dared enter his bedroom without permission? He opened one eye, murderous thoughts bouncing nonsensically in his mush-filled brain, all his attention focused on a much firmer part of his body.

Ranald? Eaden gritted his teeth as he fought to stall the passion threatening to burst from him. Ranald grabbed the person at his side and shoved her behind him, her chestnut hair swinging through the air with streaks of gold.

Mary?

Eaden rose to his elbows, sliding away from the grasp of the woman in his bed.

Isobel!

Across the room, Ranald fought to keep his grip on Mary as she pounded him with clenched fists, sounds of fury escaping her in shrieks and hisses. With a roar, Eaden heaved himself from the bed, snatching the sheet around his hips, uncovering Isobel's naked body. She slid along the mattress until she lay fully stretched on her belly, resting her chin on her hands. A sly, satisfied smile spread across her face as she eyed him from beneath lowered lashes, obviously aware of the havoc she'd wrought.

"Witch!" Eaden snarled at the raven-haired seductress. He wrenched his gaze to the doorway, but Mary was gone. The door hung open with Ranald at the threshold, staring into the chamber. Disgust twisted his brother's lips as he glared from Isobel to Eaden.

"Ye *amadan!*" Ranald shook his head in disbelief. "Ye cannae be such a fool ye thought ye'd no' get caught?"

"I dinnae think such a thing." Eaden cast an evil look at Isobel. "I dinnae know she was in the bed."

Ranald blinked, glancing from his brother to the empty doorway and back. "Who'd ye think . . ? Nay, spare me the details. There's no way of fixing *this*."

"Get out of my way," Eaden snarled, brushing past Ranald and through the door. He was back in a moment, shredding the sheet from his hips, disregarding both his brother and his former mistress as he snatched up his breeches and pulled them on, taking only a moment longer to shrug into his shirt. He turned abruptly to Isobel as he finished dressing.

"Get out." Eaden's voice rumbled low in anger, causing Isobel to scramble to her feet, her shining black hair swinging like a curtain about her.

"No. You are mine, now," she declared with a triumphant smile. "She will not return after this."

Eaden strode to the door, tossing Ranald a brusque command. "Bind her and leave her tethered in the great hall. I will deal with her later."

Without another glance at either Isobel or Ranald, Eaden chased after Mary.

* * *

Isobel stared at the open doorway, her skin pale with shock. Suddenly, her cheeks pinked vividly. Clenching her fists, she stormed across the floor, stopping only a few inches from Ranald. He eyed her warily.

"*Amadan!*" she hissed. "I warned him no one would ever love him as much as I. He thought himself bound by honor to that little bitch. But I made certain she feared his touch."

She paused, chest heaving, her black hair tossed wildly about her shoulders. Ranald stared dispassionately at her, unmoved by her nakedness. She snarled, "I convinced her Eaden would think her a whore if she responded to his lovemaking. But he couldnae see beyond her pretty face."

Spite twisted Isobel's lips. She paced a few steps away. "I fired the stables to entice him from her bed, knowing he would blame The Barde's soldiers. A piece of white silk was all it took to convince her the ghost of Lady Fenella called her to leap from the walls. She nearly went over the edge when she saw Eaden fall. It would have been simple to give her a shove."

Ranald clenched his fists, furious. Isobel's eyes blazed with hatred and she spat, "But you showed up! You saw me and I had to *save* her instead."

Filled with disgust for the woman before him, Ranald took up the sheet lying discarded on the floor and rent a long strip from its length. He twisted the fabric into a thin rope and motioned for Isobel to turn around.

She tossed her head defiantly and Ranald glimpsed the first signs of fear in her eyes as she glanced furtively about, seeking escape from the room. The open door lay behind him. He positioned himself between her and the portal, determined she'd not slip past him.

With a grim set to his lips, he advanced on the woman, his makeshift rope dangling loose and ready in his hand. "Dinnae make this hard on yerself, lass," he cautioned, edging closer.

She stared at him with the feral eyes of a trapped animal and darted to one side. Ranald countered the expected move with ease, hands spread low at his side, the rope swaying gently from his fingers. She whirled and leapt onto the bed, her hands flat against one of the massive bed posts.

Ranald considered it a perfectly secure place to tie her, but discarded the notion, not relishing the thought of Mary entering the room and finding her rival thus bound.

"Wheesht, lass," he sighed, motioning for her to come to him. "Let us be done with it."

Isobel ran two paces to her right, her bare feet sinking into the mattress, slowing her pace. Ranald feinted to his left. She turned and jumped to the floor, angling past him to the open door. With a sigh, he countered her move. Isobel threw him an anguished look, and for the first time, Ranald glimpsed the madness in her eyes.

"Stop yer runnin', Isobel. I willnae leave ye tied naked before the others. Ye will have to accept yer punishment, but I willnae humiliate ye."

Isobel choked on a sob. "I cannae have him, can I?" she mewled, her voice curiously thin and childlike.

Ranald shook his head, letting his hands fall to his sides. "Nay, lass. He doesnae belong to ye."

She dropped her gaze, nodding as her shoulders drooped in defeat. Suddenly, she whirled to the narrow, open window and Ranald gave a shout as he realized her intent.

With the casing ajar, it took only a slight twist to fit her slender body through the narrow opening. She crouched for an instant, her feet balanced on the ledge, toes gripping the ancient stone. Rising to her full height, she stared at the courtyard below. The morning sun pierced her translucent skin, outlining her with a blinding radiance.

"No!" Released from his momentary shock, Ranald lunged toward her. Isobel spread her arms wide and fell forward, her body a graceful arc as it toppled from the ledge to the ground below.

Chapter Thirty-Two

Blinded by panic, Mary fled down the stairs. Her arms outstretched for balance, she skimmed the wall with her fingertips as she ran. Pausing at the bottom of the steps, she brushed hot tears from her face, her lungs aching.

The great hall was empty but for a few servants setting out food and drink for the morning meal. She slipped around the edge of the room, avoiding all but the most curious looks, and walked briskly through the open doorway as though she knew exactly what she was doing. Nothing could have been farther from the truth. More tears gathered in her eyes and she wiped them away impatiently on the sleeve of her robe.

Where to go? What to do? The scheming, lying bastard hadn't even been satisfied to wait until he could go to the witch's room! She closed her eyes against the memory of Eaden lying on *their* bed, his head thrown back in his pleasure, and Isobel . . .

Mary's eyes flew open, her face flaming hot as she realized what Isobel had been doing. Lurching across the bailey, she clutched her stomach against the sharp pain of betrayal. *He is my husband! Isobel has no right to him!* She stifled a sob.

She would not share her husband. If he was not satisfied with her, Isobel could have him, and good riddance to both of them. Stumbling to a stop, she made a quick decision to return to Bellecourt where she belonged. She would not stay in this sordid castle a moment longer where the laird played on her innocence and trust, betraying her with another woman.

But, how to leave? Surely Eaden would follow her. Mary's heart skipped a beat. Or would he?

She glanced around the bailey. People milled about, caught between waking and the beginning of their workday. Few looked her way. She strode to the paddock, coming to a halt beneath a gnarled oak tree. Concealed in its shadow, she clucked her tongue softly at the horses awaiting their morning grain. Starnie trotted over, nickering happily. Mary patted the long bone of his face.

"There's a good lad." She mimicked Eaden's words of encouragement to the horse. "I'll get your tack and we'll be off."

The armory door swung open and the master armorer stretched as he stepped through the doorway, pausing to blink against the sunlight. He scratched his crotch in an absent manner before strolling toward the great hall. Mary waited another minute to see if anyone else was about, then darted across the yard and slipped inside the building.

The odor of metal and oil mingled with the earthier scent of leather, and Mary wrinkled her nose as she peered around the room. Tack lay scattered everywhere and she eyed the array of leather goods with dismay. How to tell which fit Starnie? She slipped a bridle from its peg on the wall, then tried to lift a saddle from the rack, but found it too heavy for her. She would have to do without.

Her heart pounded. She had wasted far too much time in the armory and even now Eaden could be searching for her. Through the open doorway, she saw an old woman sitting in the morning sun in the bailey, carding wool with slow sweeps of her gnarled hands. She heard a commotion on the far side of the bailey, but the sounds did not appear to come closer so she dismissed it from her mind.

Mary slipped through the door to the paddock where Starnie waited, his ears pricked forward at her approach. He accepted the bit without a fuss, though Mary's hands trembled, clinking the metal sharply against his teeth. Slipping the headstall behind Starnie's ears, she was relieved the bridle fit securely. She led the horse through the gate, closing it carefully behind them.

"Good lad," she told him, her teeth clenched to keep them from chattering with nervousness.

She guided Starnie against the fence, clambering up the rails to gain the level of his back. Clinging precariously from her perch on the fence, Mary gathered her skirt about her knees and said a quick prayer. With a little hop, she slid onto his back, grabbing at his mane to keep from slipping off the other side. Surprised to find herself sitting on Starnie's broad back and not sprawled in the dirt, Mary gathered the reins. Gripping his sides with her knees, she turned him toward the castle gate.

Head bent, looking neither to the right nor the left, she did not wave to the guard who glanced briefly down on her from the parapet. Much too interested in the milling crowd beyond the doors of the great hall, he let her pass.

Starnie ambled agreeably down the path from the castle. The morning sun slipped through the mist, lightly kissing Mary's right shoulder, and she knew she headed north. She would wait until she traveled far beyond the sentry's sight before she turned Starnie around and rode south.

Despite leaving the castle unchallenged, Mary knew she'd been watched, her description, if not her actual identity, noted. Eaden would learn of her departure soon, if he hadn't guessed already. She should have changed her clothes, disguised herself in some way. She had been too hurt, too angry and focused on leaving as quickly as possible to think through all the difficulties of running away. She also had no provisions and no covering beyond her heavy velvet robe.

The watery sun, peaking through the evaporating mists, made her hope for clear weather.

* * *

Ranald hurried down the stairs, looking for Eaden. It was pointless to check on Isobel. As the crowd thickened around her, there was no question in his mind that she was dead. It was more important to let his brother know the woman had jumped to her death from his bedroom window. Ranald cursed under his breath. As bad as the morning had begun, things were quickly headed downhill.

"Did ye no' see yer mistress this morning?"

Ranald heard Eaden's voice, tight with worry, and hurried through the kitchen door. Eaden looked up, and Ranald saw the strain in his brother's eyes. Pivoting on his heel, Eaden turned away from the girl, shoving a hand through his hair—a typical gesture that bespoke his frustration. Ranald opened his mouth to speak, but Eaden motioned curtly for him to follow.

"Eaden." Ranald let out a gusty sigh, weary of talking to his brother's back.

"Not now." Eaden's voice rumbled low with irritation. "Now!"

Eaden whirled. "What?" he snapped.

Ranald jerked his head over his shoulder, indicating the growing crowd a short distance away. Eaden took in the scene with a deepening scowl. He cut his gaze to his brother and Ranald sighed, not looking forward to breaking the news.

"Isobel jumped."

"What do you mean, *Isobel jumped*?"

Ranald's temper snapped and scorn ripped through his voice as he crossed his arms over his chest. "Two words, Eaden. Which do ye no' understand?"

"Dinnae fash with me, Ranald. I've no' the time to waste."

"All right. Is this easier?" Ranald gestured toward the crowd. "There, on the yard next to the castle, lies Isobel, who leapt to her death from yer bedroom window." He pointed to the casement two stories above. "Clear?"

"How could ye let that happen!"

"Ye left the window open." Ranald checked the urge to pick a fight with his brother.

"Is she . . ." Eaden shook his head. "Nay. Forget I asked. I dinnae have time to discuss this."

Ranald extended a hand, stalling Eaden's move. "Ye'll to have deal with it, brother." He nodded toward the milling crowd. "There's more than one person asking how the naked lass, who isnae yer wife, but known to have been yer mistress, managed to fall from yer bedroom window."

Eaden glowered at his brother. "I havenae found Mary. I willnae waste time dealing with a dead woman."

"As laird ye must." Ranald sighed, his loyalty to his brother strong. He gripped Eaden's shoulder. "We will find Mary. I swear it."

* * *

Eaden was certainly no stranger to death, but the sight of Isobel's ruined body hit him unexpectedly in the gut. This should never have happened. He should have been more direct with her, insisted she leave the castle days ago. He should have made it perfectly clear she was no longer a part of his life—and never would be again. A string of *should haves* flew through his head, damning him for Isobel's death.

The murmurs grew, and he saw for the first time the wary looks of the people gathered near. Eaden parted his lips to speak, but his words were forestalled by an accusing voice from the crowd.

"She fell from *yer* window, Laird!"

Eaden scanned the faces, but could not determine who had spoken. A ripple of sound rose and fell, bringing with it an edge of hostility.

"Tha's Paedrus' wife."

"Aye. But the laird's mistress."

The gaze of the crowd grew speculative and Eden clenched his jaw. He stood next to Isobel's body, sensing Ranald's presence beside him, his eyes gauging the crowd's growing restlessness. Faces looked from Isobel to the window above, their gazes lingering only a moment before sliding back to Eaden. His jaw clenched tight, Eaden stood firm against the dark conjecture.

"Where is Lady Scott?"

"Aye!"

". . . havenae seen her . . ."

". . . saved my Ailie, she did . . ."

The mood of the crowd shifted again—this time dangerously—at the reminder of Lady Scott's selfless heroism. And Eaden had no answers for them.

Ranald strode forward. "Lady Scott is in the castle," he said, his voice pitched to carry across the sounds of the mob. Eaden's gaze burned into Ranald's back, wondering how far the prevarication would fly.

The crowd's grumbling rose as Eaden raised a hand for silence. "Bring blankets," he directed.

The men shuffled their feet and one man leaned over and spat on the ground. His gaze locked with Eaden's for several seconds before his gaze finally dropped and he sidled judiciously behind another clansman.

Two women broke away and hurried into the castle, returning a few moments later, their arms laden with heavy linens, one obviously a tablecloth pulled hastily from one of the long tables in the hall. Eaden nodded briefly, and the women knelt beside Isobel, gently rolling her body onto the makeshift shroud.

As they eased Isobel onto her back, Eaden forced himself to look at the ruin of her face. Features shattered and bloody, she was still recognizable, and Eaden crossed himself as he considered the depth of despair or madness that made her choose certain death over living outside the castle. In disgrace.

He knelt and gently closed her eyes, her body already leaching the warmth he'd once known. Her skin had begun to lose its resiliency and the gray hue of death crept up from her fingers and toes.

The thunder of pounding hooves broke into his thoughts and he pushed to his feet. He looked sharply at the two men who jerked their horses to an abrupt stop. People scattered out of their way with cries of protest. Eaden's gut clenched as he recognized one of the men. Isobel's husband had arrived.

Chapter Thirty-Three

Paedrus, *baillie* of Craigievar, slid heavily from his horse, his figure not as nimble as it once had been. Soft living had taken its toll, his girth already impressive for a man his age. Scarcely a pair of years older than Eaden, Paedrus, with his pasty skin and loss of muscle tone, seemed much older.

His black velvet cloak, draped with a double-linked gold chain and seal of his office, swirled about him. He grasped the edges of the midnight cloth, holding the voluminous garment in check as he approached his wife.

Eaden stood, impassive, as Paedrus knelt at Isobel's side, brushing the white linen aside. He stared at his wife for several moments before he turned to Eaden, fury in his eyes.

"Ye've killed her!" His voice resonated, low but forceful, and carried easily through the silent crowd.

"Nay, Paedrus. I wasnae there when she fell."

"Ye killed her!" Paedrus repeated, his accusation gaining volume as he lurched to his feet. "She married me an' ye couldnae keep yer foul hands from her!"

"Hold, Paedrus!" Eaden thundered, a warning edge to his voice. For all the man was apparently crazed with grief, he would tolerate only so much. "Ye go too far."

Paedrus flung an arm up, finger pointing accusingly at Eaden. "All of Craigievar knew ye were lovers! Even after yer marriage, ye wanted her in yer bed!"

Eaden's quick perusal about the bailey told him he had but to say the word and the man would either be clapped in irons or dead at his feet. The men-at-arms along the wall had responded to Paedrus and the other man's arrival by notching their arrows and training them on the two men. On the ground, Eaden spied at least four soldiers elbowing their way through the crowd, Ian among them. They would be at his side in a matter of moments.

The crowd grew restless beneath Paedrus' harsh words. Eaden turned back to the distraught man, noting the wild eyes, how the morning breeze whipped his hair into a frenzy and snarled his cloak about his legs.

Eaden spoke firmly. "I will have a word with ye, Paedrus. In private. There is nothing to be gained by this, here." Eaden jerked his head toward the great hall's doors. "Take yerself inside."

"I'll no' go inside the castle with ye, *Laird Scott*." Paedrus tossed his head scornfully as he spat out Eaden's title.

Eaden sighed. He'd not wanted to put Paedrus in irons, but 'twas obvious the man needed time to cool down. He nodded once at Ian who now stood but a few feet away. Ian and his soldiers advanced silently on Paedrus, encircling him with their bodies and the still-sheathed threat of steel.

"Paedrus, ye leave me no choice. We will speak of this later." Eaden watched dispassionately as Ian ordered his soldiers to take Paedrus in hand. No match for the trained soldiers, Paedrus nonetheless resisted, pulling a dagger from his belt in a ridiculous display of defiance. Finlay, Ian's second-in-command, burly and completely loyal to Eaden, knocked the weapon to the ground with less trouble than batting away a pesky fly.

Finlay grunted. "An' ye no' want to accidentally fall on tha' wee pricker, ye'd best leave it in thc hands of someone who understands its use." He kicked the dagger to one side, out of Paedrus' reach, and jerked the man's arms behind his back. Holding both of his wrists in one enormous hand, Finlay gave the man a gentle push.

Paedrus tried to wrench away, but Finlay held him easily. With an irritable frown, he shoved Paedrus' wrists upward, nearly dislocating his shoulders. Paedrus yelped but gave way to the pressure, stumbling in the direction Finlay pointed him.

"Ye'll no' get away with this," Paedrus flung over his shoulder. His cloak slipped from his shoulders and hung askew, trailing its hem in the dirt and causing him to trip. Lurching suddenly forward, he fell from Finlay's grip and landed face-down on the ground, unmoving. Silently, Finlay yanked him to his feet and Paedrus hung limp in the burly soldier's grasp.

Turning to Laird Scott with a rueful shrug, Finlay grimaced. "Puir lad. An' him drunk at this time 'o day."

Eaden gave the soldier a quelling look as the man hoisted Paedrus onto his shoulder. When Finlay disappeared behind the doors of the castle, Eaden turned to the two women at Isobel's side.

"Cover her and see she is laid out properly." They curtsied to him and set about their task. At a nod from Ian, two soldiers stepped forward to help carry Isobel's wrapped form to the chapel to await the arrival of the priest.

* * *

Maighstir Nevin's hands were clasped inside the deep sleeves of his cassock, giving him the appearance of a man of immense patience. From past experiences with the priest's refusal to tolerate willful disobedience, both Ranald and Eaden knew otherwise.

As the priest approached, Eaden edged him from the crowd, seeking privacy. After retreating a distance away, he nodded to *Maighstir* Nevin. "Ye will see to the burial."

"An' ye will tell me what this young woman was doing, unclothed, in yer room."

"Ask her," Eaden retorted, refusing to let the priest intimidate him.

"Ye have an obligation as laird to uphold the moral precepts . . ."

"An' ye have an obligation as spiritual leader of these people to absolve them of their sins. Though I admit I have my share of sins to confess, I will swear adultery is not among them." Eaden pinned the priest with a glare. "And neither is murder."

"Explain to me what happened," Father Nevin commanded, surrounded by the curious gazes of the crowd as they strained to hear the conversation.

"I will no' discuss this now," Eaden said. "And neither will Ranald. We have more pressing things. See to the lass."

He turned his back on the priest and motioned for Ranald to join him. For once his brother did not waste time arguing and hurried past the crowd.

Eaden tried to disregard the men and women still gathered in the bailey beneath the open window, but the stain of blood on the ground drew his gaze.

"See to it they disperse," he murmured to Ian as his steps slowed. The captain nodded and approached the crowd.

". . . murder . . ."

". . . mistress . . ."

Eaden did not flinch at the muttered words. Despite the fact he was their laird, an earl by the king's own command, Isobel's actions today would cost him dearly. It would take time to dispel the rumors, and some would persist no matter the truth.

There remained enough for him to straighten out. Sorting through this mess would have to wait. He turned to speak to Ranald, but a cry from a sentry on the wall sounded across the bailey. Eaden jerked his gaze upward, following the wave of the guard's arm. Through the open castle gates, he saw riders advancing at a moderate pace, banners waving boldly in the wind, their colors declaring them from the king.

Eaden swore under his breath. Could anything else go wrong this day?

The contingent from King Robert rode into his keep. Eaden took stock of his circumstances. His wife had fled, the stain of a dead woman lay a few feet away, her body in the chapel, her grief-stricken husband cooling his heels in a secure room in the castle. Eaden ground his teeth and waited for the king's messenger.

Outwardly placid, his insides churned impatiently as the king's men stopped before him. They reined in their horses and Eaden inclined his head in greeting.

"We are here under direct orders from King Robert tae escort ye and yer wife to Troon. Our Sovereign bids ye come with all haste."

Eaden's jaw clenched and he took a steadying breath. "I am most grateful for the king's thoughtfulness in providing an escort. Take yer rest. My wife and I will be ready to travel on the morrow."

The king's spokesman rose in his stirrups, his gaze traveling over the lingering crowd. "Where is yer wife? The king is most anxious to meet her."

Eaden forced his lips into a smile. "She is about, undoubtedly attending to unfinished business."

He jerked his head at Ian. "Send men to disperse this crowd and have the blood washed away," he murmured. "Make sure the king's men are fed and their horses tended." He dropped his voice even lower. "And see the lady Isobel receives a proper burial."

Chapter Thirty-Four

Searching the castle turned up no trace of Mary. Few people had taken heed of Lady Scott, who was often found about the castle early in the mornings. Eaden's questioning at last revealed she had been seen walking into the bailey. Furious to think she'd left the castle unescorted, Eaden immediately roused the sentry, a young soldier who'd had the bad luck to draw the last watch of the night.

He quickly recalled a young woman riding out an hour or more earlier. Being restless and bored with his watch, the sentry had not questioned anyone leaving the castle. He'd only been interested in those entering the gates — and the commotion on the far side of the bailey.

"Damn!" Eaden swore fervently as he caught Duff and led him from the paddock. He'd wasted precious time earlier searching the castle for his wife. Knowing her to be angry and hurt, he'd expected her to hide away until she calmed and demanded an explanation. He hadn't thought she'd be so upset or brave to take a horse and leave. She knew the dangers of a woman alone beyond the castle walls.

Eaden slammed the wooden gate, unable to find a more convenient outlet for his growing anger. Without comment, Ranald caught the gate as it rebounded from the force of Eaden's hand, and deftly latched it shut.

Isobel's death and the king's men had further delayed him. Eaden cursed himself for teaching her to ride, though it certainly had not occurred to him at the time such a skill would be to his disadvantage.

"Damn it! Where could she be headed?" He shot a glare at Ranald, daring him to comment. His brother lifted a shoulder in silent response and slung his saddle to his gelding's back, forestalling a pointless argument.

The soft slap of leather against leather pierced the strained quiet as they silently readied their horses. Giving Duff's saddle a final tug, Eaden shook out the reins and prepared to mount.

"D'ye think Sorcha would help?" Ranald ventured.

Eaden shook his head. "She's come into heat and I've closed her in a pen. I dinnae want her bred."

"But she might be able to track Starnie . . ."

"All right. We can try." It wasn't he feared Sorcha would breed—worse things could, and had, happened. But her mind would be on one thing only during this time, and he feared it would not be the scent of Mary's horse.

Eaden crossed to the kennel and released the hound. She leaped through the gate and danced around him for a moment, obviously thrilled to be out of her pen. The deep howl of a thwarted male boomed deep within the building. Sorcha whirled and bounded back inside.

Eaden huffed in disgust and followed Sorcha to where she sniffed eagerly at a well-fortified gate. Taking her by her collar, he dragged her back to her kennel and shut the door tightly.

As Eaden silently gained his horse, Ranald gave a nod of assurance. "We will find her," he vowed.

* * *

Mary stared at the ground. Starnie's hoof prints were clear in the dust and she sighed with despair. She shifted wearily on the horse's broad back, her legs and back aching with the effort to stay astride. With no saddle or stirrups for support, she'd tired quickly and longed to find someplace to rest. But with her path clearly marked by Starnie's hooves, it was too easy for Eaden to follow her.

Sliding from Starnie's back, she groaned as her feet touched the ground, the muscles in her legs and back bunching stiffly to hold her upright. She straightened slowly against the strain, searching for a leafy branch. Within moments she found what she sought.

She grabbed the stick, ignoring the bark scraping her hands. Leaving Starnie to graze, his reins tied to a nearby limb, she retraced her steps on the path. At last she stopped and waved the leaves gently through the fine dust of the trail, teasing the hoof prints from sight and smoothing the blades of grass flattened beneath Starnie's tread.

Swinging the branch as she backed to the horse's side, she finished erasing the hoof prints and surveyed her work. She'd never before tried to hide her trail from men who were almost certainly excellent trackers, and she had no idea if this would work or not. Or even help.

Mary dusted the tiny particles of dirt and bark from her hands. Releasing Starnie's reins, she led him from the trail into the tall grass and yellow broom covering the expanse of ground from the road to the river.

* * *

Eaden reined Duff to a halt. Somehow he'd lost the trail. He turned the horse about, searching the ground for hoof prints, but they seemed to have disappeared. Surely Mary wouldn't have thought to hide her tracks?

Rubbing a hand across the back of his neck, he stared at Ranald. "If she rides north, where could she be heading?"

Ranald took a moment to consider the question. "The abbey?" he ventured.

"To seek solace or sanctuary?" Eaden returned bitterly.

"A chance to reflect, perhaps."

Eaden bent again to study the ground. "Do ye think she knows how to hide her trail?"

Ranald shrugged. "The lass has surprised me more than once."

Eaden nodded. "We must split up. If she rides to the abbey, she is almost there. If she seeks to deceive me, she may already be heading south."

"To Bellecourt Castle?"

"Aye."

"We dinnae pass her on the road." Ranald pointed out. "If she has left the road, she could be anywhere, or . . ." One forbidding glance from Eaden, and Ranald did not finish his statement.

"Head south. I will continue to the abbey." Eaden urged Duff forward until even with Ranald. Grabbing his brother's forearm in a firm grip, he gave him a hard look. "If she goes to Bellecourt, she is not going to reflect. If ye find her, bring her home. Peacefully or kicking and screaming, I dinnae care. But bring her home."

* * *

Mary led Starnie down the bank of the river. Tying him to a sturdy limb in a copse of trees, she retraced her steps. With the leafy branch, she did what she could to erase their tracks to the water, but the mud at the very edge held the footprints firm, and she could think of no good way to disguise the deep casts. A sudden roll of thunder caused her to scan the sky. If it rained, it might wash the hoof prints away.

She returned to Starnie and led him from the bank and into the river where the current rinsed away their tracks almost instantly. She steeled herself against the cold bite of the water but even so, her legs grew quickly numb, and the chill steeped into her body. Within a short time, she was shaking uncontrollably with cold. To further her misery, a wind, racing ahead of the storm, picked up speed, plastering her wet robe and shift against her skin.

She stumbled and fell. She was now completely soaked by the river. Her hair clung to her neck and face in icy coils and she tried vainly to brush it back with trembling fingers. Tracking the edge of the river southward, she knew she would soon be within sight of Scott Castle. She could not afford to stop now. She needed to be south of the castle, on the road to the border, before dark.

Gritting her teeth, she pushed on as the wind kicked up white-topped waves around her, raising the water nearly to her waist. She stumbled again, grasping Starnie's reins tight to keep from falling. He tossed his head and whinnied.

"I don't like it, either," Mary muttered, her teeth clenched to keep them from chattering. She missed her footing again. Tears streamed unchecked down her cheeks.

"I should have killed him while I had the chance," she stormed at the poor horse, thoroughly frightened and upset. "I'm cold and wet and miserable and dragging you through a damn river and he's probably at the castle warm and dry. I'll die out here and wash up on the bank somewhere downstream and you'll find your way home . . ."

She brushed at the tears on her face. Starnie balked. Planting his feet firmly on the rocky bottom of the river, he refused to go further. Mary tugged at his reins. "You stupid beast! You cannot stop!"

But Starnie had had enough of trekking through the water and he reared, lifting his forefeet high, pulling the reins from Mary's grasp.

"No!" Mary grabbed wildly for the flapping leather reins, terrified of losing him and being left on her own. Even with Starnie, she was quite likely to be caught, and not just by Eaden or his brother. Once remounted, she would feel safer and be able to cover the distance to Bellecourt much faster than if on foot.

Snagging the reins before he could bolt, she led him to the bank. He followed her eagerly, nearly treading on her heels in his hurry to be out of the river.

"I hope we've managed to lose them," Mary muttered grimly as she spied the footprints the horse left in the muddy bank. Starnie shook himself like a big dog, sending water flying from his coat. Mary raised an arm to ward off the flying droplets.

The noonday sun hovered directly overhead behind wispy grey clouds racing before the wind, affording her the illusion of warmth. It also illuminated her, and could potentially betray her to the curious eyes of any who passed by.

Mary patted Starnie's neck nervously. "Don't whinny. There will likely be other people on the road now the threat of rain is past. We need to be far away from here before anyone sees us." She swallowed hard against her next thought.

A woman alone on the road is helpless. It was imperative she elude reivers and other miscreants — as well as Laird Scott.

* * *

Ranald bent his attention to the edge of the road. For such a well-traveled route, the dust appeared remarkably free of tracks. He sat on his haunches, letting his gaze travel slowly up and down the road, searching farther out with each pass.

There! A clump of roots showed white against the new green of the early spring grass. Could Starnie have snatched a bite as Mary led him from the road? Ranald rose to his feet, absently drawing his horse along behind him. He knelt beside the uprooted grass, fingering the broken stems. Dry soil fell from the clump.

She's a fair distance ahead. Ranald glanced up, searching for Eaden. The dust from Duff's hooves already settled and even a shout would not bring his brother back. Ranald frowned. Unless Mary was more clever than he thought, Eaden was headed in the wrong direction.

But they had not passed her on the road. Ranald rose to his feet again, looking outward. The glint of the river lay ahead. Did she think to lose her trail in the water? Or did she merely use a well-known landmark to guide her toward Bellecourt?

A rumble of thunder reached his ears. Wherever she was, she was about to get wet. He remembered the robe she wore as she ran from Eaden's room. Had she thought to get other clothing? A disguise? His blood ran cold. She could find herself fair game for miscreants roaming the roads. The question was not where she was headed, but along what route.

And would he find her before she ran afoul of those who would not care she was the lady of Scott Castle?

Chapter Thirty-Five

Mary's knees quivered. Her feet, slippers long ago shredded and lost, were bruised and bleeding. Muscles unused to riding bareback and trekking through cold, wind-tossed rivers, clenched in protest. Too miserable to do more than stand next to Starnie, hidden in the dense foliage of the glen, Mary focused on simply existing.

Fading sunlight lit the mist rising from the river. Golden-hued fog crept along the ground, promising protection if she could elude any who followed her a little longer. Her pale green robe hung in ruins around her, no longer a potential beacon to curious eyes, its tatters and stains blending with the mist and trees surrounding her. Praying Starnie would not call out, she slowly stroked his nose to keep him settled.

Starnie stamped a foot, shuffling his weight. Mary jerked her head up, horrified to discover she'd slipped into a light doze. She hauled his head down, hugging his nose against her chest. Impatient, Starnie wrenched free, tossing his head as he whickered a greeting. Mary grabbed frantically at his reins, jerking his bit.

"Ye'll injure his mouth an' ye keep that up."

Mary whirled, slipping in her exhaustion, splaying her hands against the horse for support. She crumpled in relief as she recognized Ranald's voice, though she could not pretend to be glad to see him.

"Go away."

Ranald stepped out of the mist and into the weak moonlight casting haphazard beams into the little glen. "Ye've led us on a merry chase," he chided her gently.

Mary bristled and looked past him, expecting to see Eaden on his heels. Ranald shook his head as though reading her mind. "Nay. Eaden and I parted north of Craigievar. We werenae sure if ye headed north to the abbey or south to Bellecourt. As the abbey was closer, Eaden chose that way. He is anxious to find ye."

"I'll not go back, Ranald. I've made up my mind."

"Have ye, now? And why is that?"

"How can you ask me? You were there! You saw . . ." Mary blinked back tears and turned her head away.

"'Twas no' what ye think, lass. Eaden was no' a part of it."

Mary whirled, her face twisted in fury. "Don't speak to me as though I am a fool! I was there! I saw them together!"

"Ye saw what Isobel wanted ye to see."

"Do not ask me to believe Eaden was not enjoying himself with her."

Ranald grimaced. "In all truth, I cannae say. But I can tell ye he dinnae ken it was her in his bed."

Mary choked. "So, any warm body will do?"

"'Tis no' that simple. Come back with me and let the two of ye settle this."

"Don't you mean the three of us?" Mary retorted bitterly.

Ranald said quietly, "Isobel is dead."

Mary's eyes widened as Ranald's unexpected announcement forced a gasp from her. "What?"

"Eaden told me . . . well, never mind what he said. He wanted me to restrain her, keep her until her punishment was decided. She dinnae want it. She saw Eaden's anger and at last understood he would never turn to her. 'Twas but an instant's decision, and I dinnae see it coming. She ran to the window and leapt to her death."

A cry of distress tore from Mary's lips. Ranald took a step toward her, but she threw out both hands, warning him away. Tears welled in her eyes and she fought the overwhelming urge to collapse to the ground and let everything fall apart around her.

Slowly her tears abated. "I am sorry. If only . . ." Her voice trailed off. What, exactly, could she have done differently? She had been shocked and horrified to discover Eaden in the throes of passion at Isobel's hands. All the woman's hateful taunts had risen in her mind, cackling, taunting, telling her Isobel had been right — Eaden would ever turn to her, unable to withstand his attraction to the black-haired witch.

"I must bring ye back." Ranald spoke firmly.

Mary glanced up, jarred from her thoughts. "No."

"Ye will. Even sprawled across my horse, ye will come."

"No. I will not." Mary stiffened, her hands fisted at her sides.

Ranald looked at her askance. "Ye think to fight me?"

Mary stiffened her spine. Her best gambit was to bluff, for she knew she had not the strength to win should he decide to drag her back to the castle. "Tooth and nail."

Ranald scowled. "Ye're acting like a child."

"Threats didn't work, so you resort to flattery?" Mary tossed at him, sarcasm coloring her words. She did not believe he would lay a violent hand on her, but couldn't be sure how far she could push him before he simply tossed her into his saddle.

"Get on yer horse, Mary. Ye're going home."

"I'm going to Bellecourt."

"Ye willnae."

At an impasse, they glared at each other. A breeze slipped through the trees and Mary shivered with the cold.

"Ye'll catch yer death, ye will." Ranald dragged the plaid from his shoulders and tried to place it in Mary's hands, but she shrank back, skirting Starnie's powerful hindquarters, placing the horse between herself and Ranald.

"Put this around ye. 'Tis warm," he insisted.

When she didn't move, he swore under his breath and tossed the plaid over the horse's back. "Here. Ye dinnae have to come to me. Just put it on. I'll not drag ye home just to watch ye sicken."

Mary stared at the plaid, longing to feel its comforting warmth, but afraid to accept anything from him. Sharing anything, even the meanest hospitality, would put her in his debt. Instead she vowed firmly, "I've made up my mind. I will not go back with you."

"I am to bring ye home."

"I cannot. I believed him true to me." She sighed. "You cannot erase the sight from my mind. I would never be able to touch him, to see him, without seeing her. I would shrink from his touch, hating him for his betrayal." Her shoulders drooped dejectedly. "We have no life together."

"Ye willnae try?"

"What would you have done to find your wife in bed, pleasuring another man?"

Even in the shadows Mary knew his face darkened. "I would have killed him."

Mary tilted her head. "It was very tempting. But I do not know who I would have killed."

"Ye have my word, Mary. Eaden wasnae a part of it."

"You don't understand. You would do anything to protect your brother. With Isobel dead, Eaden can say what he likes, with no one to contradict him. I must go to Bellecourt and think this through, away from the lies and accusations."

"I dinnae lie to ye, either."

"No, I don't believe you lied. I believe you told me what you deem to be true."

He seemed to consider her words. "If I allow ye to go to Bellecourt to take the time ye need, will ye promise to send word in a few days?"

"I cannot say when, but I will send word."

"Eaden willnae be pleased I dinnae bring ye back."

Mary's lips twisted in a wry, humorless smile. "I suspect he'll let you live."

"I wouldnae be so sure."

* * *

Bone weary and vowing she'd never ride again, Mary at last reined Starnie to a halt before the gates of Bellecourt Castle. Her early morning appearance before the guard had given her some difficulty, but Ranald's clenched jaw and challenging stare sent the sentry scurrying to alert the warden. Moments later the man appeared at the closed gate, scowling as he jerked his breeches closed. He raked her with an insolent stare, equally disdainful of her bedraggled state and her bristling Scottish guard.

"What is your business here?" he asked, as though she had unconscionable nerve to believe she had any right to expect entry into the castle.

Mary arched an eyebrow coolly, too tired and disillusioned by the past hours to put up with his rudeness. "I am Mary Marsh. I have come home."

Chapter Thirty-Six

Ranald spied the silhouette of a lone rider racing toward him and reined his horse to the side, in no mood to risk a challenge by a miscreant on the road.

Please don't let it be Eaden. He'd ridden hard for more than six hours to make it this far, and he still didn't know how to tell his brother he'd let Mary go to Bellecourt—or that he'd left her there.

Scott Castle's rock tower rose above the curtain wall, stark against the mid-afternoon sky. It would be good to be home. He was tired and hungry, the anticipation of a warm bath and clean clothes the only things keeping him on the road.

The rider approached rapidly, his horse beating out a furious tattoo as his great stride devoured the distance between them. Ranald recognized them both.

"Damn." Ranald swore under his breath and kicked his horse forward to meet his brother.

Eaden jerked Duff to a stop, bringing the horse down on his haunches as he slid to a halt. Mud slinging from beneath his flashing hooves, Duff pranced in a tight circle, champing his bit against the command.

"She was no' at the abbey, though it took me time enough to get a straight answer," Eaden growled, reining Duff to a standstill. He eyed Ranald narrowly. "Have ye seen her?"

"Aye."

"Damn it, Ranald! Where is she?"

"She's at Bellecourt."

"You *left* her at Bellecourt?"

Duff tossed his head, sensing his rider's anger.

"She asked for time to think." Ranald grimaced at the memory of their conversation. "Well, she dinnae *ask* as much as declare."

"I told ye to bring her home. Kicking and screaming, as I recall, *was* an option."

"Eaden, she only asked for a few days . . ."

"I dinnae have a few days! What I *do* have is a nicely worded command from the king to appear at Troon in five days' time. With my wife."

Ranald blinked. "Five days? 'Tis no' possible."

"It is. I've done it in less." Eaden sighed and patted his horse's sweat-soaked neck. "But I've pushed Duff hard enough this day and he deserves a good feed and a night's rest."

He looked beyond Ranald in the direction of Bellecourt, and following his brother's gaze, Ranald could easily picture the towers and turrets of their enemy's keep.

Eaden sighed heavily. "We should have left yesterday. 'Twill be tomorrow before I'll take Duff out again." He turned his horse back toward Scott Castle. Ranald followed, his hands jerking on the reins at Eaden's muttered words.

"God save the king."

* * *

Sunlight from the bailey splashed into the room as the heavy wooden panels swung outward, casting her shadow across the stone floor. Rushes lay scattered about, and the familiar scent of rosemary drifted in the air. Slippers shuffled on stone to Mary's right and she turned in response. Recognition flooded her as Agnes' round form bustled into the hall.

"Heavens, lass!" A gasp of burst from the woman's lips as she caught sight of Mary. Her hand flew to her breast in a dramatic gesture, pale and plump against the coarse black silk of her gown. Mary hid her own grubby hands in the tattered folds of her ruined velvet robe, wincing in embarrassment at her bedraggled state, remembering the rule the woman had wielded over Miriam and herself since her mother's death three years earlier.

"Mary, what has happened to ye?"

Blinking back sudden tears, Mary staggered beneath the agonies of the past two days. Agnes hurried to her, hands outstretched to cup Mary's cheeks between the warmth of her palms. She turned Mary's pale face from side to side, assessing her former charge.

"Ye must have a hot bath and clean clothes," she announced. "Whatever were those men thinking?" She grasped Mary's hand, dragging her along in her wake. "Men are barbarians — simply barbarians! To see what they've done to our little Mary. Makes a body wonder, it does!"

Bemused with the unprecedented attention, Mary allowed herself to be hauled to the kitchen. The warmth of the enormous hearth slipped beneath the clinging wetness of her robe to her skin, producing a belated shiver she had been too tired and cold to generate before.

Agnes guided her toward the small storeroom next to the kitchen. Adjacent to the massive fireplace that framed the kitchen's main cooking source, the constant fire in its stones made this room warm and cozy. The herbs drying in bound clusters hanging from the rafters lent their mingled scents to the dry air. Mary watched with detachment as Agnes bustled about, ordering a bath to be readied.

Moments later, Mary slipped from the ruined remnants of her clothes and into the warm water that rocked gently against her clammy skin. The cloying scent of roses wafted in the steam. Slipping deep into the sheltering warmth, she drifted into a state of dreamy exhaustion, left in a young maid's watchful care.

The room shimmered around her and sound echoed eerily in her head. Groggy from her short nap, Mary struggled to awaken, aware hands pulled at her, the water she sat in no longer the warm haven she'd originally entered.

"Come, Mary. We've a room prepared for ye and fresh clothes. Come out where ye can dry and dress."

Leaning heavily on Agnes' stout arm, she dragged herself from the tub and stood passively for a moment while Agnes patted her skin dry. Yawning, Mary reached for the linen in Agnes' hands. "Thank you. I can finish," she told the older woman, her words soft but firm.

Giving her an assessing look, Agnes relinquished the drying cloth. "There is a new gown and robe for ye." She pointed to the clothing draped across a nearby chair. "When ye finish, come into the kitchen and someone will see ye to your room."

"I know where my room is . . ."

Agnes harrumphed and frowned as she pursed her lips. "'Tis not there I've been told to put ye. Ye are to have your mother's room." With another snort of displeasure, she bustled from the room, leaving Mary to dress herself.

Mary stared in shock as the door closed behind Agnes. Why would she be put there? Surely her old room would be adequate.

With no answers readily available for her questions, Mary wiped the remaining moisture from her body and draped the damp fabric over the lip of the tub. Reaching for the gown left for her, she missed the familiar swing of her pendant against her skin. Her hand flew to her chest where the chain normally lay. Memory washed over her as she realized she had left it on her dressing table the day before.

Mary sighed dejectedly. Though the necklace was safe and not lying on the bottom of the river, it was, nonetheless, lost to her.

Would she ever return to Scott Castle, to Eaden? Her heart still ached at the memory of seeing him in bed with Isobel. The betrayal—no matter Isobel arranged it to suit her needs—left an empty spot inside. What had she given up to rage over the unfairness of Isobel's actions?

Mary's eyes pooled with tears and she blinked irritably at her weakness. Pressing a hand to her stomach to quell its flutters, she paused, uncertain. Had there always been that slight mound, low in her abdomen?

Her hand rested against her belly, fingers tracing the tiny curve. Her mind replayed the past few days and nights with Eaden and the frequency of their intimacy. If one such occurrence could produce a child as she'd been warned, then there was a more than excellent chance . . .

She snatched her hand away. It wasn't possible to know this soon. Assuredly, there would not be a noticeable change in herself in only a few days. How could she be certain? Who could she ask? She touched her belly again, allowing herself to wonder. A child?

What good could come of it? Abruptly Mary turned from her musings, anger replacing the curiosity. Difficulties of unimagined proportions would result from such a thing and she dared not dwell further on it. To be saddled with an unwanted marriage was bad enough. The reality of a child born into such a union seemed unthinkable. She grabbed the shift and dragged it over her head.

The scrape of a booted foot alerted her she was not alone, and she whirled.

"Laird Barde!" she gasped, recognizing the red-headed man framed in the portal. Dark eyes met hers and Mary's skin crawled as his gaze roamed slowly over her.

"'Tis good to have ye back, Mary. Ye look well." He brought his gaze back to hers, the gleam in his eyes showing obvious interest.

Mary shuddered. How could he look at her so? He was Miriam's *father*. She took a step back, her legs bumping against the chair, until she could retreat no further. "Please leave me."

Laird Barde gave her a brittle smile. "Ye ask for the hospitality of my house. I would like to know what has driven ye back to my doors."

Mary swallowed convulsively. Laird Barde had always been a source of undefined terror for her. Stern and quick to anger, his mere presence had been enough to keep her quiet and obedient as a child. Had she not known Miriam was again living at Bellecourt Castle, Mary would have thought twice about seeking refuge here.

"Miriam wrote me, explaining her marriage, and told me she and her husband lived here. She also told me I could return if I ever needed to."

"And why would *Lady Scott* need to find succor at Bellecourt Castle?"

Heat rose to her cheeks. "I wish to visit Miriam and seek peace in my childhood home."

Laird Barde gave a bark of laughter. "I heard of yer Scott escort to my doors. 'Twas not yer husband who brought you here. Tell me, *Lady Scott*, is yer man so cruel to drive ye away? Is he so foolish, to allow another to escort his wife, alone over the night, and not think of the stain on her reputation?"

"He is neither cruel nor foolish, m'laird," Mary retorted, lifting her chin defensively. "'Tis no concern of yours if I travel with or without an escort."

"And what of yer reputation, my sweet?"

Revulsion at his endearment sent a shudder over her skin. "My reputation is my own concern," she whispered past the fear tightening her throat.

"Then have a care, Mary. That brat ye think ye carry may need his father—whoever he is."

Chapter Thirty-Seven

Dundonald Castle, Troon

Eaden entered the main hall, his eyes fixed on the king seated on his throne. The scent of candles hung heavy in the air, thickening in his throat. Fabric whispered as people moved about the room, the sound mingling with the murmurs of speculation only partly hidden behind sheltering hands. Deep inside, Eaden's instincts shivered in alert response, sharpening his senses like those of a hart pinned beneath the steady eye of the huntsman.

His eyes locked on those of his king, though whether he'd found friend or foe remained to be seen. The enmity in the room left a silvery taste of threat in his mouth.

Eaden halted before the dais, head bowed, though he peered upwards through his lowered lashes. King Robert's frown covered his face from his downturned lips to his gathered brow, wrinkling his aged skin further into lines of displeasure.

Minutes stretched endlessly and a muscle in Eaden's jaw twitched in response to his rising temper. Stretching his jaw as unobtrusively as possible, he loosened the tight muscles and schooled his expression into one of acceptance. Subservience was, at this moment, clouded by his anger at being so summoned, and completely out of the question.

Finally, King Robert shifted in his chair, though he continued to favor Eaden with a look bordering on anger. "Where is yer wife, Scott?"

Eaden's eyes narrowed at the growl in the king's voice and the implication he was unable to produce his wife when bidden. "My wife has returned to Bellecourt Castle."

The king's face paled, taking Eaden aback. "Could ye no' keep her in yer bed?"

Eaden's pulse raced as he battled his ire at the king's words. "She is *my* wife, Sire . . ."

The king exploded to his feet, slapping his palms against the wooden arms of his throne. "She's *my* daughter!"

Eaden's breathless *whoosh* of surprise echoed loudly in the resulting, shocked silence.

King Robert glared around the room and the courtiers instantly averted their faces, though the speculative sound of their voices rose in the hall like the thrum of angry bees. With a jerk of his head, the king motioned for Eaden to follow him, and they retired to a chamber beyond the hall.

The king pointed toward the door. "Close it."

Eaden did so, still reeling from the king's words a moment before. King Robert seated himself behind a massive desk on the far side of the room. Then, restless, he regained his feet and paced across the floor to stand before Eaden.

"Is she well?"

"In truth, Sire, I last saw her several days ago, but she appeared in a fine mettle."

"Why did she no' come with you? My men reported she had fled the castle."

Eaden gritted his teeth, condemning the gossiping fools to a painful existence. "There was a misunderstanding and she asked for time to herself. She looked forward to visiting here, but it apparently slipped her mind at the last."

"Have ye no' resolved yer differences? I thought ye would have convinced her to see reason long ago."

"Ye give me too much credit, Sire," Eaden replied, flicking his fingers in the air in a frustrated gesture. "We had reached an arrangement of sorts. There was a problem we had yet to work out. I will see it resolved as soon as I return to Craigievar."

"I want to meet her, Scott."

"Why do ye think she is yer daughter?"

"Do ye remember the necklace ye asked me about when we met last?" the king asked.

Eaden's hand drifted to his chest. Entering his room at Scott Castle, he had noticed the pendant lying on the dressing table. Drawn by a need to have something of Mary next to him, he had slung the length of chain over his head, settling the pendant beneath his shirt. After a moment's hesitation, he drew it from his neck and offered it to his liege.

King Robert's lips parted in surprise at the sight of the pendant, and he stared intently at the green stones. Gold filigree curved possessively around the jade, lending a mysterious glow to the opaque gems. His eyes clouded as he cupped the pendant in one large palm, his attention seemingly focused on some memory too precious to share.

At last the king spoke, his fingers closing gently around the cross. "I met her mother almost twenty years ago. She was newly widowed and my wife was unwell and could not tolerate the cold winter air in Edinburgh. I was negotiating the release of David from the English and there was much strife in the court. I often slipped away, seeking my own counsel, and one night I met Eilean in the snow-covered garden at Edinburgh Castle."

King Robert's mouth turned up gently at the corners. "We each had our own challenges, and we found our company to be compatible." His smile deepened. "Very compatible."

He stirred from his introspection and glanced at Eaden. "We both knew there could be no future for us, but for a while we found each other a comfort. When time came for me to hand control of Scotland to David, Eilean and I parted as I was no longer welcome at court. I gave her a green jade pendant. The color matched her eyes and I was pleased to gift it to her. I believed she traveled to the Highlands where her father's people were, to live with a cousin. She never told me she was with child."

"Mayhap she dinnae know at the time."

King Robert nodded slowly. "Mayhap." He thought for a moment, then said, "Ye know I have many children. They are a weakness of mine." He emitted a gusty sigh. "Legitimate or no, I want the best for each of them."

Eaden managed to keep his expression bland. The king's marital arrangements had led to much conflict after the validity of his first marriage had been brought into question years earlier. It wasn't the lack of an heir posing the problem. 'Twas the existence of too many.

"I well remember Eilean. I would like to know her daughter." The king moved to the hearth and plucked a slender length of kindling from the box near the fire. Lighting the end, he placed it against the wicks of the candles on the table, bringing a golden glow to the room.

Satisfied, he tossed the flaming remnant into the fireplace and leaned his hip against the edge of the desk. "Ye said she went to Bellecourt Castle. Do ye expect her to return to ye?"

Eaden's brow creased in an uncertain frown. From the grim look on the king's face, if Mary was kept from him or harmed in any way, there would be more than mere boundary lines in contention along the Scott and Barde border.

* * *

Mary slept fitfully, tossing and turning in her unfamiliar surroundings. She had expected to feel comforted to be in her mother's old room, but many guests had stayed in the room over the years and nothing remained to remind Mary of her. The heavy bed, the chest beneath the window, the dressing table where her jars and brushes and mirror once resided, all were there, but her mother's essence had dissipated long ago.

Scurrying sounds in the corner brought a shiver of distaste, raising goose bumps on her skin. She clutched the blanket around her and resolved to rethink her problems on the morrow. Learning Miriam and her husband had departed for the Melville estate several days earlier for a visit, Mary's enthusiasm to tarry for a while at Bellecourt Castle had taken a severe blow. Agnes seemed happy enough to have Mary around, and willing to settle back into the relationship they'd shared only a few weeks back. Mary smiled fondly as she drifted back to sleep. *Bossy old woman.*

Later, Mary slipped silently into the hall. She'd deliberately waited in her room until she was certain most of the castle folk had finished breaking their fast before she ventured downstairs. Servants moved a few of the long tables against the wall, clearing space for the activities of the day. Dinner would be the main meal, taken at noon, and Mary hoped to miss that particular gathering as well. She craved anonymity, not a chance to be on display for all to see. She'd eat scraps from the kitchen if necessary to avoid being held up for speculative scrutiny.

"I trust ye are well-rested?"

Mary jerked at the sound of Laird Barde's voice. She faced him, assessing his scornful gaze, giving him a carefully blank stare of her own. Not only would she refuse to answer the smoothly mocking question, but she found his intense regard too unsettling to form a coherent response.

Laird Barde beckoned to her, and years of conditioning did not allow her to disobey. With wooden feet, Mary preceded him to a private chamber a few feet down the hall. Prodded further into the room, Mary flinched at the snug snick of the door as it latched behind her.

She forced herself to look around the room, trying to steady her nerves but remembering all too readily the fear Miriam's father had always inspired in her. She pinned her gaze on the scarred wooden desk, piled high with parchments and bound ledgers. A flask held place of honor in the middle of the desk, and Mary's unease grew when she detected the scent of well-aged whisky drifting from the mug beside it.

Her eyes flickered over him. "Are you ill, m'laird?" she asked, some of her spunk returning. If her presence in the castle had driven Laird Barde to drink this early in the day, perhaps he would state his piece and allow her to retire without further comment.

With a trace of guilt on his face, Laird Barde released the mug he'd picked up, settling it with a thump on the stained desk blotter. He stomped around the desk and yanked his chair out with a grinding scrape of wood against stone.

Seating himself, he stared at Mary over the top of his steepled hands. "Ye do favor your mother," he murmured.

"Sir?" Mary lifted a brow. *What do my looks have to do with anything?*

"She and my late wife were cousins, ye know," he commented, ignoring Mary's query. "She never told ye who yer father was, did she?"

Mary blinked, confused. His words came too fast. She reeled from his abrupt change of subject, from the known, but never discussed, relationship to Miriam's mother, to the biggest question of all . . . *Who is my father? And what does Laird Barde know?*

Chapter Thirty-Eight

Mary steadied the rapid beating of her heart. Even when she'd grown old enough to ask her mother a direct question about her father, the best answer she'd gotten had been a sharp admonition to appreciate her circumstances. The worst answer had been silent tears.

For a long time, Mary had known what *illegitimate* and *bastard* meant. Growing up, her mother's position as castle chatelaine and Mary's own place as Lady Miriam's companion had shielded her from the worst of the children's taunts. But the words still carried the ability to touch her with shame. She clenched her fists, surprised at the sticky sweat on her palms.

Laird Barde smiled—a narrow-eyed, evil half-lift of his lips that made her shudder and caused her stomach to lurch. "Yer lady mother did not like to be reminded of it, but she once was Lady Barde. She and my elder brother met at court. They married, but it only lasted a few weeks. Colin died in a stupid accident before they could return to Bellecourt Castle."

Mary bit the inside of her lip, tasting the tang of blood as she steeled herself not to react to Laird Barde's revelations. She hated to admit she knew nothing of the tale of her mother's brief marriage, and she feared he would stop, from spite if nothing else, leaving her at some critical point in the story.

"Yer mother lived at court for a time after my brother died. King David resided in London at the pleasure of King Edward, while Robert, then Steward of Scotland, occasionally negotiated for King David's release." Laird Barde leaned back in his chair, fingering his chin as he regarded Mary. "She remained there for some time and I took my place as Laird Barde. I married her cousin, and soon after Giselle took to bed following Miriam's birth, yer mother arrived with ye, here at Bellecourt."

Mary felt behind her surreptitiously for the door or some solid substance to lean against. Lightheaded, her vision faded around the edges. Touching the rough wood of the door, she sank against its oaken strength, too overwhelmed to care if Laird Barde noticed.

"'Twas agreed the two of ye could reside here. Eilean proved a great comfort to Giselle, and 'twas thought ye would make an acceptable companion to the baby. Neither yer mother nor Giselle ever revealed where she had been all those months, though I suspect Giselle knew."

"Am I your brother's daughter?" Mary ventured hesitantly.

Laird Barde gave a derisive snort. "Ye think I would have kept you around to usurp my daughter's position as heiress? There was no chance ye were Colin's brat. It had been nearly three years since my brother died when yer mother arrived on my doorstep with ye in her arms." He raked her with an insulting stare. "It appears history does repeat itself."

Mary's cheeks flushed hotly and she straightened, pushing away from the door's support. "I will not accept hospitality from you other than that of a guest. I wished to visit with Miriam, nothing more." She angled her chin defiantly, staring down at Laird Barde.

"And what of the child ye bear?" Laird Barde smiled slowly, bringing Mary's instincts to full alarm. "I cannae imagine Laird Scott letting a lovely young woman such as yerself live as his wife and not take advantage of the situation. I'm sure he has plowed yer belly enough times to ensure himself an heir."

"What my relationship is with Laird Scott is none of your concern," Mary flung coldly at him, anger overriding her normal sense of caution. "Things appear to have changed much around here. If you cannot offer a guest more hospitality than this, I will leave."

She snatched at the front of her skirt, lifting it from the floor as she whirled about. Grabbing the heavy latch, she tugged at the door, feeling it drag against the stone floor. Behind her she heard Laird Barde's grating laugh.

"And go where, milady?" he mocked. "Ye have confirmed the Scotts' opinions. Barde women are a spineless, unworthy lot." He rose from his chair and strode to her side, leaning over her shoulder to push the oaken panel closed. "Yer husband is no longer at Scott Castle. He has gone to visit the king, leaving ye to your own ends. His mistress lies dead, and ye have run away."

Laird Barde touched his lips to her hair. "Laird Scott did not want ye when he married ye. Ye have done him the great service of leaving his household without having to toss ye out himself. Ye are a bastard, Mary Marsh. Yer life was ruined the day yer mother spread her legs for her lover. A bastard cannae become a lady. But ye could have other purposes."

With a low screech of fury, Mary whirled. Her fisted hand came up, its arc fueled by the force of her turn. Caught off-guard, Laird Barde made no move to evade her and her fist connected with an audible crack against his jaw. Tears sprang to her eyes as pain shot through the jarred bones in her hand.

Laird Barde's face flushed dark with rage and he grabbed her fist before she could pull away. Mary cried out as the grip of his fingers forced the bones together and he dragged her against him.

"If ye ever raise a hand to me again, ye little bitch, ye will wish ye had died along with yer mother." Laird Barde rubbed his jaw with his free hand. "I can play as rough as ye like."

"Unhand me," Mary spat at him, pulling against his grip. "I will not remain here a moment longer."

Laird Barde sneered at her. "Did ye not hear me? Ye have nowhere else to go. There is a rumor something ye possess is wanted by the king. Ye will stay here until I discover what it is."

* * *

Mary raced upstairs, her feet slipping in her haste as though ice coated the stone treads. She grabbed at the railing, blinking through tears of anger and fear. Reaching her room, she jerked open the door and stumbled inside, slamming the panel shut behind her. She leaned against the door, breathing erratically, trying to block the sound of Laird Barde's mocking laughter.

Her hand clutched the empty spot at her breast where her mother's pendant usually hung. Could the necklace be what Laird Barde meant? She had no other mementos from her mother. Mary's gaze sought and lingered on each item in the room. Any personal effects belonging to her mother had disappeared long ago, though in truth there hadn't been much, other than items such as her brushes and clothing. Her mother had worn a slender silver wedding band which Mary had insisted she be buried in, but the cross was her only other piece of jewelry.

What does it represent?

Mary walked across the room and opened the chest beneath the window. A fur-trimmed cloak lay on the bottom beneath two silk dresses she did not recognize as any her mother had worn. She would need the cloak if she meant to leave tonight. The light-colored gown Agnes had loaned her would mark her beneath the full moon as readily as if she carried a lighted torch.

I will not stay here a moment longer.

Her hands trembling with emotion, she pulled the cloak from the chest and shook out the folds. The fur rippled, luxuriously thick and rich beneath her fingers. Mary settled the heavy fabric about her shoulders. It quickly caught the warmth of her body, and the chill running through her from her encounter with Laird Barde faded.

She strode to the bed and sat on the edge, kicking her feet out before her. Where would she go? If she returned to Scott Castle, what then? Was she ready to forgive Eaden? She flinched. Would the image of Isobel ever leave her mind?

There was no reason the king would give her sanctuary because of a jade pendant. More likely he would have her thrown in jail for possessing something of his. How had it come to her mother? Laird Barde said she had gone to court for a time. Had she become entangled in the loss of the necklace? Mary rubbed her aching forehead with trembling fingers. She simply could not see her gentle mother stealing anything. And the stone was of no great worth. At least her mother had said so. But, her mother had apparently kept a good many secrets. Could the cost of the pendant be yet another one?

Her stomach rumbled, reminding her if she wanted to slip away this night, she needed not only food to keep up her strength, but enough for the journey as well. She rose to her feet and crossed the room, catching the door handle and slowly releasing the latch, listening for the slightest sound of protest. Relieved at the silence, she pulled the door open and stepped to the portal . . .

And reeled backward, gaping at the sight of the well-armed guard looming over her. A forbidding look on his face, he crossed his arms over his chest and planted his feet firmly in her path.

"Who are you?" she managed, her voice squeaky with fright.

"I am Gilbert. You will stay in your room until Laird Barde sends for you."

Flustered to find her way barred, Mary grasped for the first excuse that came to her mind. "But I wish to go downstairs to eat."

"Someone will bring you a tray."

Her face heated and she huffed, "I want to eat now. Move out of my way."

The guard's expression did not change. Neither did his stance. Mary tossed her head and took one step toward him, intending to slip through the tiny space between his side and the door frame. Gilbert unfolded his arms and grabbed the neck of her cloak. He turned her around and, with a slight push, propelled her back inside the room. She stumbled into the room, coming to a halt as she landed against the bed.

She whirled, furious, but the door closed with a firm snick of the latch. She slumped against the soft mattress and slid down its side, landing with a soft thump of her fanny on the floor. Wrapping her arms around her knees, she stared at the closed door.

Now what was she to do?

Chapter Thirty-Nine

The tray of food sat untouched on the chest beneath the window. Mary had automatically taken it when thrust at her, peering around Gilbert's huge body to see if anyone lingered in the hall behind him that she could enlist to her aid. Scarcely had the food left his hands, Gilbert slammed the door shut again.

It had taken all of her control not to hurl the tray at the closed portal. She knew she needed the nourishment, but her stomach churned in queer butterfly motions, and the smell of the roasted meat on the platter made her set it aside.

Damn him!

Mary sat, hunched on the bed, the hem of her cloak tucked about her feet. Her borrowed slippers, noticeably too big for her, lay piled together on the floor. The single candle in its sconce by the bed flickered close to guttering, and she stared into its dancing flame, trying to keep from succumbing to dismay.

She must have dozed, for the next time she opened her eyes, the room was dark and the candle cold. Her stomach rumbled and she rose groggily to her feet. Padding across to the chest, she lifted the linen napkin covering the tray and studied its contents of grouse, bread and something that appeared stewed. She poked the bread and found it somewhat dry. The grouse, however, did not seem affected by its entombment beneath the napkin, and she bit into it hungrily.

The grouse vanished forthwith, and Mary decided the bread wasn't so bad after all. She turned to the pitcher on the washstand and lifted it to her nose, testing the quality of its contents. Smelling nothing but stale water, she drank, washing down her meager meal.

Wiping her fingers on the scrap of linen, she walked to the window. Ranald's words whispered through her mind as she gazed at the ground three stories below. How could Isobel have jumped? A chill ran down her spine, raising goose bumps in its path.

The moonlight filling the bailey gave her no answer and Mary turned back to the room. Shedding her cloak with a weary shrug, she slid beneath the coverlet on the bed and slept.

* * *

Two more days passed, repeating the same pattern. Anxious to be away, Mary spent much of her time pacing the room, replaying her conversation with Ranald the day she left Scott Castle. Remembering the plan to visit King Robert, she slowed her step and sank absently to the top of the wooden chest beneath the window. Was there something to Laird Barde's story? Had King Robert asked for her, specifically? Or had he just politely mentioned meeting Laird Scott's new wife?

A noise beyond the door broke her concentration. Leaping from her seat, Mary ran to the portal. Voices sounded on the other side, and her heart quickened as she recognized the high-pitched, demanding tone.

"Miriam!" The pitch of the voice grew, accompanied by the low rumble of a man's voice. Laird Barde had chosen her guard well. Apparently, Gilbert remained unaffected by Miriam's imperious demands. Most unusual.

"Miriam!" She beat on the door, bruising her fists as she fought to make herself heard. Pausing, she pressed her ear to the wooden panel, straining to make sense of the sounds beyond her room. She heard nothing. The hallway was quiet as the grave.

"Argh!" Giving the door a final fierce thump, she flung herself back into the room. Her gaze darted around, coming to rest on the window. Its frame was narrow, but not impassable. Mary ran to the bed and flung the coverlet to the floor. She grabbed the sheet and stripped it from the bed, running its length through her hands until she encountered an edge. With quick jerks of her hands, she rent the fabric into narrow strips, then tied the pieces together.

Gathering the newly made rope, she attached one end to the leg of the bed and let the other end fall from the window. Steeling herself, she leaned out the window and stared dizzily to the ground below as the makeshift rope swung gently against the side of the castle.

The rope was too short.

Saint Andrew's teeth! She clenched her hands in frustration. A glance around the room for a way to lengthen the rope yielded nothing. The coverlet was too heavy, and without a knife or scissors, she could not use it as she had the sheet. Several feet of her makeshift rope stretched from the window to the bed. Mayhap, if she could push the bed to the window, the added length might bring the rope closer to the ground.

She grasped the bed by a corner post and planted her feet. It moved. An inch. The accompanying screech of the heavy frame dragging across the wooden floor made her glance up nervously. She held her breath for a moment, watching the door latch, half-expecting someone to have seen the rope and alerted the guard, or worse, Gilbert had heard the bed move. Seeing nothing of alarm, she released her breath and closed her eyes in relief. She braced herself again to pull against the bed, and heard the soft whoosh of a well-oiled door.

Jerking upright, Mary stared in surprise. Miriam stood against the far wall, her hand against the edge of a door so cleverly hewn that she'd had no idea of its existence.

"Miriam?"

"Shh!" Miriam motioned frantically for Mary to be silent. She spied the rope trailing through the window and gasped. "What are you doing?"

"Escaping."

"I can see that. You'll break your neck trying to climb down from this height!" Miriam ran to the window and began hauling the rope upwards.

"Stop!" Mary was at Miriam's side in an instant, batting at her hands as they reeled in the rope.

"Do you want someone to see?"

"I want to leave here."

Miriam eyed Mary with sadness and laid a hand on her arm. "I know, Mary. I know. But not this way."

Mary nodded at the hidden door. "Can you get me out through there?"

Miriam finished pulling the rope in, dropping it to the floor as she closed the window. "I could, but where will you go?"

"I don't know." The admission sighed from her, unwilling to claim Craigiever Castle as her destination, though she knew she had no place else to turn.

Miriam kicked the knotted length of sheet beneath the bed and smoothed the coverlet across the mattress. She patted the bed beside her. "Come, sit beside me and tell me everything."

Mary tossed her a wry look. "The last time I climbed into a bed at your bidding, I found myself married to the Scott laird."

Miriam's eyes danced with sudden humor. "Oh, Mary, can you ever forgive me?"

Mary sighed. "If you help me get home, I will forgive you anything."

"So, Craigievar is now your home?"

Mary lowered her gaze, her fingers nervously pleating the fabric of her gown. After a moment, she shook her head and looked at her friend. "No," she whispered. "Eaden is."

Silence filled the room. Mary gestured toward the secret door. "How did you know about this?"

"I discovered it by accident, really. This has been used as a guest room since . . ." Miriam's voice trailed off and she gave Mary a sorrowful look.

Mary nodded. "Since my mother died."

"Well, yes. A few weeks ago, I searched for my father and could not find him." Miriam shrugged. "I heard a noise in this room and thought perhaps a servant was cleaning in here and might have seen him. I'd observed him not long before, climbing the stairs, to retire for the night, or so I thought." She stopped, a pained look on her face.

"Yes?"

"He was in here, all right. With a servant girl. The secret door stood ajar." Miriam pursed her lips in disapproval. "They did not notice me."

"You think he used the door to meet women secretly in here?"

Miriam nodded. "I came back the next day and figured out how to open the door. I followed the hallway behind the wall."

"Well? Where does it lead?"

"To his bedroom."

Mary's eyes grew wide with dismay.

"I don't dare lead you through until I know for certain he is not there."

Mary crossed to the bed and sank beside Miriam. "We can do this."

"Of course we can." Miriam patted Mary's leg comfortingly. "I only have to be certain."

"How long do you think it will take? Surely there isn't someone in his room all day?"

"No, but he has given orders you are to not leave the castle. We can only do this at night, and only when he is not there." Miriam turned to Mary. "I know you want to leave. I know what my father is capable of. But if you escape and he captures you again, he will lock you in a cell beneath the castle. And I do not know if I can release you from there."

"I must get word to Eaden. He is in Troon, but will return home shortly. I told his brother I was coming here to think. He waits for me to send a missive when I wish to leave. I do not want them riding here, expecting to rescue me." Mary swallowed her fear. "I must let him know I am all right."

Miriam nodded. "Of course."

"I can write a letter."

"Two letters," Miriam replied firmly.

"But, I only need to write one."

Miriam smiled serenely at Mary. "You write two. One saying you are being held prisoner and need his help. That's the one you give to Gilbert to send to Laird Scott. The other one, saying you love him and will be home soon, you give to me."

"I don't understand."

This time Miriam laughed. "Trust me. Gilbert will not send the letter you give him—he'll bring it to my father. He'll think he's intercepted your letter, thus allaying his suspicions. The second letter will slip past him, unnoticed."

"However did you think of this?"

"Oh, Mary. How do you think I managed to steal away and marry Bennett?"

* * *

Mary kept vigil by the window. How had she been able to condense the past few momentous weeks of her life into the passage of an hour's conversation? It seemed impossible.

She regarded her hands, two fingers on her right stained with smudges of ink. Rubbing them against her skirt, she glanced at the writing desk where a folded piece of parchment lay. With Miriam's help, she'd written a letter to Eaden, imploring him to rescue her, afraid of Laird Barde and his intentions. She prayed it would convince Laird Barde it was the only letter.

A rap sounded against her door and she moved away from the window. Knowing the single knock was the only warning she would receive, she didn't bother opening the door or responding. Gilbert pushed the panel open, her evening meal tray in his hands.

Her mouth quirked in a cautious smile. "Gilbert." He looked at her with suspicion and she quickly turned aside so he wouldn't see the trepidation on her face. She strode to the desk and stopped, staring at the letter resting there. Stretching her hand out, she let it hover above the parchment as though hesitant how to proceed.

Just before she reckoned Gilbert's patience would fail, she snatched the letter and spun around, clutching it to her breast. She raised her eyes to meet his gaze, chewing her lip as though in indecision.

"I really shouldn't ask you this," she began, letting her voice trail off. Silence ensued as she waited for Gilbert to make the next obvious move. His narrow look of suspicion turned into a scowl of impatience.

"Ask me what, milady?"

"I wrote a letter to . . . to my husband." She swallowed hard and lowered her eyes. "Laird Barde is holding me here against my will. I do believe he will release me when he has learned what he wishes to know. However . . ." Mary raised her face to Gilbert, this time allowing trepidation to show. "I do not wish my husband to come looking for me. I fear he will take this amiss." Her voice dropped to a whisper. "I do not want bloodshed."

"What is it you wish me to do?"

As though suddenly convinced of the rightness of her actions, Mary rushed to Gilbert's side. "I want you to take this letter and see it gets to him. I cannot pay you now, but I swear to you, I will see you amply recompensed for your trouble as soon as I am released." She rested a hand on his arm, holding the letter out for him. His arm twitched at her touch. Mary swallowed another smile.

Gilbert made a show of settling the tray on the desk. He took his time, obviously marshalling his thoughts. Finally, he turned back to her. "I must ask you what is in this letter, milady."

Mary's hands flew to her breast, clutching the parchment to her again. "It is my most urgent request he remain at Scott Castle whilst he awaits my return. Must you know the exact contents?"

Gilbert's skin flushed and he ducked his head. "You swear there is nothing in this missive harmful to the people of Bellecourt?"

The parchment crinkled audibly as Mary grasped the letter in fervent appeal. "You have my word, Gilbert. I wish none of you harm."

Reluctantly, Gilbert nodded his head and held out his hand for the letter. Glancing down to inspect the seal, Mary gave it to him with a beaming smile of gratitude on her face. The formalities satisfied on both sides, Mary hummed to herself as she turned to the food tray.

Canting a look over her shoulder, she watched Gilbert stow the missive within his shirt, a smirk of triumph spreading across his face, erasing the earlier wide-eyed look of sympathetic virtue.

Mary nodded. The letter was certainly on its way to Laird Barde without delay. She prayed Miriam's plan was right.

Chapter Forty

Mary sat on the bed, her back propped against the wall. She tried to remain focused on the piece of embroidery she held to keep from stabbing herself with the delicate needle.

"I'm so nervous, I'm afraid I'll stitch this to my skirt on accident," she admitted with a brittle laugh, her voice shaky and low.

Miriam looked up from her own embroidery hoop and frowned. "Don't lay it across your knees, or you really will," she chided.

"The dragon looks like an embarrassed chicken, anyway." Mary flung the fabric to the bed beside her and sighed in frustration.

Gaining her feet, Miriam crossed to the bed and peered at Mary's work. She laughed, "Poor thing! With such a short neck and stumpy wings, he does look rather like a chicken. Though I've never seen a silvery-blue one before."

Mary glowered at her friend. "Are you certain we sent the right letter? I do not want Eaden here. I fear bloodshed should he come after me. Especially since your father thinks I possess something of great value and holds me as hostage to it."

Miriam fisted her hands on her hips and sighed. "For the last time, Mary, we sent off the correct letter. You held the false one in your hand as you watched me walk out the door with the other. Don't worry. Yours is doubtless in ashes in my father's fireplace, and mine is safely on its way to Scott Castle."

She touched Mary's shoulder in sympathy. "I know how you must feel. I left Bennett at Melville Manor of my own accord. He'll finish the hunt in a few more days and return to me. Even though I miss him terribly, I cannot imagine not knowing when I would see him or my home again."

Mary patted Miriam's hand. "Thank you. I fear things between Eaden and I are so fragile they may completely fall apart if I do not return home soon."

"Don't worry. I've already given your letter to the stable lad who carried my last missive to Bennett. He is very trustworthy. It should arrive at Scott Castle within the next few days." Miriam looked at Mary's stricken face and tilted her head in sympathy. "Mayhap sooner."

* * *

Laird Barde leaned over his desk and spread out the letter Gilbert had brought to him. He read the missive again, absently noting the elegant handwriting.

Eaden, my love, Laird Barde is holding me at Bellecourt. He says I have something belonging to King Robert, but I cannot imagine what it could be. He says he will not release me until he discovers what it is. I am at his mercy.

Please come quickly! He frightens me so!

Mary

Lifting his gaze, Laird Barde nodded to the folded parchment in Gilbert's hand. "That is the other one?"

Gilbert held out the letter. "Yes. The stable lad seemed most anxious to bring it to my attention."

Laird Barde took the second missive. Unfolding it, he laid it next to the first. "After his last *mistake* helping my daughter, I can hardly see otherwise. The lad learns fast." He furrowed his brow and turned his attention to the second letter.

Eaden, I promised Ranald I would send word. I will return soon, but beg your indulgence a little longer. I am well and Miriam is here with me. Her husband is away on a hunt, so she and I are able to spend time together.

   Do not worry about me. I will write again soon.
   Mary

Laird Barde glanced up. "Ye read both of these?"
"Aye."
Straightening from his position at the desk, Laird Barde slowly paced the room, fingering his jaw thoughtfully. "Laird Scott has been summoned to King Robert's court where he was to present his wife. In that, he was stymied, as she is here. If the girl has something the king wants, she did not bring it to Bellecourt with her. She came here in rags and wore nothing beneath." He waved a hand in the air, brushing aside the tantalizing memory. It could wait.

   "Holding her ransom would be a slap in the face to Eaden Scott." Laird Barde shrugged, not necessarily disliking the idea. "If I send the intended letter, he might linger at Scott Castle and I would have time to question Mary further. If I send the other, he will almost certainly ride on Bellecourt."

Laird Barde pivoted on his heel, his cloak swirling about his boots, liking the thought of that very much. He raised his gaze to Gilbert who answered with a grin of comprehension.

"Send the first letter, m'laird."

* * *

A lone rider appeared on the horizon, traveling fast, and Eaden reined Duff to a stop, signaling his men to halt. Unconcerned with a single rider headed their way, the men sat at their ease, sipping from water skins and nibbling on oatcakes left from their meager breakfast.

As the rider approached, Eaden recognized young Alan, a braw lad who trained under Ian. Eaden's unease sharpened. Within minutes Alan reined his sweating horse to a stop next to Duff.

"Laird," he said, bobbing his head. Eaden nodded curtly and opened his mouth to question the lad, but shut his jaw with a snap as Alan pulled a folded piece of parchment from his sporran and handed it over.

Eaden stared at the seals on the letter. One, stamped with an elaborate 'B,' had been broken and replaced with wax embossed with his own seal.

"Where did ye get this?"

Alan gulped for breath, as winded as his horse. "It arrived at the castle a day or so ago. It was handed to one of the servants and told it was to go to your hands and none other. No one could truly say whence it came. Yer brother read it. He gave it to me and told me to find ye with all haste." Alan patted his horse's neck ruefully. "'Tis glad I am ye were on yer way home from Troon. I dinnae want to travel so far."

Eaden nodded absently, his attention already distracted by the letter in his hands. Sliding his thumb beneath the wax, he broke the seal and unfolded the parchment with a snap of his wrist.

As he read the fine, elegant handwriting gliding across the page, the muscles in his neck grew taut and his heart pounded in his chest. For a long moment he did not move, fighting the urge to destroy something. Little wonder messengers were considered immune from the actions of their job. As if sensing impending danger, Alan tucked his hand on the reins, causing his horse to back away.

Bringing himself under control, Eaden reined Duff to face his men. "Gavin, go with young Alan. Those of ye who can keep up, ride with me to Bellecourt. The rest of ye head to Craigievar and tell my brother to ready the castle."

The men looked at each other uneasily, clearly confused by this turn of events. "Ready the castle, Laird?" one man ventured. "For what?"

Eaden shot the man a dark look. "For war."

* * *

Eaden met Ranald on the road just before he crossed the border onto Barde land. The last of his guard had fallen away an hour earlier and even Duff's great heart was failing him. Still he rode.

Ranald broke the cover of the trees well in advance of Eaden's arrival, positioning himself clearly on the trail in the moonlight.

Duff stumbled, yanking the reins in Eaden's hand as his head lunged forward in an effort to keep himself from falling. Eaden righted him with a jerk, feeling the jar of the horse beneath him in every weary muscle. His back ached, his fingers twisted into claw-like shapes, and he knew his legs would tremble with fatigue if he dismounted. The long hours in the saddle had not cured his anger one bit. Pulling Duff to a halt, he glared at Ranald.

His brother frowned. "I knew ye'd be this way. And ahead of the rest, too. As captain of the guard, Ian wanted to meet with ye, but I said I'd come." He eyed Eaden's foam-flecked mount as Duff champed the bit in nervous exhaustion. "Though whether to save yer horse or yer own disreputable hide, I dinnae know."

"Get out of my way, Ranald," Eaden growled warningly.

"I'm going with ye, Eaden. At least as far as Duff'll carry ye."

Duff shook his head tiredly and snorted. His body quivered beneath Eaden's legs and foam dripped from his mouth. With a sigh, Eaden swung a leg stiffly over Duff's neck and slid to the ground. Hiding his grunt of pain as his feet hit the ground, Eaden grasped the reins beneath the shanks of the bit and led Duff beside Ranald.

"The puir lad willnae make it to Bellecourt," Eaden agreed, giving his horse a quick pat. He placed a hand on Ranald's stirrup, steadying his own weary limbs. So braced, he leveled his gaze on his brother. "'Tis why we're exchanging mounts."

Not giving him a chance to realize his intent, Eaden gripped Ranald's boot and shoved upward as hard as he could. With an outraged cry, Ranald flew sideways from his saddle, landing heavily on the ground. Eaden snatched the reins from his brother's numbed grip and swung into the vacated saddle with a grunt of effort. Wrenching the horse's head around, pointing him toward Bellecourt, he spurred him into a run, leaving Duff and Ranald staring after him—one with mild interest, the other in palpable frustration.

Chapter Forty-One

Streaks of pink and gold tinted the horizon. Still cast in shadows, the earliest risers of Bellecourt Castle crossed the bailey to the great hall, huddled anonymously against the morning mists in their blankets and cloaks. A single shepherd, a small flock of ewes and lambs surging ahead of him, exited through the man-door beside the massive main gate, which was still closed against the night. With bleats loud in the silence, the sheep veered away to the grazing lands. The shepherd, intent on keeping his flock headed in the right direction, spared only a nod in greeting to the weary man who entered the narrow gate behind him.

Mary leaned her elbows on the windowsill, chin in her palms. Her thoughts roamed far beyond the hills to the north. She watched the play of the lambs as they bucked and kicked in high spirits, following tight against their dams' sides. The odor of cooking fires drifted through the mist and her stomach grumbled approvingly.

She turned from the window, her gaze pulled to the inviting softness of the bed. She longed for sleep, for peace from the unanswered questions running through her head. But she was unable to rest knowing there would be no rescue attempt once Eaden received her missive. Unable to close her eyes knowing Laird Barde could enter her room and none in the castle would be the wiser.

Exhaustion consumed her. A quiver of dread, just as strong as her need for oblivion, rippled through her body as she spied the nearly invisible outline of the secret door hiding the tunnel leading to the bedroom where Laird Barde . . .

She gripped her hair at the scalp and tugged hard to clear the thought. If Laird Barde had made use of the passageway while her mother lived, she would rather not know. Right now Mary carried all the guilt she could manage. With a sigh, she crept to the bed. Pulling the coverlet back, she burrowed beneath the sheets and found oblivion as the sun climbed behind the building clouds on the horizon.

* * *

Eaden limped across the bailey, only partly acting for the amused benefit of the guards on the parapet. His entire body ached from the hard ride and he remembered the way Mary's body had stiffened the day he'd taught her to ride. And the way she had softened beneath his hands as he'd rubbed her muscles to relieve the soreness. Pride rose in him to recall how quickly she'd overcome her fear of horses to become a competent horsewoman. A horsewoman who'd used her new-found skills to run from Scott Castle.

Shite. He scowled, cursing under his breath as his foot struck a partially-buried stone. Time to dwell on those things later. Wool-gathering like an ancient crone would only get himself killed. Hobbling to the side of the yard, he leaned against one of the stone buildings and massaged his ankle, letting his gaze roam over the castle's façade.

Comparing the structure against the memory of the interior of the great hall, he recalled the night he'd kidnapped Mary, thinking she was Miriam. Before, anger had driven him to Bellecourt for the woman he didn't want. Now, anger fueled his need for revenge against Barde for holding his wife against her will.

Morning was coming on, and he needed to either breech the castle or find a place to hide until nightfall. Pushing away from the wall, he slipped around the bailey, looking for an unwatched opening into the castle.

It was still fairly simple to move about and not attract attention. Clouds built, hiding the sun, leaving the morning partly cloaked in shadows. With the promise of a stormy day, Eaden perceived the weather could be a much-needed help. He crept along the edge of the bailey, halting in the shadows of various buildings clustered in the yard along the way.

"And a good skelpin' ye'll get if the stew is ruined when I get back!"

A rather buxom woman, carrying a woven basket, bustled from the bailey, a frustrated look creasing her face. Eaden straightened from his slouch and watched her curiously as she strolled to what appeared to be the kitchen garden.

Would she know where Mary is? Would she tell me? Does she even know Mary is being held against her will?

His jaw clenched. He'd run similar questions through his mind for the past day and a half, with no better answers now than when he'd headed for Bellecourt. Would he find Mary in the prison beneath the castle, or in her room? Or in another, more secure place?

As the woman snipped herbs and stacked them carefully in her basket, Eaden glanced about to reassure himself of the usual activity one found in a bailey. Though he heard no cries of alarm, he hesitated. Instinct told him something was not right. The woman in the garden did not seem to share his concern, but why would she? Castle gardening was not usually considered a risky occupation.

Eaden hunched his shoulders, as much for concealment of his true height and stature as to loosen his muscles in preparation for whatever was brewing. He was in his sworn enemy's castle, about to approach an innocent woman to obtain information. He had no illusions what would happen to him if captured. It was a certainty Mary would suffer, too.

He broke cover and strode quickly toward the garden, reaching for the dagger at his belt. Within seconds he realized he'd walked into a trap.

* * *

Both Eaden and the woman in the garden heard the war cry, warning him an instant before he located the source of the sound. The jerk of her head told him she'd spotted something alarming to his left. He whirled, crouching as he moved, spreading his hands wide, his dagger in one hand, reaching for the knife in his boot before he came to a stop.

A sword swung viciously above him, perfectly aimed to separate his head from his body, had he still been standing. Eaden rolled to the side, coming to his feet between the outbuilding and the outer wall of the bailey. Using this as a shield, he slipped quickly into the narrow opening and took stock of his situation.

"Come, Laird Scott. Come taste our steel."

Several soldiers loomed in an arc before him, smiling grimly, beckoning him into the open. The flash of meager sunlight on steel struck his eyes and he sank deeper into the shadows. One of the guards, an enormous man with an arrogant swagger, advanced on Eaden, waving his sword before him.

Eaden hefted his boot knife in his hand, testing its weight, its balance.

The guard grinned widely, flexing his arm muscles to the jeers and shouts of his friends. Eaden retreated further, forcing the giant to lurch inside the passageway to approach close enough to engage.

"Fight me, Scott," the man challenged, beckoning Eaden with his sword. With a short lunge, Eaden threw his knife at the guard. The narrow blade flashed through the air and sank to the hilt into the base of his throat. Caught mid-stride, the soldier halted as though snatched by an invisible rope, poised a moment in mid-air. His hands opened wide and his sword clattered to the ground as blood spewed from the wound. He collapsed, a look of pained surprise caught on his face.

The jeers of contempt from the Barde soldiers skidded into cries of anger. Obviously, none had considered their companion so vulnerable. Eaden flexed his hands, adjusted his balance as another guard, less arrogant, appeared in the entrance.

"Ye cannae remain here forever," he shouted. Eaden ignored him.

The guard leapt over the body, closing the distance between himself and Eaden. Eaden hefted the dagger in his hand, and the soldier eyed him warily, lifting his short sword as he advanced.

Eaden waited for him. The man's gaze darted to the side, betraying his next move. Leaping forward, Eaden landed behind the soldier's guard. With a vicious jab, he drove his dagger between the man's ribs, angling it upward, the tip piercing his heart. He twisted the blade, widening the dagger's path, hot blood cascading over his hand as the guard fell to the ground at his feet.

Eaden immediately crouched in readiness, watching the entrance, listening for the guards' next move. Suddenly, three soldiers barreled through the opening, shouting loudly as they charged down the aisle. Eaden braced himself, letting them come to him.

At the last second, he feinted to the side, ducking beneath the first soldier's blade, slashing at the back of the man's leg as he rushed past him. With a cry of pain, the soldier crashed to the ground, tendons severed, his leg forever useless.

The next guard fell upon Eaden before he recovered, and his blade caught Eaden's arm, leaving a trail of fire racing down its length. Eaden jabbed at the guard, but his dagger was slick with blood and as it snagged on the chain mail at the man's neck, it broke from his grip. With a grunt of pain, Eaden switched his knife from his left hand to his right. The guard stumbled backward over his fallen companion as the third guard charged past.

Eaden sensed a movement at his back. Something flashed at the edge of his vision and he stiffened for a blow. He ducked and raised his right arm, ready to parry with his knife, but a truncheon clipped his shoulder, stunning the nerve in his arm. All feeling gone in his hand, his knife fell to the ground.

A thin noose dropped over his head, jerking hard against his neck. His good hand grabbed the rope, but it was already too tight, and it bit deep into his throat. Eaden clawed frantically, gasping for air as the world darkened around him.

* * *

Water surged like fire through his nose and Eaden snorted and coughed, certain he was drowning, coming to consciousness in a violent convulsion of movement. Pain burst behind his eyes and tightened every muscle, and he gritted his teeth. Something thick and wet threatened to choke him and he rolled to his side, spitting the coppery-tasting liquid from his mouth onto the wet stone floor.

His ribs grated, and he groaned. Laughter rang out above him, and he gingerly tilted his head toward the sound. To his disgust, only one eye would open, but the lack did not prevent him from recognizing the red-haired man looming over him.

"Enough, Gilbert," Laird Barde said with a chuckle, a hand raised to stop the man's action.

Gilbert scowled at Eaden as he set aside the bucket in his hand. At the size of the puddle he lay in, Eaden imagined Gilbert had been trying to rouse him for quite some time.

"Welcome to Bellecourt Castle, Scott. I hoped ye would respond to our invitation," Laird Barde said.

Eaden's head ached and a ringing sounded in his ears. His entire body throbbed painfully, witness to the fact the angry guards had vented their frustration on him once they'd taken him down. He scowled derisively at their cowardly conduct, but a split in his lip opened with fiery warning. The muscles in his abdomen screamed in protest as he straightened his body enough to sit, and he feared some internal injury.

He tried to pull his hands in front of him, but rope cut into his wrists, holding them securely behind his back. He glanced at his feet and found them likewise secured.

"Ah, yes. I believe ye had a tussle with my guards. They were not aware how dangerous ye could be, but the less wary served as a warning to the others." Laird Barde shrugged. "Ye received quite a beating, but it did not kill ye, more's the pity."

Barde's words made no sense. Eaden knew the man toyed with him, but he hated any loss of control, and he couldn't resist replying. "What the hell are ye talking about?"

Laird Barde favored him with a patronizing smile. "Yer pretty wife was most accommodating. I needed ye here, at my mercy, and she supplied the perfect bait." He idly perused his fingernails, as if considering his next words. "She writes most elegantly, and with such emotion! I knew her heartfelt letter would bring ye here." He crouched beside Eaden, dropping his voice to an evil arrogance. "Lady Scott helped set my trap. She is, ye will agree, a most remarkable lady."

Chapter Forty-Two

Mary stirred, not certain what had woken her, too groggy to make sense of her thoughts. The half-light of a stormy day room bathed the room, and the low rumble of thunder reached her ears. She sighed. Doubtless the storm invaded her sleep. She grabbed the pillow next to her and hugged it close, trying to recreate the dream of Eaden beside her, but the memory fled beyond her recall.

With the sun scarcely visible, she couldn't determine the hour. Her head ached as though she had only slept a short time, perhaps only a few minutes. Her thoughts were fuzzy, her eyes swollen and scratchy. Pursuing sleep proved useless as the storm continued to announce its imminent arrival.

Irritably, she yanked the covers back and swung her feet over the side of the bed. She rubbed the palms of her hands over her eyes, trying to ease their strain, and slowly rose to her feet. Crossing to the wash table, she poured water into the bowl and splashed her face.

Feeling somewhat revived, she blinked in the pale yellow light. The shutters stood open and she leaned out the window for a breath of fresh air.

Shouts from below caught her attention. Something was amiss. Two soldiers raced across the bailey yard and disappeared from view. Alarmed, Mary glanced at the parapet, partly reassured by the remaining guards standing steadfast at their posts, though they watched the bailey with interest.

The bedroom door opened and Mary pivoted, taken by surprise.

Miriam's voice floated through the doorway. "No, we do not require assistance." She swept into the room, a breakfast tray in her hands. She placed the tray on the desk, then slapped her hands on her hips and glared at the guard following on her heels. A ruddy flush crept up the boy's neck as he scowled and retreated into the hallway, closing the door firmly behind him. Miriam gave a *humph* of satisfaction and turned a sunny smile on Mary.

"Stupid boy," she announced cheerfully. "Thinking he could come in here and stare at you. They all remember you, you know. You've not been gone so long. Only now you're Laird Scott's woman, which gives you a certain, um, notoriety."

She set about unwrapping Mary's breakfast as she talked. "Gilbert is strict, but at least he knows his place."

Mary poured a goblet of water and picked an apple from the tray as she nodded in agreement. "Which is right at your father's side," she noted wryly. She set her drink down and crossed to the window, munching on the apple. "Do you know about the commotion outside?"

Miriam joined her and leaned out the aperture to look. "I'm not certain. The men have been on alert the past day or so. I think there's been a miscreant hanging about. Perhaps they've caught him."

Clouds, traveling on a brisk wind, abruptly blotted the weak sunlight. Rain fell, slowly at first, then in silver sheets. Miriam ducked back inside, closing the shutters firmly against the pelting rain and the smell of wet earth wafting in the air. She caught Mary's hand and led her back to the desk.

"Have you discovered what it is your father thinks King Robert wants from me?" Mary asked.

"I cannot broach the subject with him. He has no time for me. The thought of besting Laird Scott absorbs him." Miriam paused. "Other than your mother's clothes and creams and salves, what could she have? Did she give you something special? A memento, perhaps?"

Mary frowned. Hiding the jade cross from Miriam had been her only act of defiance against her friend her entire life. It at last seemed safe enough to mention it.

"She wore a cross beneath her gown. It was a pendant of gold set with four pieces of jade and a diamond at their juncture. It is now mine. I have kept it hidden as she did."

Miriam's face grew animated. "A jade cross? Let me see!"

"I don't have it with me. I left it on my dressing table at Scott Castle."

"Well, is it fabulous? Why would your mother not show it?"

Mary gave a dispirited shrug. "I think it is pretty, but not worth a king's ransom." She smiled faintly. "I tried to ask her where she got it, but she would not tell me."

Miriam's eyes widened. "Do you think it was stolen?"

With an irritated sigh, Mary rolled her eyes. "You remember my mother. Do you think she'd steal a necklace?"

Miriam's face fell. "No, I suppose not." Another thought struck her. "Do you suppose it was a gift from your father?"

"Most likely."

"Did she ever tell you who he is?"

"No. The subject upset her too much. I suppose he could have been anyone."

Miriam gasped. "You're going to think I'm crazy . . ."

"What is it?"

"Well, the king supposedly wanted to meet you . . ."

"Yes. Because I married Laird Scott and you didn't."

"No. Because you have something he wants."

Mary nodded reluctantly. "Yes. I have thought of that."

"I think it is your necklace."

"Why would the king want my necklace?"

Miriam leaned forward in her chair. "Because, what if, eighteen years ago, *he* gave it to your mother?"

* * *

Mary sat in silence as the shadows of the storm chased across the walls of her room. Miriam had left her to her thoughts hours ago, and still Mary could not get past her words. Laird Barde had said her mother went to stay with relatives at court after her husband's death. Though he would have only been Steward of Scotland at the time, Robert would have been much younger and a known womanizer. Chances were good they had met, though Mary's imagination stopped there. The idea her mother and the king could have been lovers was too incredible to consider.

Dazed, Mary rose to her feet, pushing her heavy hair from her shoulder as she rubbed the back of her neck. Her fingers snarled in the dank tangles of her hair, but the air touching her skin felt refreshingly cool. Collecting a square of linen, she crossed to the table where the pitcher of water sat. She filled the wash bowl and untied the laces of her gown, allowing the loosened bodice to fall to her waist.

She wrung excess water from the linen and washed her face and neck, the slow actions soothing her troubled mind. Closing her eyes, she inhaled deeply, the hair on her arms prickling as the cool air touched her damp skin. With a shiver, she reached for the larger length of linen, drying herself with brisk swipes. She pulled her bodice over her thin chemise and reached for the lacings.

A rustle in the corner of the room disturbed her and she spun about, dreading the sight of a rat. She was partly right, though the rodent seated on a chair in the corner was of the two-footed variety.

"Don't stop on my account, my dear."

With a jerk of her hands, she managed to get her laces tightened. "How long have you been there?"

"Long enough," Laird Barde replied, an amused smile on his face.

Mary's face heated angrily. "You're Miriam's father. You're old enough to be *my* father! In fact, you're my uncle," she flung at him.

"By marriage, only. Not by blood."

"It doesn't matter. You're a lecherous old man!"

"Mind yer manners, lass. Yer very existence here depends on whether I get what I want."

"You'll not get *me*," Mary shouted, crossing her arms defiantly over her chest.

Laird Barde chuckled. "Mary, ye mistake me. Right now, I want only what the king does."

Mary's blood ran cold.

"I see ye know more than ye are willing to tell." Laird Barde rose to his feet and swaggered to her side. "I assure ye *will* tell me what ye know. What is so important to the King of Scotland, that he would request an audience with our little bastard, Mary?"

"Don't call me that," Mary growled.

"But 'tis the truth. Ye have no value. Only that which the next man sees in ye." He twined a finger in a lock of her hair. "I could be that man."

Mary slapped his hand away and darted across the room. She grabbed the door latch and tugged. It was locked tight. Laird Barde gave a mirthless laugh and she set her back against the panel, hands fisted so tightly her fingernails dug into her palms.

Laird Barde stalked her, the leer on his face a promise of retribution. Mary's chest heaved and she swallowed against the lump in her throat, her gaze darting about, seeking an escape.

She spied the nearly invisible lines of the secret door and realized it stood slightly ajar. He'd slipped in without the guard knowing? Mary judged the distance to the door, but the bed stood in her path, and she was not willing to risk letting him catch her there.

Shoving away from the door, Mary plunged past Laird Barde, angling in a feint away from the secret door. Taking the bait, he grabbed wildly at her as she rushed by. His back now to the hidden passage, Mary changed direction, slipping between him and the wash table in a straight line to the door. Elation surged through her, ending on a gasp of fright as Laird Barde's hand closed on her arm. He jerked her to a halt, spinning her around to face him.

She stumbled backward into the washstand, her free hand grasping for support as her legs twisted in her skirts. Her fingers closed on the handle of the metal pitcher and as she regained her balance, she swung the empty jug at his head. The ewer connected with a terrible thud, and blood spurted from Laird Barde's temple. He dropped to the floor like a sack of sand and lay there, eyes unfocused, limbs twitching. Blood masked his features as it poured from the split in his scalp.

Fighting the urge to retch, Mary stared at the man at her feet. Gathering her wits, she realized she was free. She fled across the room and grabbed the edge of the narrow door. Heavier than she'd anticipated, it swung open silently at her impatient tug. She hesitated at the sight of the dark tunnel beyond. A choking, gurgling sound behind her spurred her on and she slipped inside the passageway, pulling the door firmly shut behind her.

Hands out to her side for guidance, Mary took a step into the unknown.

Chapter Forty-Three

Mary crept forward, completely blind in the dark. The musty smell of the passage nearly overpowered her, but she dared not sneeze, not knowing who or what would alert to her presence. She held a hand before her, recoiling each time she touched the cold stone wall. Her nerves strung tight, the sticky gossamer spiders' webs she encountered increased her anxiety. Resolutely pushing away the thoughts of the eight-legged inhabitants of those webs, and their unfortunate victims, Mary forged ahead, step by hesitant step.

Her hand touched stone in front of her. A dead end. Cautiously, she turned, feeling for the opening to tell her which way to continue, finding walls on three sides. Relief washed through her. This must be the door into Laird Barde's room. If only she could figure out how to open it. She placed her palm on the stone, praying it wasn't latched.

The door swung open silently, and Mary sent a fervent thanks to the ancient stonemasons who'd done their job well. And to whomever kept the hinges oiled. She eased into the room, glancing about to be certain she was alone. A single lit candle cast a yellow light near the center of the room, leaving the corners in shadows. The room appeared empty.

The flame caught the draft from the open door and danced wildly on the wick. The shadows flickered and jumped, giving them life, and Mary clutched her chest as though she could steady her heart's sudden frantic beating.

She closed the secret door behind her, relieved to see the candle's flame return to a normal flickering glow. Crossing to the room's main door, she dusted what she could of the tunnel's filth from her skirts before turning the latch.

Opening the door, Mary pulled up short, surprise on her face. Miriam stood in the portal, her fist raised, an angry scowl on her face.

"What are you doing here?" Miriam recovered first and looked past Mary into the room.

Mary could only stare, slack-jawed with shock. Even if she could make sensible words form on her tongue, how could she tell Miriam she might have just killed her father? "I must leave, Miriam. I cannot stay here any longer." There. That much was the truth, anyway. *Please don't let her ask further.*

Miriam grabbed her arm, looking quickly over her shoulder before hurrying her down the hallway.

"You took an awful chance coming here. But I was going to get you, after I spoke to my father, anyway. He has done a terrible thing."

Mary heard the snarl in Miriam's voice and drew her arm away. "I know he is deceitful . . ."

Miriam beckoned Mary to keep up. "He's going to get us all killed," she continued in a low voice. "He has let his obsession with Laird Scott overrule his better judgment. He plans to kill him and keep you here." She stopped and stared at Mary, pained disbelief in her eyes. "And not as his wife."

Mary gasped, trying to form the words to confess her deed.

"He's not already . . ." Miriam's voice begged for reassurance.

"No, but he tried." Slowly, she raised her gaze to Miriam's and felt the sting of tears. "I hit him, Miriam. I know I knocked him down. 'Twas how I escaped. I think I hurt him badly."

Miriam's face blanched white. "Oh, Mary!" she whispered. "I've come to know of his cruel ways more and more in the past few months. I'd always thought him brave and stern, and felt safe knowing others feared him. No one dared attack our keep. Even his deliberate cruelties somehow seemed right at his hands. But I've come to see him differently of late and I know if he can, he'll use you until he tires of you. He has captured your husband and I have no doubt he will torment you with his torture and death before long."

Miriam reached into a small bag hung from a cord at her waist. Pulling forth an iron key, she pressed it into Mary's hand. "Come. I will get you as far as the gates, but you will have to manage on your own after that."

"Eaden is here?"

"Yes. I told you. They captured him."

"Where?" Mary demanded, reeling from Miriam's confession of her sire and Laird Scott's imprisonment.

"The jail. You must rescue your husband."

* * *

Mary had never been in this part of Bellecourt Castle before, though the threat of it was familiar to all the castle children who got into trouble from time to time.

The torch-lined walls were streaked black with soot that soaked up the light and added to the overall gloom. Rats scurried across their path, burrowing into the filthy rushes on the floor. The reek of unwashed bodies and a sickly sweet odor Mary could not name, competed with the heavy smoke from the torches, leaving a bad taste in her mouth. She gagged, but went doggedly forward, staying as close as she could to Miriam.

The soldier at the entrance to the jail had been indifferent about allowing two unescorted women inside. The burly guard in the antechamber was not so quick to let them pass. "Wot do we have 'ere, now?" he called in a loud voice.

The other guard in the room slid his chair back from the rickety wooden table and sauntered over. Though hooded and cloaked, Mary could feel their boldly assessing stares upon her, and she drew the edge of the hood further forward over her face.

"We are here to see the prisoner." Miriam's voice was firm, brooking no interference.

The burly guard snorted, picking his teeth with a slender twig. He spat onto the floor. "Cannae."

"You will. Or I will see to it my father knows of your treatment of me and my companion."

The guard raised his brow. "The laird's brat, er, daughter? What d' ye want with the prisoner?"

"I am here to see to his welfare. I heard he is injured. If he is to be held for ransom, he must not be allowed to die." She nodded to Mary. "She is a healer."

"He killed three of our men. Th' bastard deserves what he got."

Miriam drew herself up imperiously and gave the man a cold look. "Open the gate."

The man scratched himself, glowering. Finally, he nodded. "Right. He's in there." Tilting his chin over his shoulder, he called to the other guard. "Bring th' key and let milady and her crone in t' see th' prisoner."

Muttering something unpleasant about *wimmin*, the younger guard snatched an iron key from a hook on the wall and sauntered forward. The hallway beyond the anteroom led to three cells. All were empty but the third. Absent a cot or chair of any kind, a solitary figure lay on the floor amid the squalor of the jail.

Mary shuddered, suddenly anxious to be near him, to rescue him from this level of hell.

Iron clanged as the lock turned. Miriam grasped Mary's hand, pulling her close to whisper in her ear. "Go inside. I will send the guard on an errand. You must be quick."

Mary nodded and followed the guard to the door of her husband's cell. She cast one last look over her shoulder and saw the sad look on Miriam's face.

For an instant she feared a trap, but calmed. Surely Miriam would have no need for such an elaborate deception. If Laird Barde had ordered her imprisoned, his soldiers would simply have dragged her down here and locked her away.

The guard swung the door open and moved back to allow her to pass. Mary scarcely noted the smirk on the lad's face as she passed him, her skirts held tightly in her hands to avoid touching the noisome floor. A single, narrow window, high in the wall, allowed watery sunlight to cast a pale beam into the cell, hardly enough for her to see the shape slumped at her feet.

Legs showed plainly in the light, and she followed their length to the shadowed torso and nearly invisible head. Though she could not make out his features, she knew he watched her. She knelt at his side, stoically ignoring the odor wafting up as her knees crunched through the layers of soiled rushes.

"Are you all right, m'laird?" she whispered.

Eaden grunted. "I'll no' say I've been in worse places."

Despite his words, the sound of his voice sent Mary's spirits soaring, and she glanced over her shoulder at the guard. He was gone, and she could hear Miriam's high-pitched voice, ordering the men to more industry than they'd probably shown in the last month or so.

Her eyes grew accustomed to the dim light and she realized Eaden's hands were manacled to chains in the wall behind him. Remembering the key Miriam had given her, as well as her admonishment for haste, she reached for the heavy locks. Hands trembling, she released him.

"Hurry!" She grabbed his arm and tugged hard. His groan of pain alarmed her and she sat back on her haunches to stare at him. "What is the matter?"

This brought a harsh bark of laughter, swallowed by a swift intake of breath. "No' much."

"You're lying." Mary stood as she watched his slow, awkward attempt to rise. Eaden gave a bitter laugh and managed to get to his feet.

She glanced down. "No chains on your feet?"

"They took them off. They dinnae think I'm so dangerous now."

An ear-piercing scream bounced from the stone walls and Mary gasped, whirling toward the doorway. Shrieks of dismay reached her ears, and she nearly fainted with relief to hear Miriam's voice.

"It's a rat! A huge rat! Get it! Get it! Take it away! Oh, take it away! Now!"

She continued for some moments in the same vein, and Mary realized Miriam had cleared the guards from the area. She turned back to Eaden who swayed unsteadily on his feet.

"Come. We must make haste."

Eaden reached for her and grasped her shoulder in a claw-like grip. She staggered beneath his weight as he leaned into her.

Hitching his step, he got his balance and gave her a mocking gesture of following. "After ye, milady. If ye're sure yer friend has set no trap. I am out of patience with the lot of them right now."

"Miriam has gotten rid of both guards. We haven't much time."

"Lead on." Eaden gave her a push. They exited the cell. Miriam met them in the hallway, beckoning them to hurry.

"Follow me. You will find your horse in the stable. I did not have time to arrange to have him saddled, but the bridle is hung by the stall." She turned to Mary. "Be safe," she whispered, giving her a quick hug.

Mary's eyes filled with tears. "Miriam, I think . . ."

Miriam shook her head, pressing a finger to Mary's lips to silence her. "Whatever is done is done. I will see to my father."

Grabbing her skirts in her hands, Miriam ran down the hallway to the entrance. Her shrill voice echoed back to Mary and Eaden as she firmly berated the soldier for allowing rodents to live unchecked in her father's castle. Mary and Eaden crept behind her to the doorway and saw the guard, Miriam's finger stabbing emphatically at his chest, backed in the corner of his post, obviously unnerved by the young woman's harangue.

Eaden urged Mary forward and they disappeared silently around the corner. They held to the edge of the walls, the grey rain shrouding them in heavy mists. Mary looked back as Eaden stumbled. She raced to his side, bracing him with one shoulder beneath his arm. His quick intake of breath alarmed her, but he did not allow her to stop and ask questions. This was not the time to assess his wounds.

The stable proved a haven, fragrant with dried hay and warm horses. Mary and Eaden passed the partly closed door of the tack room. Glancing inside, they glimpsed the recumbent forms of three stable lads taking full advantage of the dreary day. Light snores mingled with the steady sound of rain overhead and the low nickers from the horses as they passed each stall. Mary found Starnie and pulled his bridle from its peg.

She slipped the headstall over his head, seating the bit in his mouth. She led him from his stall and over to a mounting block near the door of the stable. Not waiting for Eaden to help her, she scrambled atop Starnie's broad back and settled herself on his furry hide.

Eaden mounted behind her, though she flinched in surprise to see him use the mounting block, one arm tucked tight against his side. She longed to ask if he was all right, but his gaze caught hers and his furious glare shut her mouth, question unasked. Pulling Starnie's head around, she kicked his sides and urged him out into the storm.

A shout of alarm arose from the jail and three soldiers rushed from the castle to the prison, hands on the hilts of their swords, urgently gesturing toward both the castle and the jail.

Eaden slid to the ground. "Go through the small gate. Walk and keep your head down. They are looking for two people who have escaped, not one. I will join you shortly."

Mary opened her mouth to protest, but he slapped Starnie's wet rump.

She slipped out the gate, waiting for the cry marking her escape. Blood pounding in her ears, she forced herself to keep Starnie at a plodding walk. A short way down the road stood a copse of trees and she guided him to its shelter. Her heart had taken permanent residence in her throat by the time Eaden joined her in the trees beyond the castle gates, on foot and limping badly.

With a struggle, he mounted behind her and took the reins. The pelting rain made for poor conversation, though Mary didn't think he wanted her questions right now. Silently, Eaden turned the horse into the woods beyond the road, following an unseen path until they reached Ranald's horse, still tied beneath an overhang of stone and shrubs, only mildly discomfited by the weather. Eaden slid carefully to the ground and mounted Ranald's horse. With a nudge of his heels to the horse's flanks, they faded into the forest, and he and Mary were soon well away from Bellecourt.

* * *

The rain stopped as they approached the river. Almost within sight of Scott Castle, the clouds broke apart and the afternoon sunshine was a welcome blessing.

"I need a moment, Eaden," Mary said. As he reined his horse to a halt, she slid from Starnie's back and vanished into the bushes. When she returned, she paused, staring at her husband. He leaned wearily over the horse's back, his gaze focused on something in the distance. Sunlight filtered through the leaves, dappling his skin with shadows and light. She remembered the guard's words. He'd killed three men? And deserved what he got?

She searched him for signs of injury, and noted again the careful way he held himself. A dark area stained the skin above one eye, but she couldn't tell if it was bruising or dried blood. Or both.

"If ye are finished staring, ye can get back on yer horse, now."

Uneasy, Mary stepped forward. "Eaden, I'd like to talk before we gain the castle."

"There may be men from Bellecourt following us, my love. Perhaps later."

Mary stiffened at the mocking way he said *my love*, and she faced him. "You have no reason to be so angry. I wrote you a letter . . ."

"Aye. I got yer letter."

Mary stomped her foot. "Then, why did you come?"

"Ye begged me to."

"I begged you to come?" she repeated. "I told you to stay away!"

"Yer letter said ye were afraid."

Mary's face paled and her eyes grew wide. "Oh, no. You got the wrong letter."

"Ye wrote two?"

"Yes. I mean, no. Laird Barde had to know I'd try to send a missive to you. So I wrote one for him to intercept. The other was meant to keep you away until I could try to escape. I knew if I told you the truth, you'd come after me."

"Aye. I did."

"Oh, Eaden. I wrote to tell you I was unharmed and I would write again later. But the one meant for Laird Barde said he was holding me against my will. How did they get mixed up? We were so careful."

Eaden grunted. "I would imagine he intercepted them both and sent the one guaranteed to bring me to ye."

"Why did you come alone?"

"There wasnae time to form an army," he replied. "I suggest ye mount up. We are likely to have company soon, and I'm no' so firm on my horse today."

Mary eyed him closely. "Where are you hurt?"

Eaden snorted. "Where am I no' hurt?" He dismissed her concern impatiently. "Climb up here."

They both caught the sound of hoof beats coming from the north and glanced up. Eaden nudged Starnie to a large rock and Mary scrambled onto his back. Standing just off the trail, they waited as the riders drew near.

A bark alerted them as Sorcha bounded into the glen and danced gleefully about Starnie's legs. The horsemen rode right behind her, Ranald at their head. At his command, they reined to a stop.

He gave Mary a nod of reassurance, then stared at his brother. "Ye look like hell."

Eaden grimaced. "I've improved, then."

"Ranald, I am so glad to see you," Mary gushed.

"Now there's a proper greeting." Ranald turned his attention to her. "I trust ye are in better shape than Himself?"

"I am fine, Ranald. But I would like a moment alone to talk to Eaden. Now you and your soldiers are here, perhaps we could have a bit of time? He's been worried about being followed."

Ranald shrugged. "Of course. He's in no shape to beat ye or act on any of the other murderous thoughts running through his head right now."

"What do you mean?"

"Well, from the way he's sitting on his horse, I'd wager a few broken ribs. And from the cut above his eye, he's probably seeing at least two of ye right now." Ranald tilted his head in assessment. "By the color of those bruises, it looks like someone has worked him over good. I'd no' be surprised if he pisses blood for a bit."

"Enough!" Eaden growled. "Watch the road and leave yer comments behind yer teeth or see if I don't keep them there for ye."

"Braw words," Ranald tossed over his shoulder as he reined his horse around. "Ye have an hour. 'Twas all I could get the king to agree to before he sets siege to Bellecourt Castle. Look to the road," he ordered his soldiers. They spread out, leaving Mary and Eaden alone.

* * *

"Well, my dear. Ye have my undivided attention. What is it ye wish to discuss?"

Mary jerked her gaze from Ranald. "Did he say the king is on his way to Bellecourt?"

"Nay. He said the king is waiting, however impatiently. I would guess he has made himself at home at Scott Castle."

"Why would the king lay siege to Bellecourt?" Mary asked cautiously.

"It seems the king once knew yer mother."

Mary looked away. Eaden sighed. "Mary. Look at me. The king gave yer mother the necklace ye wear when they parted. 'Twas a chaotic time between him and King David. After David's release by the English, Robert was relieved of his station and returned home. Yer ma had already left Edinburgh and they never saw each other again. He told me she left to live with a cousin. She never told him she carried his child."

"Would it have mattered?" Mary asked bitterly.

"The king has many children. Several are no' legitimate. He acknowledges all of them." Eaden gently took Mary's chin in his hand, forcing her to look round at him. "Yer ma did what she thought was right. She may have felt she had no choice. But she raised ye, and 'tis what matters right now."

"You aren't still angry with me?"

Eaden sighed. "Ye dinnae trust me and ye ran away. The king has threatened me with my land and title yet again—this time should I no' bring ye home. I've had the hell beat out of me and spent the past several hours in Laird Barde's stinking prison. Right now, I'm tired and wet and hungry." He flashed her a tired grin. "I'm no' still angry."

Mary nodded slowly. "Ranald told me Isobel is dead."

"Aye."

"Did you love her?"

Eaden made a rasping sound in the back of his throat. "There was never love between us. We had an arrangement, nothing more."

"*We* have an arrangement," Mary said softly.

"Nay. We have a marriage."

"I can still see her . . ."

"'Twas no' my doing. I dinnae invite her there."

Mary sighed. "I see that now. I think I knew from the beginning, but I was too shocked and upset to realize it. Why did it hurt so much?"

"Perhaps ye love me a wee bit, though ye've no' said it."

"Is that what fills my heart each time I look at you?"

"Aye. And I would know. I dishonored ye by forcing ye into this marriage, though at the time it was no' a choice for me, either. No matter had the king said *aye* to yer request for a divorce, I could no' allow it. And my heart twists painfully inside to recall it."

"Why?"

"'Tis hard to explain. I think it's called *love*."

Mary smiled. "I like the sound of that. Can we go home now?"

"Nay."

Mary blinked at him in surprise.

"Ranald gave us an hour. I intend to use a few more minutes of it."

"But you're injured," Mary protested, though a streak of warmth and excitement flashed through her.

Eaden motioned for her to dismount, following to stand before her. "Nay so bad as I cannae kiss my wife."

He gathered her carefully in his arms and slid his lips tantalizingly across hers. Mary curled her arms about his neck and returned his kiss with fervor, opening her mouth and twining her tongue in a welcoming dance with his. Shaken to her very core, she lost herself in his hungry caresses. Running her hands through his hair, she brushed against the side of his face, and recoiled as she touched the caked blood. But Eaden simply pulled her closer, ignoring the wound.

Finally, he broke the kiss, leaning his forehead against hers, his breath coming fast between his parted lips.

"I'm so sorry they did this to you," Mary murmured achingly. Eaden winced as he shrugged. She touched his face. "Does this hurt?"

"Nay so much. But yer fingers are setting fires in me that will be a long time putting out."

Mary smiled knowingly. She ran her fingers lightly over his ribs. "How many are broken?"

"I'd guess one or two are cracked."

"Am I hurting you, now?" She cupped her hands around his arms and slid them up to his neck, massaging the taut muscles.

Eaden closed his eyes. "Nay."

"And this?" She kissed his chin. He grinned but did not open his eyes. She pulled her hands down the front of his chest. "Here?"

"Ye ask a lot, lass."

Her hands dipped lower and he grabbed her wrists. She glanced up and found his smoldering gaze locked on her.

"I'll answer ye after the healer binds my ribs."

* * *

They approached Scott Castle, Eaden, Mary and Ranald at the front, the soldiers fanned out in a vanguard behind them. Above the tower, the king's standard flapped in the breeze, and Mary's heart quickened in anticipation. The gates opened wide as they crossed the double moat. Reining Starnie to a halt in the middle of the bailey, they dismounted, Eaden leaning awkwardly against the beast until a stable lad caught his reins.

A troop of soldiers marched from the castle, forming a double line that parted to form a protective path. A man, instantly recognizable in his finery as the king, strode toward them. Mary's stomach flipped to realize she laid eyes on her father for the first time. She dropped into a curtsy, bowing her head. Eaden remained standing, canted to one side to relieve the pressure on his ribs.

"Ye took yer time, Scott," the king grumbled.

Eaden gave a pained shrug. "'Twas easier the first time."

"Looks as though someone laid a truncheon to ye."

"Sire," Eaden said formally, giving the king a quelling look. "May I present . . ."

"I ken the lass," King Robert replied. He turned to Mary, the hard lines of his face softening instantly. "She has the look of her ma."

He moved closer, taking Mary's hands in his, drawing her to her feet. Acutely aware of her bedraggled appearance, she looked down in embarrassment. The king patted her hands reassuringly. "Nay, lass. I know ye've had a hard time of it. We'll discuss it later. Ye make me feel young again to see ye. 'Tis as though I am seeing yer ma again for the first time."

Mary peered at him and saw the smile on his face reflecting, not her appearance, but some blissful memory, and her resentment against him for her mother's years of longing fled. However it had ended, there had once been happiness for them both, and she found forgiveness in her heart.

"We have much to speak of, lass. Tell me. When will ye be able to return to Troon with me?"

Mary gently eased her hands away and moved to her husband's side. Leaning lightly into him, she laid a hand on his chest. "I'm sorry, Sire, but I do not wish to go to Troon."

She looked at Eaden who regarded her with an unreadable expression. "My home is here. If he'll have me."

Eaden's arm slipped around her waist and he pulled her close. His grunt of pain sounded low and Mary chose to believe it reflected her weight against his injured ribs and not the anticipation of their life together. He tucked her against him, his mouth settling on hers with a swiftness she'd not thought possible in his condition. He shifted his weight, bringing her full against him as he kissed her thoroughly in front of the king, driving away any lingering reservations she may have had that he wanted her. She wrapped her arms about his neck and answered his kiss with a passionate promise of her own.

The subtle cough of a guard reminded they had an audience and Mary gently pulled away, a smile on her lips.

King Robert sighed, though his eyes twinkled merrily. "So, 'tis the way of it?"

Mary regarded the king. "Aye, Sire. I belong here."

"Then I will remain a few days and we will talk." He tossed Eaden a stern look. "I want to hear of grandbairns soon, Scott."

340

Eaden gave an amused grunt. "We will make it a priority, Sire."

Mary's hand slid around to lightly touch her tummy. A quick glance at her husband caught his speculative look, and a slow smile spread across his face. His hand covered hers as he turned back to the king.

"Our very first priority."

Epilogue

Mary patted her swollen belly, a smile on her lips as she felt the bairn kick. Eaden sent her an anxious look.

"Do not worry about me, love," she told him. "There are weeks left before you get to meet your son."

"Or daughter," he corrected automatically. "Are ye certain? I can send someone else to Ranald's wedding."

"You've sent Finlay already," she reminded him. "And the king has requested your help. I only wish I could travel with you. The young woman he is to wed must be heart-broken over her father's passing."

"Aye. And with her brother missing on the battlefields of France and presumed dead, this is a difficult time to consider a wedding. But the succession must be sealed and the lands and people protected."

"At least she has a good man to soon call husband."

Eaden gave a short laugh. "She will remember Ranald from the times he and I visited Scaurness as lads. We dinnae always treat her as well as we should. She tagged along no matter what we were about, and I am afraid she likely has poor memories of our pranks."

Mary rolled her eyes. "Our son will treat the fairer sex better."

"Our *daughter* will know how to stand up for herself," Eaden countered, a twinkle in his eye, happy to tease his wife. His look, however, turned pensive as he considered the magnitude of the responsibilities Ranald now faced as laird of the Macrory clan.

"What is it, Eaden?" Mary asked, laying slender fingers on his arm. He covered them reassuringly with his hand, pleased at the easy way she touched him. "What do you fear?"

He raised his eyebrows. "Other than my brother is about to wed a young woman who may or may not wish to be married to him?"

Mary tilted her head in sympathy.

Eaden lifted the fingers on his hand one by one. "He has taken command of a clan he has faint blood ties to, amid people divided between his rule and that of the laird's absent son. And the clan is a sea-faring one."

"Why is that a problem?"

"My brother cannae tolerate boats. He gets seasick just looking at the waves."

Mary smiled. "Give him my love and tell him I would love to meet his bride one day. And let him know of his soon-to-be-nephew."

"Or niece," Eaden replied as he gathered his wife in his arms, thrilling to the firmness of her rounded belly against his. Tilting her chin up, he kissed her, lingering until he could push the time for his departure no longer. "Ye should have no difficulties from Bellecourt now that Miriam and her husband are in control. The feud is at an end, no matter Barde sits harmless as an auld man in his tower now. Take care, Mairi, love. I will return to ye as soon as I am able."

"I love you, Eaden. I will wait until you return to produce your heir." Her merry look met his as he squeezed her hand one last time. Mounted on Duff's back, he leaned over and placed a final kiss on Mary's lips, pointing a finger at Sorcha who whined to be at his side.

"Protect her," he commanded. He wheeled Duff about, spurring him to a gallop through the castle gates.

The End

MORE BOOKS

by Cathy MacRae

The Hardy Heroines series
(with DD MacRae)

Highland Escape (book 1)
The Highlander's Viking Bride (book 2)
The Highlander's Crusader Bride (book 3)
The Highlander's Norse Bride, a Novella (book 4)

The Saint:
World of de Wolfe Pack
(published through Wolfbane Publishing)

The Ghosts of Culloden Moor series
(with LL Muir, Diane Darcy, Jo Jones, and Melissa Mayhue)

Adam
Malcolm
MacLeod
Patrick

About the Author

Cathy MacRae lives on the sunny side of the Arbuckle Mountains where she and her husband read, write, and tend the garden—with the help of the dogs, of course.

You can visit with her on facebook, or sign up for her newsletter, read her blogs and learn about her books at **www.cathymacraeauthor.com**. Drop her a line—she loves to hear from readers!

Other ways to connect with Cathy:
Instagram
Twitter: @CMacRaeAuthor
Amazon author page

Acknowledgements

There are many people I have learned much from in this process called writing. I cannot imagine I could name everyone. And would likely take a very long time if I tried.

To Debby Gilbert and Char Chaffin at Soul Mate Publishing- thank you for taking a chance on the original manuscript. You have been a pleasure to work with and made my first dip into the publishing waters so much easier.

To the ladies of Heart of Dixie Romance Writers who welcomed my first endeavors at writing, taught me to think outside the box and helped me keep my dream alive – there are not thanks enough.

To Dar Albert for creating the new covers for the Highlander's Bride series.

To the best critique partners in the world! You have guided me, corrected me and cheered me on from the day I posted my first chapter for you to read. Derek Dodson, Cate Parke, Dawn Marie Hamilton, and Fran Redding, you are the absolute best. Remind me I owe you lunch.

Cathy MacRae

Read an excerpt from The Highlander's Reluctant Bride:

CHAPTER ONE

1377, Scotland, above the Firth of Clyde

"Fire!"

Riona jolted awake. She blinked, her eyes blearily registering the red glow that pulsed across the stone wall of the laird's bedroom. The banked hearth did little to dispel the gloom, the embers like so many pinpoints of burnished light. What shone through the window seemed much brighter.

Her head shot up. Colors of ochre and scarlet flickered through the narrow portal. The harsh scent of smoke rose on the air. Riona bolted to her feet, her stool tumbling noisily to the stones.

The door to her father's room flung open and a man leapt inside. "Lady Caitriona." His voice ground harsh and overly loud in the sickroom, but Riona did not fuss. A quick glance to her da reassured her he still slept, his breathing barely moving the blanket drawn over his chest.

She turned and stared at the man at the door. "What is happening, Fergus?"

Chorused shouts from the parapet caused her to jerk in response, but she could not pull her gaze from Fergus's pale face.

"The castle is under attack."

* * *

"Fire!"

Ranald Scott reined his horse to a halt, waving a hand to silence the dogs whining anxiously beside him, their sensitive noses twitching at the acrid stench of smoke filtering through the trees. Along the crest of the cliff, the night glowed red around the base of Scaurness Castle and Ranald could see dark forms scurrying back and forth like misshapen ants in the glare.

He spoke to his captain. "Keep it silent, Finlay. We dinnae want to alert the attackers."

Finlay nodded to the men riding behind them. "Ride with haste but caution. The rocks are treacherous."

Ranald unleashed the dogs to save them from the danger of being stomped. They would follow with caution, having been raised in his stables and accustomed to the great beasts. With his soldiers falling into line, he spurred his horse forward, bolting up the mountainside. Hearn's muscles bunched and surged under Ranald, fighting to keep his footing on the stony slope.

Beside him, Finlay's horse stumbled to its knees, a well-timed jerk of the reins giving the steed back his balance. Their shod hooves rang on the rocks, but the shouts from the castle had grown louder and hid the sound of their advance.

Ranald stifled a curse as Hearn slid on a loose stone, nearly pitching him to the rocks. Would they reach the castle in time? Unscathed?

The harsh glow of the fire dimmed in the first light of morning. With a roaring battle cry, Ranald released his soldiers across the field. Three score swarmed into the unsuspecting flank of those firing upon the castle. The postern gate hung partly ajar, but the main gate remained unbreached and bowmen on the parapet held the attackers at bay.

Around the base of the walls, lingering Greek fire clung to the charred grass and soil, keeping the enemy away and at the mercy of the clouds of arrows raining down whenever they approached too closely.

At the unexpected cry of challenge from Ranald's men, the attackers split into two groups, peeling away from their attempt to broaden the opening at the damaged postern gate. Shields raised against the maelstrom of arrows left them no protection from the mounted horsemen sweeping them from behind. Quickly the forces engaged, but surprise was on Ranald's side. He and his men plunged into the fray, claymores singing in the morning air as mist rose from the water below and wafted across the bloody ground.

"Retreat! Retreat!" The cry went up among the harried attackers, and they drew back into the forest, fading wraith-like into the early morning shadows.

"Hold!"

The Scott soldiers grouped, searching the now-empty field for sight of the enemy. Ranald wiped sweat from his eyes, barely registering the gritty feel of partially dried blood caking one side of his face. At his whistle the hounds, Pol and Senga, bounded to his side.

With a jerk of his head, he turned his men to the gates of Scaurness Castle.

* * *

Riona gazed down from the parapet. The men who had routed those attacking the castle now reformed about their leader, bristling with swords and triumphant battle-lust. The field had cleared of the enemy, except for six who lay dead. She peered closely at the still forms. Though impossible to tell from this distance, she hoped the dead did not include the soldiers who had come so unexpectedly to their aid.

Men shouted in the bailey below and she heard the creak of the heavy portcullis as it lifted. Their unknown supporters approached the castle.

"I will join Manus." Handing her bow and half-full quiver to a soldier, Riona hurried down the steps to the bailey. She made her way to the gate, finding the captain of the guards deep in conversation with one of his men. Manus ended his conversation as Riona approached.

"My lady." His words were clipped, the expression on his face just short of hostile. Riona ignored the tone of his voice. He made it clear he did not approve of her assumed leadership of the clan since her father's illness. Though it rankled, Riona no longer let it bother her. It was not his decision to make.

"Do ye know these men at the gate?" Manus demanded.

"I believe they have been sent from the king." Her reply did not seem to improve Manus's attitude. Men from the king sent to rule the Macrory clan had not been his choice, either.

Riona flexed her fingers to relieve the strain of the bow. "Let them in."

Manus gave the command. The gate swung open and the bloodied soldiers rode through the narrow barbican, Macrory soldiers watching warily through the holes in the ceiling and arrow slits along either side of the passageway.

* * *

Ranald's muscles were tight, poised to react at the least provocation. Roiling battle-fury had yet to bleed away, compounded by the obvious distrust of the Macrory soldiers reluctantly allowing them into the castle and the frown on the face of the young woman standing at their head.

Tall and slender, her dark red hair bound back in a thick braid, she stood her ground. Ranald knew it was irrational, but somehow her attitude rankled. He drew Hearn to a stop several feet away from the woman. Pol and Senga pranced over to the two fallen men lying inside the jammed postern gate, sniffing the bodies curiously.

The woman eyed the enormous dogs. Hearn pawed the ground, tossing his head impatiently. Ranald made no attempt to control the beasts. His sympathy lay with those newly come from battle, not the young woman who faced him with a regal air.

"This is Lady Caitriona." The hulking, dark-haired man beside the woman took a step forward. Ranald acknowledged the woman with a brief nod, earning another frown. "I am Manus, captain of the Macrory guard."

Ranald leaned forward in his saddle, at last checking Hearn's movements. "I am Ranald Scott. I am here to secure the castle for the king."

He thought Lady Caitriona stiffened, but she inclined her head gracefully. "Welcome to Scaurness Castle, milord. Yer arrival was most timely."

Ranald swung down from Hearn's back, handing the reins to a lad who stepped forward for the duty. Finlay remained at his side as he questioned Lady Caitriona. "I want to know how they jammed the gate."

"Milord, ye are injured," she replied. "We will tend ye and then discuss this. The gate will be repaired."

Ranald favored Lady Caitriona with a half-smile. "The blood isnae mine. I'll be glad of a wash in due time. We will settle this first."

"As ye wish."

Ranald paused, waiting for her to retire to the keep. She did not.

They paced forward, Ranald and Finlay in step with Manus. Approaching the gate, Ranald noted its hinge sported a dagger jammed deep inside. Frowning, he turned to the Macrory captain. "This wasnae done by an outsider."

Manus grunted. "Nae. We will find the traitor and deal with him."

Ranald pierced him with a stare. "Do it." He stepped forward and grasped the dagger. With a mighty heave, he pulled it from its berth, and the door swung slightly with release.

"Fix it." With that, Ranald turned and jogged quickly down the shallow steps from the postern gate. He reclaimed his horse's reins and swung into the saddle. His anger communicated itself through his arms to his horse's bit, his legs tightening as Hearn danced in response. He urged the powerful horse deeper among the Macrory soldiers in the bailey witnessing his exchange with their captain.

Halting in their midst, Ranald used Hearn's antics to fully capture their attention. "Hear me! I am Ranald Scott. I come at the order of King Robert of Scotland, at the request of Laird Macrory, to secure this castle from those who would seize and hold it against the king."

Hearn's forelegs lifted briefly, then jarred to the ground as Ranald added, "I will tolerate no man standing against me or mine. If ye have issue with this, take it up with my captain. If ye canna accept it, the postern gate is still open, and ye are free to leave today. I will tolerate none who question my authority." Ranald eyed the Macrory soldiers. None offered him challenge. Their laird had requested help from the crown, bitter dregs to swallow, but they would face it, nonetheless.

Satisfied with the response, he dismounted again, slapping Hearn's rump to send him back to the lad reaching for his reins. Pol and Senga gamboled beside Ranald, and he rested a hand on Pol's broad head. He turned to the laird's daughter, expecting her to invite him into the keep.

Strands of burnished hair had torn loose from her braid, whipping in the wind. Her eyes narrowed with either dislike or distrust, or perhaps both, she appeared far more likely to usher him straight to hell.

* * *

The Highlander's Reluctant Bride – available from Amazon

354

57913659R00197